Edward Sylvester Ellis

Two Boys in Wyoming

A Tale cf Adventure

Edward Sylvester Ellis

Two Boys in Wyoming
A Tale of Adventure

ISBN/EAN: 9783337073107

Printed in Europe, USA, Canada, Australia, Japan

Cover: Foto ©Andreas Hilbeck / pixelio.de

More available books at **www.hansebooks.com**

NORTHWEST SERIES, NO. 3

TWO BOYS IN WYOMING

A TALE OF ADVENTURE

BY

EDWARD S. ELLIS

AUTHOR OF " DEERFOOT SERIES," " LOG CABIN SERIES," ETC.

THE JOHN C. WINSTON CO.,

PHILADELPHIA,

CHICAGO, TORONTO.

CONTENTS.

(iii)

TWO BOYS IN WYOMING.

CHAPTER I.

JACK AND FRED.

YOU should have seen those youths, for it gives me pleasure to say that two manlier, more plucky and upright boys it would be hard to find anywhere in this broad land of ours. I have set out to tell you about their remarkable adventures in the grandest section of the West, and, before doing so, it is necessary for you to know something concerning the lads themselves.

Jack Dudley was in his seventeenth year. His father was a prosperous merchant, who intended his only son for the legal profession. Jack was bright and studious, and a leader in his class at the Orphion Academy; and this leadership was not confined to his studies, for he was a fine athlete and an ardent lover of outdoor sports. If you witnessed the game between the eleven of the Orphion Academy and the Oakdale Football Club, which decided the championship by a single point in favor of the former, you were thrilled by the sight of the half-back, who, at a critical point in the contest, burst through the group which thronged about him, and, with a clear field in front, made a superb run of fifty yards, never pausing until he stooped behind the goal-posts and made a touchdown. Then, amid the cheers of the delighted thousands, he walked back on the field, and while one of the players lay down on the ground, with the spheroid delicately poised before his face, the same youth who made the touchdown smote the ball mightily with his sturdy right foot and sent it sailing between the goal-posts as accurately as an arrow launched from a bow.

That exploit, as I have said, won the championship for the Orphions, and the boy who did it was Jack Dudley. In the latter half of the game, almost precisely the same opening presented itself again for the great halfback, but he had no more than fairly started when he met an obstruction in his path. The gritty opponent tackled him like a tiger, and down they went, rolling over in the dirt, with a fierce violence that made more than one timid spectator fear that both were seriously injured. As if that were not enough, the converging players pounced upon them. There was a mass of struggling, writhing youths, with Jack underneath, and all piling on top of him. The last arrival, seeing little chance for effective work, took a running leap, and, landing on the apex of the pyramid, whirling about while in the air so as to alight on his back, kicked up his feet and strove to made himself as heavy as he could.

The only object this young man seemed to have was to batter down the score of players and flatten out Jack Dudley, far below at the bottom; but when, with the help of the referee, the mass was disentangled, and Jack, with his mop-like hair, his soiled uniform, and his grimy face, struggled to his feet and pantingly waited for the signal from his captain, he was just as good as ever. It takes a great deal to hurt a rugged youth, who has no bad habits and is in sturdy training.

The active lad who had downed Jack when going at full speed, and nipped in the bud his brilliant attempt, was Fred Greenwood, only a few months younger. He was full-back for the Oakdales and their best player. Furthermore, he was the closest friend of Jack Dudley. In the game it was war to the knife between them, but in the very crisis of the terrific struggle neither had a harsh thought or a spark of jealousy of the other. Fred led the cheering of the opposing eleven when Jack kicked such a beautiful goal, but gritted his teeth and muttered:

"You did well, my fine fellow, but just try it again—that's all!"

And Jack *did* try it again, as I have explained, and, tackling him low, Fred downed him. While the two were apparently suffocating under the mountain, Fred spat out a mouthful of dirt and said:

"I got you that time, Jack."

"It has that look, but——"

Jack meant to finish his sentence, but at

that moment the mountain on top sagged forward and jammed his head so deeply into the earth that his voice was too muffled to be clear. Besides, it was not really important that the sentence should be rounded out, since other matters engaged his attention. The two friends went through the game without a scratch, except that Jack's face was skinned along the right cheek, one eye was blackened, both legs were bruised, and half his body was black and blue, and it was hard work for him to walk for a week afterward. The condition of Fred, and indeed of nearly every member of the two elevens, was much the same.

But what of it? Does a football-player mind a little thing like that? Rather is he not proud of his scars and bruises, which attest his skill and devotion to his own club? And then Jack had the proud exultation of knowing that it was he who really won the championship for his side. As for Fred, it is true he was disappointed over the loss of the deciding game, but it was by an exceedingly narrow margin ; and he and his fellow-players, as they had their hair cut so as to make them

resemble civilized beings, said, with flashing
eyes and a significant shake of the head:

"Wait till next year, and things will be
different."

Fred Greenwood was the son of a physician
of large practice, whose expectation was that
his son would follow the same profession,
though the plans of the parents were in a
somewhat hazy shape, owing to the youth of
the boy. As I have already said, he and Jack
Dudley had been comrades or chums almost
from infancy. They were strong, active, clear-
brained lads, who had not yet learned to smoke
cigarettes or cigars, and gave no cause to fear
that they would ever do so. It is not necessary to state that neither knew the taste of
beer or alcoholic drinks, nor did they wish to
learn. They understood too well the baleful
effects of such indulgences to be in danger of
ruining their bodies and souls, as too many
other youths are doing at this very time.

Doctor Greenwood had been the family
physician of the Dudleys for many years.
The heads of the families were college mates
at Harvard, and continued their intimacy

after the marriage of each, so that it was quite natural that their sons should become fond of each other. The fathers were sensible men, and so long as their boys' fondness for athletic sports did not interfere with their studies the gentlemen encouraged them, and, when possible, were present at the contests between the representatives of the schools.

When Jack Dudley was presented with a shotgun and allowed to make an excursion down the Jersey coast Fred was his companion, and the two had rare sport in shooting duck and wild fowl. They became quite expert for boys, and before the hunting season set in did considerable fishing in the surrounding waters, and both learned to be skilful swimmers and boatmen.

Mr. Dudley was wealthier than his professional friend, though the large practice of the physician placed him in comfortable circumstances. In one of his many business transactions Mr. Dudley found that he had to choose between losing a considerable sum of money and accepting a half-ownership in a ranch in the new State of Wyoming. There seemed little choice between the two horns of the dilemma, for he saw no prospect of ever getting any money out of the Western land, but he accepted the ownership, the other half of which was divided among three gentlemen, one of whom lived in Cheyenne, and the others in Chicago.

It is perhaps worth noting that although the fathers of Jack and Fred were great admirers of athletics, and, as I have said, encouraged the devotion to them shown by their sons, yet neither was inclined that way in his youth.

"I never expected to own a foot of ground west of the Mississippi," remarked Mr. Dudley, when making a call upon the doctor, "and here, before I fairly knew it, I have become a half-owner in a ranch away out in Wyoming."

"Eventually it may prove worth something," suggested Doctor Greenwood, "for that section has enormous capabilities, and a tide of emigration has been moving that way for years."

"It will take a long time to fill up that

country with people. Meanwhile I'll sell out cheap, doctor, if you feel like investing."

The physician laughed and thought the joke was on his friend. He said he would think the matter over, which was another way of saying he would do nothing more than think of it.

Jack and Fred were present at this interview, and listened with keen attention to the discussion of the Western purchase. By and by Fred gave his chum a significant look, and, excusing themselves to their parents, they passed out of the room and up stairs to the sleeping-quarters of Fred. The door was carefully closed behind them, and, drawing their chairs close together, they talked in low tones, as if some dreadful penalty would follow a discovery of what was passing between them. Had any one been able to see the two attractive countenances, he would not have had to be told that the same thought was in the mind of each.

"I tell you, Jack," said Fred, with impressive solemnity, "it would be a shame; it will never do; we must not allow it."

"Allow what?"

"Why you heard your father say that he never expected to go out to Wyoming to look at that ranch he has bought."

"I could have told you that much, without waiting for him to say it. It will be just like him to give it away for a song."

"And who knows but that it contains valuable gold or silver mines? I have heard of treasures being bought in that way."

"That may be," was the thoughtful response of Jack, "though I believe most of Wyoming—that is the valleys and plains—is a grazing country."

"I don't know much about the country, but I have read enough to learn that the greatest discoveries of gold and silver have been in places where no one expected to find them. What I am getting at, Jack, is that your father should make up his mind not to part with his interest in the ranch till he knows all about it."

"How is he to learn, when he won't go near it? Of course he can write to the people out there, but likely they will not tell him the truth."

"He must send some one whom he can trust, and let him investigate."

"That does seem to be a sensible plan," remarked Jack, as if the thought had not been in his mind from the first.

"A sensible plan!" repeated the enthusiastic Fred, "it is the *only* plan; nothing else can make it sure that he is not being swindled out of a big fortune."

Jack was silent a moment, while he looked steadily into the brown eyes of his chum, who half-smilingly met the scrutiny. Then the whole scheme burst forth.

"And whom can your father trust before *us?* He must see that the best thing he can do is to send us out there to make a full investigation. We won't charge him anything like what he would have to pay other folks."

"Of course not; only our travelling expenses and supplies."

"What do you mean by supplies?"

"Say a Winchester rifle and a revolver apiece, with the proper ammunition; what sort of supplies did you think I meant?"

"I thought it was food, while we were out hunting."

Jack turned up his nose.

"If we can't keep ourselves supplied with food, when we are in a country that has the finest game in the world, we deserve to starve."

"My sentiments exactly;" and as if the co-incidence required something in the nature of a compact, the boys shook hands over it.

"What a splendid treat it would be for us to spend some weeks out in Wyoming!" exclaimed Jack Dudley, his eyes sparkling and his cheeks glowing; "it looks as if it were providential that father got hold of that ranch."

"There can't be any doubt about it; but how much more providential it will be if we are sent to learn all that should be learned about it! I wonder if that can be brought about?"

Enough has been told for the reader to understand the plot formed by these two youths. There could be no question of the grand treat it would prove to both, provided their parents could be persuaded to take the same view of the matter; *there* was the rub.

Jack crossed his legs and thoughtfully scratched his head. Unconsciously Fred did the same.

"It's a tougher problem than we ever attacked in Euclid," remarked the younger. Then a bright thought struck him.

"Don't I look a little pale, Jack?"

"You look as if a month's vacation in the autumn would be acceptable; but the fact is, Fred, I never saw you look better than you do this minute."

Fred sighed.

"I am afraid I can't work that on father. He's too good a doctor for me to worry him about my health."

"How about *me?*"

Fred shook his head.

"You look as strong as an oak knot, and you are, too; no, we can't make them think we are in need of a month in Wyoming. We shall have to try another tack. Now, there is no doubt that if we spend the month of September putting in extra work on our studies, we can stand the following month in laying off. We shall come back with new vigor and appetite, and soon catch up with our class."

"There isn't a particle of doubt about that, but it still remains that we must convince our fathers that it will be a wise course to send us away from home. We can't do it by looking pale and weak, for we can't look pale and weak. We must fix on something else or it's no go."

"Why not fall back on what we first talked about?"

"What's that?"

"Make your father think it will be a prudent thing for him to send you out there to look after his property."

"Suppose I should convince him on that point, how about *you?*"

"You will need some one to look after you, and I'm just the fellow."

"We are both satisfied in our own minds; in fact we were from the first; but our fathers are very hard-headed men."

Now, a couple of boys may be very shrewd,

but it often happens that their parents are a good deal shrewder, a fact which my young readers will do well to remember.

Unsuspected by Jack Dudley and Fred Greenwood, their parents read on the instant the momentous problem which assumed form in the brains of their sons. When the younger signalled to his chum to follow him out of the room, the two gentlemen understood what it meant as clearly as if they overheard all the conversation that followed. Waiting until they were beyond hearing, Doctor Greenwood looked at his friend and remarked, with a smile:

"They are hit hard."

"No doubt of it; their hearts are set on making a visit to the ranch, and it would be singular if it were otherwise. We can feel for them, for we were once boys."

"Yes, John, and it's longer ago than we like to recall. What do you think of it?"

"You know we have always agreed that many parents injure their children by undue indulgence."

"True, and we have been indulgent to ours,

but not improperly so. A great deal depends upon the children themselves. Jack and Fred are obedient, studious, and have good principles. If we should say 'No' to this scheme of theirs they would be disappointed, almost beyond what we can understand, but neither would protest or sulk. They would study just as hard as ever. It is that which appeals to us. If they were sullen and dissatisfied we wouldn't care; but, John, you and I have each been blessed with model sons, and they are entitled to privileges which it would not be safe to grant to other boys. I confess I feel like sending both out to Wyoming for an outing."

"Of course it would spoil the enjoyment of Jack unless he could take Fred with him, but what excuse shall we make, Doc?"

How reluctant a father is to appear weak and too conciliatory toward his child! These two men had virtually decided to grant the fervent wish of their sons, but it must be done in a common-sense way. They could not say "Boys, since you have set your hearts on this we grant it," but they must fix upon some scheme that would made it seem a necessity that they should go thither.

And now observe how ludicrously similar their thoughts were to those that were agitating their offspring up stairs.

"I have been thinking," observed the physician, "of suggesting to them that they are in need of an extension of their vacation; but what a farce it would be! School opens next Monday, and they are the types of rugged health, strength and activity. If I undertook to make such a proposition I couldn't keep my face straight, and I am sure both would burst out laughing."

"I know *I* should, if I were present."

"Parents must not make dunces of themselves before their children," was the philosophical remark of the physician; "some other plan must be adopted."

Mr. Dudley leaned forward in his chair and slapped the shoulder of the physician, his face aglow.

"I have it, Doc!"

"Let me hear it, for I admit that I am cornered."

"I will take the ground that, since I have become part owner of this large tract of land, my first duty is to learn the truth about it. I can write to parties out there, but they are all strangers to me, and there is no saying how much reliance can be placed on their reports. What is necessary is an agent who will make an intelligent and honest report; and surely we can trust our own sons to do that."

"But, John," remarked the doctor, with his pleasant smile, "there are scores of people right here at home who will do that for you. Suppose Jack reminds you of the fact?"

"If he hasn't any more sense than to make such a suggestion, then, by gracious! I'll punish him by sending some one else."

"Little fear of Jack saying anything of that nature. Even if he undertook to do so, Fred would place his hand over his mouth. But, John, let's understand the matter before we say anything to them. Your plan of sending out Jack to inspect the property is a good one. It sounds business-like, and must strike them that way; so that difficulty is removed. You and I don't know anything about the

region, nor the best time for hunting game,
but it is fair to believe that the month of
October will be suitable. Suppose we keep
them in school throughout September, and
then give them a month's leave of absence,
to examine and report upon your property.
If all goes well, they are to appear here, ready
to resume their studies on the first Monday
in November."

"I can suggest no improvement upon that.
No doubt the young rascals are up-stairs, plot-
ting how to bring us round to their way of
thinking. Suppose you call them down, Doc.
Shall you or I unfold our brilliant scheme?"

"You, by all means, since the property is
yours."

The physician opened the door of his office
and called "Fred!" There was instant response, "Yes, sir." "I would like to see you
and Jack for a few minutes in the office."

"Yes, sir; we are coming."

And a minute later they arrived, handsome, glowing and expectant.

"Mr. Dudley has something to say to you,
Jack."

Both boys turned their faces expectantly toward the gentleman named, who crossed his legs, cleared his throat and looked very grave.

"My son, Doctor Greenwood and I have been discussing that property of mine in the new State of Wyoming. We have agreed that I ought to learn something about it before selling my interest in the same. To secure such reliable information it is necessary to send some one thither whom we know to be truthful and honest. The doctor thinks, and I agree with him, that the right one to go is you, Jack—that is, if you have no objections."

The parent paused for a reply, and Jack, as if the matter was too important to be disposed of hastily, answered:

"I don't think of any objections just now, father."

"Very well; I am glad to hear it. If any occur to you, you will let me know, so that I can engage some one else."

"I'll let you know at once, if I think of any."

"Very well. Our plan is that you and

Fred shall resume your studies next Monday, and keep right at them to the close of the month. On the first of October you will start for Wyoming——"

"Alone?"

"I am surprised, my son, that you should interrupt me with that question. Do you suppose I would allow you to spend a month in that wild region without a companion to look after you? No, sir! Fred goes with you. I entrust you to his care, and expect him to bring you back in time to resume your studies on the first Monday in November. It is very kind in the doctor to consent to the arrangement. I hope you appreciate it, sir."

"I thank him very much," said Jack, looking toward the physician, who just then drew his hand across his mouth to suppress the smile that was tugging at the corners.

"Of course," continued Mr. Dudley, still with the manner of a philosopher, "in visiting such a section, inhabited by large and fierce game, you must take every precaution. I shall furnish each of you with a repeating Winchester, a revolver, and such other articles

as may be necessary. We will now excuse
you, with the understanding that if any objections occur to either, you will let us know
at once, so that you may continue your studies,
while I engage other parties to attend to this
business."

"I'll think it over," replied Jack, tremulous with delight.

And then he and his chum withdrew and
went up-stairs again to the room of Fred
Greenwood, who hastily closed the door. The
next instant they were hugging each other,
and dancing about as if their senses had for-
saken them; and indeed it may be said that
for a brief while such was the fact.

"Fred," said the happy Jack, when there
was a lull in the excitement, "we must fix
upon a name for ourselves."

"I thought our parents attended to that a
good many years ago."

"You know what I mean; we need some
title that will distinguish us from all other
young gentlemen of our acquaintance. How
does ' W. R.' strike you?"

"' W. R.'? What does that mean?"

"The 'Wyoming Rangers;' that sounds rather high-toned."

Fred shook his head.

"We are not going West to reduce the aboriginal population; I hope we shall have no trouble with the red men. When we get among the people who have always lived there, such a title will make us ridiculous. for it smacks of conceit; it assumes too much."

"Suppose *you* suggest something?"

"Let's call ourselves the 'V. W. W.'; that surely will be appropriate."

"What do those letters mean?"

"The 'Verdant Wanderers of Wyoming;' that is precisely what we shall be."

Jack Dudley laughed, and at first protested, but finally agreed to accept the title as fitting and appropriate, and it was so ordered.

CHAPTER II.

RIDING NORTHWARD.

AND so it came about that on a sharp, crisp day early in the month of October, two sturdy youths left the Union Pacific train at Fort Steele, which is situated in a broad depression between two divisions of the Wind River Mountains, themselves forming a part of the vast Rocky Mountain chain, which, under different names, stretches along the western portion of the two continents from the Arctic Ocean on the north to the extreme southern end of South America.

Like the sensible youths they were, Jack Dudley and Fred Greenwood had made the fullest preparation possible for the experience which was destined to prove tenfold more eventful than either anticipated. Mr. Dudley, in accordance with his promise, had presented each with a fine repeating Winchester

rifle, an excellent revolver, an abundant supply of cartridges, and various knick-knacks
which the hunter is sure to find are more in
the nature of necessities than luxuries.

They had tough corduroy suits, a material
which, as everyone knows, wears like leather,
though it is unpopular in the West because
of its unpleasant odor when wet. From the
knees downward the lower part of the legs
were protected by strong leathern leggings,
and the shoes were made for wear rather than
display. The coats were rather short and
gathered at the waists by a belt, while beneath
the garment it was intended to wear the cart-
ridge-belt. The revolver rested in a sheath,
instead of being thrust into a trouser's-pocket
at the hip, while their hats suggested the
sombrero pattern, so popular among cowboys
and cattlemen. The brim was broad and stiff,
so that it was not liable to bother their vision
when the wind was blowing, and it could be
depended upon to protect the eyes and face
from the sun and rain. Their whole outfit,
in short, was strong, comfortable and ser-
viceable.

The two were generously furnished with money, while Mr. Dudley arranged with a banker at Laramie City to furnish the boys with whatever funds they might need through accident or robbery. They were going into a region where there were many lawless characters, and everything was done to provide against all possible contingencies.

Their extra clothing and articles were contained in a couple of valises, which were put off the train upon the lonely platform at Fort Steele. But while this marked the farthest distance they could travel by rail, a long ride still confronted them before reaching the ranch, which was almost half-way between the railroad and the Big Horn Mountains to the northeast. Several streams had to be crossed, the country in many places was rough, and there was no stage line to help them. All this, however, had been discounted before the boys left the city of Chicago, and what they encountered was only what was expected, and only that for which they were prepared.

Word having been sent in advance of their expected arrival, the first act of the youths

was to look around for the man or men who
were to meet and conduct them to the ranch.
A few people were moving about the long,
low platform, several in the uniform of United
States infantry and cavalry, while a couple of
Indians in blankets, untidy and sullen, surveyed them with scowls. Few passengers
were in the habit of leaving the train at this
point, so that some curiosity on the part of
the loungers was natural. Perhaps the agent
at the station suspected them of being run-
aways whose heads had been turned by stories
of wild adventure, and who had set out to anni-
hilate the aborigines of the West; but if such
a fancy came to the man, it must have vanished when he noticed their intelligent appearance and the completeness of their outfit.
Boys who start on such whimsical careers are
never rightly prepared, and have no concep-
tion of the absurdity of their schemes until
it is forced upon them by sad and woeful experience.

"Are you looking for any one?" asked the
agent, respectfully.

"Yes, sir," replied Jack Dudley; "we are

on our way to a ranch which lies to the eastward of Camp Brown, not far from Wind River."

"May I ask your errand thither?"

"My father is part owner of the ranch, and we wish to visit it for a few weeks."

"Ah, you are the young men that Hank Hazletine was asking about yesterday. He has charge of Bowman's ranch."

"That's the place. What has become of Mr. Hazletine?"

"I think he is over at the fort, and will soon be here. He brought a couple of horses for you to ride. Ah, here he comes now."

The boys saw the man at the same moment. He was walking rapidly from the direction of the fort, and looking curiously at the youths, who surveyed him with interest as he approached. He was full-bearded, tall, and as straight as an arrow, dressed in cowboy costume, and the picture of rugged strength and activity. His manner was that of a man who, having made a mistake as to the hour of the arrival of the train, was doing his best to make up for lost time.

Stepping upon the long, low platform, he walked toward the lads, his Winchester in his left hand, while he extended his right in salutation.

"Howdy?" he said, heartily, as he took the hand of Fred Greenwood, who advanced several paces to meet him. "I reckon you're the younkers I'm waiting for."

"If you are Hank Hazletine, you are the man."

"That's the name I gin'rally go by; which one of you is Jack Dudley?"

"I am," replied that young gentleman.

"Then t'other one is Fred Greenwood, eh?" he asked, turning toward the younger.

"You have our names right."

"Glad to know it; I got your letter and looked for you yesterday; have been loafing 'round here since then."

"We were not sure of the exact time of our arrival and missed it by twenty-four hours," said Jack; "I hope it caused you no inconvenience."

"Not at all—not at all. Wal, I s'pose you're ready to start for the ranch, younkers?"

"We are at your disposal; we have quite a long ride before us."

"We have; it'll take us two or three days to git there, if all goes well."

"Suppose all doesn't go well?" remarked Fred.

"We shall be longer on the road; and if it goes too bad we'll never git there; but I ain't looking for anything like that. Where's your baggage?"

Jack pointed to the two plump valises lying on the platform, near the little building.

"That and what we have on us and in our hands make up our worldly possessions."

"That's good," said Hazletine. "I was afeard you might bring a load of trunks, which we'd had a purty time getting to the ranch; but there won't be any trouble in managing them; I'll be right back."

He turned away, and soon reappeared, mounted on a fine, wiry pony, and leading on either side a tough little animal, saddled and bridled and ready for the boys.

"There ain't any better animals in Wyoming or Colorado," he explained; "they can travel fast and fur a long time. We'll strap on that stuff and be off."

There was no trouble in securing the baggage to the rear of the saddles, when Jack and Fred swung themselves upon the backs of the ponies, adjusted their Winchesters across the saddles in front, following the suggestions of Hazletine, and announced themselves ready to set out on the long ride northward. The animals struck into an easy canter, and a few minutes later all signs of civilization were left behind them.

The boys were in buoyant spirits. There was just enough coolness in the air to make the exercise invigorating. Here and there a few snowy flecks dotted the blue sky, but the sun shone with undimmed splendor, the warmth slightly increasing as the orb climbed the heavens. To the northward the undulating plain was unbroken by hill or stream, so far as the eye could note, while to the eastward the prospect was similar, though they knew that the North Platte curved over in that direction, and, after winding around the upper end of the Laramie Mountains, joined the main stream far over in Nebraska.

To the westward the prospect was romantic and awe-inspiring. The Wind River range towered far up in the sky in rugged grandeur, following a course almost parallel with their own, though gradually trending more to the left, in the direction of Yellowstone Park. The snow-crowned peaks looked like vast banks of clouds in the sky, while the craggy portions below the frost-line were mellowed by the distance and softly tinted in the clear, crystalline atmosphere. The mountains formed a grand background to the picture which more closely environed them.

As the three galloped easily forward they kept nearly abreast, with the ranchman between them. He was in a pleasant mood, and seemed to have formed a fancy for the youths, who felt a natural admiration for the big, muscular veteran of the plains and mountains.

"Yes," said he, in answer to their inquiries; "I've spent all my life as a cattleman, cowboy, hunter or trapper. I left the

States with my parents, when a small younker, with an emigrant train fur Californy. Over in Utah, when crawling through the mountains, and believing the worst of the bus'ness was over, the Injins come down on us one rainy night and wiped out nearly all. My father, mother and an older brother was killed, and I don't understand how I got off with my scalp, but I did, with half a dozen others."

"Did you go on to California?"

"No; I've never been in that country, which I s'pose you'll think strange; but I was on my way there, when I met the great scout Kit Carson and several hunters. They took me along with 'em, and the next twenty years of my life was spent in New Mexico, Arizona and Texas. Since then I've ranged from the Panhandle to Montana, most of the time in the cattle bus'ness."

"At what are you engaged just now?" inquired Jack.

"The same—that is, the cattle bus'ness. You may know that after thousands of the critters have spent the summer in Texas, New

3

Mexico and Arizona, they drive 'em north into Wyoming, Montana and the Dakotas, to git their finishing touches. The grazing is so much better than in the south that in a few months they're ready for the market, and are either killed and their carcasses shipped to the East, or they are took there by train in as fine condition as anybody could ask. You observe that the grass under our feet is powerful good."

The boys replied that it seemed to be.

"Wal, there's hundreds of thousands of acres better than this; there's thirty thousand of 'em in Bowman's ranch, where we're going, and it's the best kind of grazing land."

"I believe it extends to the Wind River Mountains," said Jack.

"It takes in a part of the foot-hills; there are plenty of streams there, and some of the finest grass in the world."

Jack Dudley did not forget the real object of the coming of himself and companion to this section, and he could not gather the information too soon.

"How does Bowman's ranch compare with others in Central Wyoming?"

"You may ride over the whole State without finding a better. If you doubt it, look at the country for yourself."

"We don't doubt anything you tell us," said Fred Greenwood. "I suppose you know that Mr. Dudley, the father of my friend, owns half the ranch?"

"I've heerd that."

"He didn't intend to buy it, but matters so shaped themselves that he couldn't help doing so. Before selling it, he sent us to take a look at it and find out whether it is all that was claimed. We have come to do that, but, at the same time, are eager to have some hunting among the mountains."

"You won't have any trouble about that. As I was saying, we're close to the mountains, and when you're ready I'll go with you, and promise that you'll have something to talk about as long as you live."

The eyes of the boys sparkled as they looked across at each other, and Jack said:

"Nothing could delight us more. We need a veteran like yourself, and are happy to know you can serve us."

"How many months can you stay in Wyoming?"

"How many months?" laughed Jack. "We are under promise to be back at school in New York on the first of November."

"Whew! I wish the time was longer."

"So do we; but we had a hard enough task to get the month, so we must make the best use of it."

"Wal, we can crowd a good 'eal into two or three weeks, and I won't let you go to sleep in the daytime—I'll promise you that."

Hazletine produced a brierwood pipe and pressed some tobacco in the bowl. Although the motion of their ponies caused quite a brisk breeze, he lighted a match and communicated the flame to the tobacco without checking the speed of his animal. Then he glanced admiringly to the right and left, at his companions.

"You're a couple of as fine-looking younkers as I've seed in a long time; but you're almost as tall as me, and it seems to me you orter be through with school."

"We expect to stay in school another year

and then spend four in college, after which several years will be needed to get ready for some profession."

"Great Jiminy!" exclaimed the astonished ranchman; "you must be powerful dumb, or else there's more to larn than I ever dreamed of."

"Well," said Jack, with a laugh at the simplicity of the fellow, "there are plenty of boys a great deal smarter then we, but the smartest of them can spend their whole lives in study and not learn a hundredth part of what is to be learned."

Hank puffed his pipe slowly and looked seriously at the youth for a minute without speaking. Then he said, as if partly speaking to himself:

"I s'pose that's so; a chap can go on larning forever, and then die without knowing half of it. I never had much chance at eddycation, but managed to pick up 'nough to read and write a letter and to do a little figgering, but that's all."

"That is what you may call your book education; but how much more you know of the rivers, the mountains, the climate, the soil, the game, the Indians, and everything relating to the western half of our country! In that respect we are but as babes compared with you."

"I s'pose that's so, too," replied the hunter, evidently impressed by the fact that these youths were destined, if their lives were spared, to become excellent scholars. He was so thoughtful that they did not interrupt his meditations, and for a considerable while the three rode in silence.

It need not be said that Jack and Fred kept their wits about them and took note of everything in their field of vision. The season had been an unusually favorable one for Wyoming, the rains having been all that was required to make the grass succulent, nourishing and abundant. They could have turned their ponies loose at any point, after leaving the railway behind them, and the animals would have been able to crop their fill. It was the same over hundreds of square miles, a fact which readily explains why many portions of Wyoming rank as the best grazing country in the world.

It was not yet noon when they rode down a slight declivity to a stream several rods in width. The water was so clear that the bottom could be plainly seen from their saddles, the depth being no more than two or three feet. The ponies paused to drink, and, as they emerged on the other side and started up the gentle slope, Hazletine suggested that for a time at least they should be held down to a walk.

One anxiety began to impress itself upon the minds of Jack and Fred. They were not only hungrier than they had been for months, but that hunger was increasing at an alarming rate. Neither had brought any lunch with them, and they wondered how food was to be obtained. Jack almost fainted at the awful suspicion that perhaps their friend intended to break them in by making the two or three days' journey to the ranch without eating anything at all!

"I suppose it would be no trouble for *him*," was the lugubrious thought of the youth, "but it will be the death of us!"

Happily this dread proved unfounded.

The sun had hardly crossed the meridian
when both lads were thrilled by the declaration of Hazletine:

"Wal, if you younkers are as hungry as
me, we'll have a bite."

They were in the middle of the undulating
plain, with no wood or water in sight; but
that was a small matter. In a twinkling all
three were out of their saddles, and the guide
unstrapped a large bundle from its fastening
to the saddle of his pony. This, being un-
wrapped, disclosed a goodly portion of cooked
and tender steak and plenty of well-baked
brown bread. Furthermore, there were a
couple of bottles of milk—enough for two
meals at least.

These having been placed on the grass, the
bits were removed from the mouths of their
horses, who were allowed to graze while their
masters were partaking of one of the most enjoyable meals they had ever eaten.

"If I'd expected to be alone," explained
Hazletine, "I wouldn't have brought this
stuff with me, but we may not see a maverick
or any game all the way home. I wouldn't

mind it, but I don't s'pose you are used to it."

"I should say not," replied Jack, as well as he could, while his mouth was filled with bread, meat and milk; "I'm hungry enough to eat a mule."

"And I feel as if I could chew his saddle," added Fred, laboring under the same difficulty in speaking clearly. "If our appetites keep up at this rate, there will be a shrinkage among the cattle in Wyoming before we go home."

"What do you mean by a maverick?" asked Jack of their guide.

"It's an unbranded cow or calf that don't b'long to nobody, and consequently it don't make no difference whether nobody or somebody brands or kills it."

The rhetoric of this sentence may not have been faultless, but its meaning was clear to the boys. They ate until they wished no more, and were vastly relieved to note that something was left for another meal.

"That'll see us through till morning," said Jack, "but how about to-morrow and the next day?"

"If we don't see anything to kill, we must wait till we git to the ranch."

Fred groaned.

"You'll have to tie me in the saddle, for I shan't be able to sit up."

The smile on the face of the guide raised the hope that he was not in earnest in making this dreadful announcement, but neither Jack nor Fred were quite easy in mind.

The halt was less than an hour, when the three were in the saddle again. Hazletine, instead of pressing directly toward the ranch that was their destination, bore to the left, thus approaching the Wind River range.

"There's a little settlement off to the right," he said, "of the name of Sweetwater; we could reach it by night, but it takes us a good many miles out of our path, and there's nothing to be gained by losing the time."

"Are you following a straight course to the ranch?"

"Pretty near; but I'm edging to the left, toward the foot-hills, 'cause there's better camping-ground over there."

This was satisfactory, and the youths were

not the ones to question a decision of so experienced a guide and mountaineer. Besides, they had hope that one reason for the slight change of course was that it increased the chance of obtaining game. For the present, the question of food supply was the most absorbing one that demanded attention. Other matters could wait, but a sturdy, growing lad finds his appetite something whose cravings can be soothed only by the one method that nature intended.

CHAPTER III.

ON GUARD.

THE beautiful weather continued unchanged throughout the afternoon. As the sun declined in the sky there was a perceptible coolness in the air, but the exercise of riding removed all necessity for using their blankets.

Although the party had been edging toward the foot-hills for hours, it seemed to the boys that they were as far off as ever. They had covered many miles, but those who have travelled in the West know the deceptive character of the crystalline atmosphere, so far as distances are concerned. However, as twilight began closing in they reached a small grove of trees, which was the destination of the guide from the first. It was there he meant to camp for the night, and he could not have selected a better place had he spent a week in looking for it.

The grove covered less than an acre, the trees standing well apart, and wholly free from brush and undergrowth. Thus even the horses could pass back and forth freely. Over this shaded space the dark-green grass grew luxuriantly, with a soft juiciness of texture which made it the ideal food for cattle and horses. In the middle of the grove bubbled a spring of clear cold water, whose winding course could be traced far out on the plain by the fringe of deeper green which accompanied it.

Saddles and bridles were removed, and the ponies turned free to crop the grass until they were filled, when they would lie down for the night. The blankets were spread on the ground near the spring, and then, at the suggestion of Hazletine, all three joined in gathering dried branches and limbs with which to start a fire. It was now cool enough to make the warmth welcome, while the flame would add to the cheerfulness of the occasion.

Jack and Fred had never ridden so far at one stretch, and when they reclined on their blankets to watch Hank start the fire they were thoroughly tired out; but it seemed to them their hunger was more ravenous than ever. Each forbore to speak of it, but the deliberation of their friend in preparing the meal was almost intolerable.

The first night spent by the boys in camping out in the wilds of Wyoming was one that can never be forgotten. When the meal was finished and the last vestige of food eaten, the three stretched out where they could feel the grateful warmth of the fire that had been kindled against the trunk of a large oak. Hank had again lighted his pipe, and deeply interested Jack and Fred by his reminiscences of a life that had been filled to overflowing with strange experience and adventure. They listened, unconscious of the passage of the hours, until he abruptly asked:

" What time is it?"

Each youth looked at his watch, and, to his astonishment, saw that it was nearly half-past ten. They had supposed that it was fully two hours earlier.

" One of the rules that must always be follered," said the guide, " when hunting or away

from home, is that all the party mustn't sleep
at the same time."

"Then one has to stand watch?"

"It looks that way. Now, we'll divide the
time atween us, each taking a part, so that it
won't come heavy on any one."

"That will suit us," Fred hastened to say,
while Jack nodded his head.

"All right. You, Jack, will keep watch
till twelve—that is midnight; then you'll
rouse t'other younker, and he'll stand guard
till two; then he'll give me a kick, and I'll
run things till daylight."

"What are we likely to see?" asked Jack,
who naturally desired to learn all the points
concerning his new duties.

"How should I know?" asked Hank, with
a grin. "There may be wild animals, sich as
grizzlies, cinnamon or black bears; there
may be wolves, or dog Injins looking for a
chance to steal our ponies."

"Why do you call them 'dog Indians?'"

"A dog Injin is a tramp 'mong the other
tribes; he don't live much with any of 'em,
but sneaks round the country, looking for a

chance to steal something, and it don't matter what it is."

"Suppose I catch sight of one of the animals you name, or a dog Indian—what shall I do?"

"Shoot him quicker'n lightning."

This was a startling order, but the guide was in earnest.

"Are you afeard to do it?" he asked, half contemptuously.

"No; I'll shoot the instant it is necessary, but I don't fancy the idea of picking off an Indian without warning."

"If you give him warning you won't pick him off. If you're so squeamish, you might argufy the matter with him."

"Leave that to me; I'm on duty now; go to sleep."

Without another word the guide wrapped his blanket about him and stretched out in front of the fire, with his feet toward it. Judging from his heavy breathing, it was barely five minutes before he became unconscious.

"It strikes me this is rushing things," remarked Jack to Fred, as the two sat beside each other. "Last night the 'V. W. W.' were in the sleeper of the Union Pacific; to-night they are looking out for a chance to shoot Indians."

"I don't believe there's any likelihood of finding it. I suspect that Hank is having some sport at our expense. If there was any danger he would stay awake himself, instead of trusting two tenderfeet like us."

"It may be, but we are in a wild country, where danger is likely to come at any time, and we may have our hands full. It seems to me that it would have been better to let the fire go out, and not attract attention."

"He's running this affair; he wouldn't have had so much wood gathered if he didn't mean to keep the blaze going."

With this Fred rose to his feet and flung an armful of wood on the flames, which brightened up until their reflection was thrown against the branches overhead and well out toward the edge of the grove. A faint whinny proved that the horses had been disturbed by the increase in the illumination.

4

Before lying down, Fred looked at his chum.

"I wonder, Jack, whether there's any risk of your falling asleep?"

"There would be if I remained seated on the ground, but I shall not do that."

"It will be dangerous to walk back and forth, where the fire shows you plainly."

"My plan is to move out in the grove, where the firelight will not strike me, and stand close to the trunk of one of the trees. I have heard of folks sleeping on their feet, but there's no fear of my doing it. Since I am to call you in less than two hours, Fred, you would better get sleep while you can."

The younger lad bade his friend good-night and imitated the action of Hank Hazletine, wrapping his blanket around himself and lying down near the fire. He was not quite so prompt in sinking into slumber, but it was not long before Jack Dudley was the only one of the little party in command of his senses.

Jack, like his companions, felt the need of sleep, but the fact that he had but a brief

while to remain awake, and the consciousness
that the safety of others, as well as his own,
rested upon himself, made him very alert.
He believed he could sit or recline on the
ground and retain his wits, but, fortunately,
he had too much prudence to run that risk.
Sleep is so insidious a foe that we can never
recall the moment when it overmasters us, nor
can we fight it off when in a prone or easy
posture.

He adhered to the plan he had formed.
Winchester in hand, he moved away from the
fire until, by interposing the large trunk of a
tree between himself and the light, he was
invisible from that direction. He stood erect,
taking care not to lean against the trunk for
partial support, and concentrated his faculties
into those of listening and looking.

The stillness was profound. From the distant mountains to the westward came a low,
soft, almost inaudible murmur, such as one
hears when many miles from the calm ocean,
and which has been called the voice of silence
itself. In the stillness he heard the faint
crackle of one of the embers as it fell apart,

and, though the night wind scarcely stirred
the leaves over his head, he caught the rustle.
The fact that there was nothing from the direction of the ponies showed they had ceased
to crop the grass and were lying down.   The
safety of the camp was in his hands.   If he
forgot his duty, it might be fatal to all.

The sense of this responsibility and the
newness of his position made Jack Dudley
more wakeful than he could have been under
any other circumstances.   To these causes,
also, was due a suspicious nervousness which
made him see danger where it did not exist.
The rustling of a falling leaf caused him to
start and glance furtively to one side, and at
a soft stir of the leaves under a breath of
wind, or a slight movement of the sleeping
ponies, he started and grasped his rifle with
closer grip.

All this was natural; but there came a moment, not far from midnight, when there remained no doubt that some person or animal
was moving stealthily through the grove, near
where he was standing.   It will be remembered that his position was such that the

trunk of the large oak acted as an impenetrable screen between him and the camp-fire, which was burning so vigorously that its rays penetrated to a greater or less degree beyond him. Thus he could see anything moving within the circle of illumination, while he was as invisible to the keenest-eyed warrior as if the night was without a ray of light.

The first warning was through the sense of hearing. He had been deceived so many times that he suspected his fancy was playing with him again, but the faint *tip, tip* continued until such explanation was amiss.

"It is an Indian or a wild beast," was his belief.

The next minute he knew that, whatever it was, its position was between him and the outer edge of the grove. Since the ponies were on the opposite side of the fire, Jack was nearer the intruder than either they or his friends, sleeping by the camp-fire. Recalling that his place was the most favorable possible, he remained as motionless as the tree-trunk behind him, and to which he stood close enough to touch by moving his foot a few inches backward.

The situation being thus, it followed that if the man or beast continued its advance it must come into sight, while Jack himself was invisible. He therefore held his Winchester ready for instant use and waited.

He was standing in this expectant attitude when a remarkable thing took place. The fire, having remained unreplenished for some time, had subsided to a considerable extent, when one of the embers fell apart and caused such a displacement of the burning wood that the light flared up and penetrated with its former vigor beyond the tree which sheltered the sentinel.

Jack was as immovable as a statue, his weapon grasped in both hands, when this sudden brightening occurred. He was peering out among the dark trees, in the effort to identify the danger, when he saw the unmistakable figure of an Indian, hardly twenty feet away.

The buck had entered the grove with the silence of a shadow, and was making his way to the camp-fire, when betrayed in this singular manner to the watcher. In the reflection of the firelight, his naturally hideous countenance was repulsive to the last degree. The features were irregular, with prominent cheek-bones, a huge nose, and a retreating chin. Ugly as nature had made him, he had intensified it himself by daubing black, red and white paint in splashes over the front of his countenance. His coarse, black hair dangled loosely about his shoulders, and a single stained eagle's feather protruded from the crown. It was gathered back of the neck by a thong of some sort, so as to prevent the hair getting in his eyes when there was such imminent need for their use.

The chest was bare to the waist, and was also fantastically painted. In the girdle which encircled his waist was thrust a knife, whose handle protruded, while the leggings and moccasins were gayly ornamented and fringed. He held a formidable rifle in his right hand, in a trailing position, and was leaning well forward, with his body bent, as he drew near the camp with that stoical patience which the American race shows in the most trying crises. If necessary, he would continue this cautious advance for hours without showing haste, for it is often that his people circumvent and overthrow an enemy by their incomparable caution and care.

One peculiar feature of the unexpected flaring-up of the light was that its strongest force impinged directly upon the painted face of the Indian, which was seen as plainly by Jack Dudley as if the sun were shining. The youth felt that he could not forget that countenance if he saw it a hundred years afterward.

Had Jack followed the instruction of their guide he would have leveled his Winchester and shot the Indian dead in his tracks. The fellow was stealing into camp in such a manner that there could be no doubt the least crime he meant to commit was to steal. No ranchman or hunter would hesitate a moment, under the circumstances, to give him his eternal quietus.

But Jack Dudley could not do such a thing. To him it was an awful act to shoot a person, even though a savage, and his conscience would never permit him to do so until there was no choice left to him. He would much prefer to frighten away this intruder than to kill him.

The youth was so confident of his command of the situation that he would have felt hardly a thrill of alarm, but for the fear that the redskin belonged to a party near at hand who had sent him forward as a scout. Manifestly the right course for the sentinel was to discharge his gun, thus scaring the Indian and awaking Hazletine; but, while debating the question with himself, he became aware that the hostile was advancing.

The fellow did this with such marvellous cunning that Jack perceived no movement of his legs or feet. The latter were partly shrouded in shadow, but the Indian himself suggested a statue set up among the trees. Nevertheless he was inching toward the camp-fire, and was already a couple of yards nearer Jack than when the latter first noticed him.

Had he approached from the other side the youth never would have discovered his danger; but now he had his eye on the enemy, and meant to keep it there until the crisis was over. It was perhaps ten minutes later that the buck was within six feet of the youth, who, noiselessly bringing his Winchester to a level, took one step toward him and asked :

"*Well, my friend, what do you want?*"

CHAPTER IV.

VISITORS OF THE NIGHT.

IT takes a good deal to startle an American Indian, but if there ever was a frightened red man it was the one who heard himself thus addressed, and, glancing like a flash to his right, saw Jack Dudley step forward, with a Winchester rifle leveled at him.

In the language of the West, the youth " had the drop" on the intruder, and he knew it. Had he attempted to raise his own weapon, or to draw his knife and assail the youth, that instant the trigger of the rifle would have been pressed and the career of the buck would have ended then and there, and he knew that, too ; but the fact that the gun was not fired, and that a direct question was addressed to him, told the Indian that his master was less merciless than he would have been had their situations been reversed.

The camp-fire was still burning brightly, and the reflection showed on the painted visage. Jack, having stepped forward into the circle of light, was also plainly discerned by the Indian, who, turning his black, serpent-like eyes upon him, said, without a tremor in his voice:

"Me good Injin; me friend of white man; me no hurt him."

"It doesn't look as if you would; but what is your business? Why do you steal into our camp like a thief of the night?"

"Me hungry—want somethin' eat."

This was too transparent a subterfuge to deceive one even so unaccustomed to life in these solitudes as Jack Dudley. An Indian wandering through a country so well stocked with game as this portion of the new State of Wyoming never suffers for food; and, were such a thing possible, the present means was the last that he would adopt to procure it.

"If you want something to eat, why did you not come forward openly and ask for it?"

The fellow did not seem fully to grasp the question, but he repeated:

" Me hungry."

Jack recalled that there was not a mouthful of food in camp. Had there been, he probably would have invited the visitor to walk to the fire and partake. It was fortunate for the youth that their larder was empty, for had the two started among the trees in the direction of the camp, the opportunity for which the Indian was doubtless waiting would have been secured. There would have been an interval in the brief walk when the advantage would have been shifted to him, and he would have seized it with the quickness of lightning.

The manifest duty of Jack was to shout to Hank Hazletine and bring him to the spot. He would read the truth on the instant and do the right thing; but the situation, as the reader will admit, was peculiar, and the motive which prevented the youth from adopting this line of action was creditable to him. He believed that the moment the guide appeared he would shoot the intruder, and that was too frightful an issue for Jack to contemplate. He did not want this warrior's life,

and would not take it except to save his own
or that of his friends.

Jack believed that enough had been gained
in thoroughly frightening the Indian, and the
thing desired now was to get rid of him with
the least possible delay. He did not think
he would intrude again, even if he had companions within call.

"We have no food; we can give you
nothing; you must go elsewhere."

"Then me go;" and, as if the business was
concluded, the buck turned about and began
walking toward the edge of the grove. Yielding to a whim which he did not fully understand, Jack Dudley followed him with the
warning words:

"If you stop, or turn about, or make a
move to shoot, I will kill you."

It is probable that the savage contemplated
some movement of the kind, but he must
have known the fatal risk involved. Quick
as he was, he could not whirl about and
bring his gun to a level before the young
man would pull the trigger of the Winchester, which was held pointed toward him. He

knew that so long as he obeyed orders he would be unharmed, and he would have been a zany had he hesitated to do so.

He did not hesitate, but with a deliberate step that was not lacking in a certain dignity he walked slowly between the trees, with his captor only a few paces behind and keeping pace with him.

Almost on the edge of the grove Jack Dudley made an interesting discovery. A pony, smaller than the one he had ridden from Fort Steele, stood motionless in the shadow, awaiting the return of his master. He was not tethered or tied, for he was too well-trained to make that necessary. He showed his fine training further by merely pricking his ears and elevating his head upon the approach of his master and companion. A whinny or neigh might have betrayed both.

The two were now so far removed from the glow of the camp-fire that they could see each other only dimly. There was no moon in the sky, though the stars were shining brightly. The Indian, from the force of circumstances, was compelled to hold his disadvantageous position, inasmuch as he had to move out from among the trees, while Jack remained within their shadows.

Realizing that this was a critical moment, he stood motionless, with his weapon still at a dead level.

"My gun is aimed at your heart," he said, "and I am watching every movement you make. Go in peace, and you shall not be harmed, but on your first attempt to injure me you die."

The words, perhaps, were unnecessary, for it may be said that the action of the youth was more eloquent. Be that as it may, the redskin showed a commendable promptness in all that he did. He vaulted lightly upon the bare back of his pony, whose bridle consisted of but a single thong, and turned the head of the brute outward. He did not speak, for it was not required. The pony knew what was wanted; and, with his nose pointed out on the prairie, he emerged from among the trees into the open, with the warrior astride.

Even in that trying moment Jack Dudley was surprised at one fact—that was the wonderful silence of the animal. It would seem that his hoofs should have given out sounds that could have been heard for a considerable distance in the stillness of the night, but it was as if he were treading on velvet. The noise was so faint that it was easy to understand how he had come to the spot without betraying himself to the intently listening sentinel. No wonder that the Indian ponies sometimes display a sagacity fully equal, in some respects, to that of their masters.

The Indian showed in another direction his perception of the situation. Had he been leaving the presence of one of his own race, or of a veteran white scout, he would have thrown himself forward on the back of his animal and ridden off on a dead run, for, despite the unexpected mercy shown him, he would have expected treachery at the last minute; but he had seen his master and knew that he was a young tenderfoot, inspired by a chivalrous honor which is the exception in that section of the country. He would not

5

shoot until good cause was given, and therefore he took care not to give such cause.

As if in harmony with the spirit of his rider, the pony walked away in a direct line, until the figure of himself and master disappeared in the gloom. When he could see him no more, Jack lowered his gun, and stooping down, pressed his ear against the earth. He could hear the soft hoof-beats of the horse growing fainter and fainter, until at the end of a minute or two the impressive silence once more held reign. Then the youth arose to his feet.

"I suppose Hank will tell me I did wrong," he mused, "but my conscience does not; it would be a woeful memory to carry with me that on my first night in Wyoming I took the life of a human being. Perhaps it will be as well that Hank should not know it; I will think it over."

Now, while Jack Dudley had conducted himself in some respects like a veteran, yet he had shown a dangerous short-sightedness in another direction. It will be noted that he had busied himself wholly with the single intruder, and at the moment of losing sight of him the young man was a comparatively long distance from the camp-fire. Had it been that there were two or more hostiles stealing into camp, they could not have asked a better opportunity, for it was left wholly unguarded. A single warrior would have had no trouble in creeping undiscovered to a point from which he could have sent a bullet through the unconscious forms of Hank Hazletine and Fred Greenwood. This probability never occurred to Jack until he started on his return to the fire, from whose immediate vicinity he should never have allowed himself to have been tempted.

Even then his strange remissness would not have impressed itself upon him but for a startling discovery. The fire was beginning to smoulder once more, but enough of its glare penetrated the wood for him to note the black, column-like trunks of the trees between it and him. With his gaze upon the central point, he saw a figure moving in the path of light and coming toward him. It looked as if stamped in ink against the yellow background, and, like the former intruder, was advancing without noise.

An awful fear thrilled Jack Dudley as he abruptly halted and partly raised his Winchester.

"While I have been busy with one Indian, another has entered the camp and slain Fred and Hank! He is now after me! There will be no hesitation *this* time in my shooting!"

Before he could secure anything like an aim, the other stepped behind one of the trunks on his right. Jack waited for him to reappear, ready to fire, but unwilling to do so until the truth was established.

While waiting thus, a low, faint, tremulous whistle reached his ears. It was the most welcome of all sounds, and raised him from the depths of woe to blissful happiness, for it was the familiar signal of Fred Greenwood that had been employed many times in their hunting excursions nearer home.

Instead of an enemy, it was his chum and dearest friend who was approaching him. Jack instantly answered the guarded hail, and the next minute the two came together.

" How is it you are awake?" was the first question of Jack.

" Because it is *time* for me to awake; it was agreed that I should go on duty at a little after twelve, and it must be near one o'clock."

" But what awoke you?"

" Nonsense! Haven't you and I travelled together long enough to know that when you go to sleep with your mind fixed on a certain time to awake you are sure not to miss it by more than a few minutes?"

" You are right; I had forgotten that. How was it you knew where to look for me?"

" I didn't. I've been prowling around camp for fifteen minutes, groping here and there and signaling to you, without the first inkling of where you were. I didn't want to awake Hank, and therefore was as careful as I could be. I began to suspect you had sat down somewhere and fallen asleep."

" I have had enough to keep the most drowsy person awake."

And thereupon Jack gave the particulars of all that had occurred while he was acting as sentinel. It need not be said that Fred

Greenwood was astonished, for the manner of their guide before lying down convinced them that no danger of any nature threatened them.

"Do you think I acted right, Fred?"

"Most certainly you did. Hank and the like of him out in this country talk about shooting down an Indian as if he were not a human being, but they have souls like the rest of us, and we have no more right to take the life of one of them than I have to take yours. I am sure I should have done just as you did."

"I am glad to hear you say that. I wonder whether, if we stayed out here a few years, our feelings would change?"

"No; for the principle of right and wrong cannot change. Do you remember what that old settler told us on the train, a couple of days ago?"

"I do not recall it."

"He said that at a little town in Montana they had a great moral question under debate for a long time without being able to decide it. It was whether it was wicked for the men to go out hunting for Indians on Sunday. It was all right on week days, but most of the folks seemed to think it was a violation of the sanctity of the day to indulge in the sport on the Sabbath. But, Jack, you are tired and in need of sleep. I'll take charge of matters until two o'clock."

"I wonder whether anything will happen to you? It does not seem likely, for I must have given that fellow such a scare that he will not show himself again."

"But you mustn't reason on the basis that he is the only red man in Wyoming. However, I shall do my best. Good-night."

Thus summarily dismissed, Jack returned to the camp-fire in quest of the slumber which he needed. Fred had thrown additional wood on the blaze, and that accounted for the increase in illumination. Hank Hazletine did not seem to have stirred since lying down. He breathed heavily, and doubtless was gaining the rest which men of his habits and training know how to acquire under the most unfavorable circumstances. The youth wrapped his blanket about his figure, for he was now sensible that the air was colder

than at any time since leaving the railway
station. He was nervous over the recollection
of his experience, though it would have been
deemed of slight importance to one who had
spent his life in the West. The feeling soon
passed off, however, and he joined the veteran
in the land of dreams.

And thus the burden of responsibility was
shifted to the shoulders of Fred Greenwood,
the junior by a few months of Jack Dudley.
No one could have been more deeply impressed with his responsibility than Fred. He
knew that a hostile red man had entered the
grove while two of the party were asleep, and,
but for the watchfulness of the sentinel, might
have slain all three.

"I don't know much about Indians," reflected Fred, "but I have been told that they
are a revengeful people. That fellow must
be angered because he was outwitted by Jack,
and it will be just like him to steal back for
the purpose of revenge. It won't do for me
to wink both eyes at the same time."

This was a wise resolution, and the youth
took every precaution against committing

what was likely to be a fatal mistake. Although his sleep was broken, and he could have consumed several hours additional with enjoyment, he was never more wide-awake. The temptation was strong to sit down on the ground with his back against a tree, but he foresaw the consequences. The man who yields only for a few minutes to the creeping drowsiness is gone.

Fred was more circumspect, even, than his chum. Instead of taking his position beside the trunk of one of the trees, he walked silently around in a circle, keeping the camp-fire as a centre. By this means he not only kept his senses keyed to a high point, but made his espionage nearer perfect than his friend had done.

That the night was not to pass without a stirring experience to the younger lad was soon evident. As nearly as he could guess, without consulting his watch, it was about one o'clock, when he became aware that some person or animal was astir in the grove. He heard the faint footfalls on the ground, though for a time he was unable to catch so much as a shadowy glimpse of the intruder.

"I believe it is that Indian, who has come back to square accounts with Jack for getting the better of him. The wisest thing for me to do is to not allow him to see me."

This was wise; and, to prevent such a disaster, Fred adopted the precise tactics that had been used by his friend. He stationed himself beside a friendly trunk, which so interposed between himself and the fire that he was invisible, no matter from what direction approached. Standing thus, he peered into the surrounding gloom and listened with all the intensity of which he was capable.

Suddenly he caught a glimpse of the intruder. The relief was unspeakable when he saw that it was not an Indian, but some kind of a wild animal. It was but a short distance off, and between him and the outer edge of the grove.

There being no one to replenish the fire, the light had grown dimmer, but a quick, shadowy flitting told Fred the brute was moving briskly about, only a few paces from where the lad was straining his vision to learn its nature.

"We might as well wind up this business," reflected Fred, as, with his hand on the trigger of his Winchester, he started abruptly in the direction of the stranger. The latter was quick to perceive him and whisked away. The lad followed, breaking into a trot despite the intervening trees. The beast continued fleeing, for nothing so disconcerts an animal as the threatening approach of a foe.

It was but a few paces to the edge of the timber, when the brute leaped out into full view in the star-gleam.

One glance was sufficient for the youth to recognize it as an immense wolf, which had probably been drawn to the spot by the odor of the meat that composed the dinner of the party. Fifty feet off the wolf stopped, turned partly about, and looked back at his pursuer, as if to learn whether he intended to follow him farther.

Fred did not, but the opportunity was too good to be lost. The aim was inviting, and, bringing his rifle to his shoulder, he sighted as best he could and pulled the trigger. He could not have done better had the sun been shining. The bullet passed directly through the skull of the wolf, which uttered a sharp yelp, leaped several feet into the air, and, doubling up like a jack-knife, fell upon his side, where, after several convulsive struggles, he lay still.

Naturally enough, the boy was elated over his success, for the shot was certainly an excellent one.

"There!" he said. "Jack frightened off the Indians, and I think I have given the wild animals a good lesson. At any rate, *you* won't bother us any more."

He supposed that the report of the gun would awaken Hazletine and bring him to the spot to learn the explanation, but nothing of that nature followed. If the report disturbed him, he merely opened and closed his eyes, and continued to slumber, after the manner of one who appreciates the value of rest.

In truth, it was always a matter of wonderment to the boys that their veteran guide adopted the course he followed that night. That actual danger impended was proven by the incidents already narrated, and yet he entrusted the safety of one of the boys, as well as his own life, to another, who, until then, had never been in a similar position. Why he did so would be hard to explain, but he never admitted that his course was a mistake. Sometimes, as is well known, a boy is taught to swim by flinging him into deep water, where he must choose between keeping afloat and drowning; and it may be the guide believed that, by tossing his young friends into the midst of danger at the very beginning of their experience as Western hunters, they would acquire the needed skill the more quickly.

CHAPTER V.

"NOW FOR THE RANCH."

ONE of the singular features connected with the experience of our young friends during the first night they spent in Wyoming was that all the danger which threatened them came from one Indian and from one *lupus*. After Jack Dudley had expelled the prowling buck, the intruder took good care to remain away. Neither he nor any of his companions troubled the campers further. The presumption, therefore, was that this solitary specimen was a "dog Indian," or vagrant, wandering over the country on his own account. Such fellows, as already explained, claim no kinship with any tribe, but are, like the tramps of civilized society, agents for themselves alone.

Had the season been winter, with the snow deep on the ground, the trouble from the wolves would have been more serious. Those gaunt creatures, when goaded by hunger, become exceedingly daring, and do not hesitate to attack even armed bodies of men ; but it was autumn time, when the ravenous brutes, who seem always to be hungry, find the least difficulty in procuring food, and they remained true to their cowardly disposition and refrained from everything in the nature of true courage.

The curious fact, as we have remarked, was that, as in the case of the Indian, only a single wolf intruded upon the little company. The animals generally travel in droves, and when one is seen it is quite safe to count upon a dozen, or a score, or even more. It is possible that the victim of Fred Greenwood's Winchester was also a sort of tramp, prospecting for his own benefit. It is more likely, however, that he was what might be considered a scout or advance agent of others. His pack was probably waiting among the foot-hills for him to return with his report. If so, the report is now considerably overdue.

Fred was a model sentinel for the remaining hours that he continued on duty. He continued circling about the camp-fire, silent, stealthy, peering here and there, and listening for the first evidence of danger. Nothing of the kind was seen or heard, and he finally came back to the smouldering fire and looked at the face of his watch.

Could it be possible? It lacked a few minutes of three o'clock. According to agreement, he should have called Hazletine an hour before.

"I don't suppose he will object," said Fred, aloud; "I'm sure I shouldn't, if allowed to sleep an hour beyond my time——"

"I ain't doing any kicking, am I?"

Looking around, he saw the guide had flung aside his blanket and was sitting erect, with a quizzical expression on his face.

"What made you fire your gun 'bout two hours ago?" he asked.

"Did you hear me?"

"How'd I know if I hadn't heard it?" was the pertinent question.

"A wolf was sneaking among the trees. I followed him out to the edge of the timber and let him have it between the eyes."

" Did you hurt him?"

" Since he flopped over and died, I have reason to believe he *was* hurt."

" Good! That's the style—always to shoot. Never waste your ammunition. You didn't kill any Injins?"

" I saw none at all."

Hank looked at the unconscious figure of Jack Dudley.

" Wonder how it was with him?"

" He did not fire his gun at anything."

Fred did not wish to tell his friend about that alarming visit earlier in the evening. That was Jack's concern.

" But he may have seed something. How-sumever, we can wait till morning. Wal, younker, if you've no 'bjection you can lay down and snooze till morning. I go on duty now."

There was vast comfort in this knowledge. It relieved the youth from the last remnant of anxiety, and he lost no time in abandoning himself to slumber. The man who was now acting as sentinel was a past master at the art, and there need be no misgiving while he was

6

on duty. Thus it came about that neither Jack Dudley nor Fred Greenwood opened his eyes until the sun was shining into the grove.

Each had had a refreshing night, but it cannot be said that their awakening was of the most pleasant nature. The hunger that had been twice satisfied the day before was not to be compared to that which now got hold of them. With the insatiate craving was the knowledge that there was not a scrap of meat, a crumb of bread nor a drop of milk in camp.

"We can fill up on water," remarked Jack, after they had bathed faces and hands and quaffed their fill.

"But what good will that do? We might bubble over, but we should be just as hungry as ever."

"It seems to me that when a fellow is chock-full of anything he oughtn't to feel much hunger."

"I've often thought that, but you can't fool nature that way."

"If it gets any worse we can shoot the ponies and devour them."

" Why both of them?"

" Because it would take a whole one to satisfy me. I don't know how *you* feel, Jack,
but if we are to have appetites like this I
shall go in for buying a drove of cattle and
spending the few weeks we have in these
parts in eating."

The youths looked in each other's face and
laughed. Truly they were ahungered, but
could never quite lose their waggishness.

" I wonder what's become of Hank," suddenly exclaimed Fred, looking beside and
behind them; " the fire is nearly burned out,
and he is nowhere in sight. HALLOO!"

The hail was uttered in a loud voice, and
was responded to, but from a point a considerable distance out upon the prairie, in the
direction of the foot-hills. The open nature
of the wood permitted the boys to see quite
clearly in that direction.

" Yonder he comes," said Jack.

" And, by gracious, he's carrying something on his shoulders. I wonder if it is that
Indian you chatted with last night."

" Better than that. It's *something to eat!*"

Jack Dudley was right. The guide was laden with the carcass of some animal. Its bulk was proof that he possessed an accurate idea of the appetite of these young gentlemen.

"How careless in him to leave us thus alone," remarked Fred, with mock reproof.

"Do you wish he hadn't done so?"

"Don't name it!" exclaimed Fred, with a shudder; "he knew the only way of saving our lives. It wouldn't have done for him to postpone it another hour."

Hank Hazletine was never more welcome than when he entered the grove and let fall from his shoulders the carcass of a half-grown calf, plump, juicy, tender, and in the best of condition.

"I don't s'pose you care much 'bout it, but I feel like having something worth while for breakfast," he remarked, proceeding to prepare the coals, for he had dressed the veal before starting on his return.

"Well," said Fred, with assumed indifference, "I suspect that since you intend to partake of food yourself, we may as well join you for the sake of sociability."

Men like the old hunter are adepts at preparing a meal. The smouldering fire was in good condition for broiling, and when raked apart afforded a bed of live coals, over which generous slices were suspended on green twigs, cut from the nearest trees. It took but a few minutes to prepare the meat. Hank always carried with him a box of mixed pepper and salt, whose contents were sprinkled over the toothsome food, of which the three ate their fill.

"Are there any more of these animals left in the neighborhood?" asked Jack, when their appetites were fully satisfied.

"S'pose you go out on the edge of the timber and larn for yourselves."

The lads followed the suggestion. Looking off in the direction of the Wind River Mountains, it seemed to them that tens of thousands of cattle were browsing among the foot-hills and on the grassy plain, while many more must have been beyond sight. This was one of the choicest regions of Wyoming, so widely celebrated for its grazing facilities.

It was an impressive sight, and the boys,

each of whom was provided with a good spy-glass, surveyed the scene for some minutes in wondering silence. The cattle were several miles distant, and seemed to be brown, undulating hummocks of dirt, kept in constant motion by some force beneath. On the outer fringe they were more scattered, but were constantly moving, as if the pasturage was so excellent that they were continually tempted to give up that which was good for that which looked better.

"Are they left wholly to themselves?" asked Fred, as the youths came back to where the guide was saddling his pony.

"No. There are always two or three men looking after them. I seed Bart Coinjock, one of our own cowboys, 'tending our animals, and he told me to take my ch'ice from the lot. You mustn't forgit that we're purty close to the Wind River Injin Reservation, where the Government has several tribes under charge."

This was news to the boys. Hazletine explained that a large tract of land to the northwest and close to the mountains had been set apart some years before by the United States

Government for exclusive occupancy by several tribes of Indians. They owned the land, and no white man had the right to intrude upon them.

In the Southwest, where the Apaches were placed on reservations, there had been the most frightful trouble, for those Indians are the worst in North America. All our readers know how many times the fierce Geronimo and a few of his hostiles broke away from their reservation, and, riding swiftly through Arizona and New Mexico, spread desolation, woe and death in their path. Not until Geronimo and his worst bucks were run down in old Mexico and transported bodily to the East was the danger to the Southwest terminated.

Nothing of the kind has taken place in Wyoming, Montana, the Dakotas and other reservations further east, but there is always a certain number of malcontents on the reservations who cause trouble. They steal away unnoticed by the authorities, and engage in thieving, and, when the chances are favorable against detection, commit graver crimes.

"That Injin that come into the timber last night was a sort of dog Injin that had come down from the Wind River Reservation to find out what he could steal."

The boys looked at each other in astonishment. They had made no reference to the visitor in the hearing of the guide, and could not understand where he had gained his knowledge. He noticed their surprise, and smiled.

"I seed the tracks of his pony, as well as his own. It was as plain to me as the words of a printed book. Why didn't you shoot the chap?"

Thus appealed to, Jack told the story. Hazletine listened with an expression of amused contempt on his bearded face.

"You'll git over that afore you've been here long. I think I know who he was. Tell me how he looked."

Jack was able to give a good description of his visitor, and before it was finished the guide nodded his head several times.

"It was him, Motoza, one of the worst scamps west of the Mississippi."

" What do you suppose he was after ?"

" He'll steal anything he can lay his hands on. If he'd found us all asleep he'd shot every one of us. That's the kind of a feller Motoza is. You played it well on him, catching him as you did, but you'd played it a hanged sight better if you'd put a bullet through him afore you asked any questions."

" What tribe does he belong to ?"

" That's a queer part of it. Gin'rally it's easy to tell from the dress, paint and style of an Injin what his tribe or totem is, but there's nothing of the kind 'bout Motoza to guide you. I think he's a Sioux."

" I understood those red men live further to the eastward."

" So they do ; but Motoza has wandered from his people. He was under Sitting Bull, and went with him into British America when it got too hot on this side of the line ; but Sitting Bull come back, and Motoza follered. He tries to make b'leve he's a good Injin, and sometimes he is for months at a time on the reservation. Then the devil gits into him, and he's off somewhere."

While this conversation was going on the three had mounted their ponies and were galloping northward, this time trending to the right, so as to draw away from the mountains and follow an almost direct line to Bowman's ranch, their destination. The animals were so fresh and spirited that Hazletine said he was hopeful of sleeping that night in the ranch itself, as he called the low, flat building where he and several cowmen made their home when in that part of the country attending to their duties.

It would take hard riding, and would lead them into the night to accomplish the long journey, but the guide saw no reason why it should not be done. If a storm came up— and they break with amazing suddenness at times in that part of the world—or if any mishap befell their ponies, a stop would have to be made for the night before reaching the ranch.

Jack Dudley decided to ask a question that had been in his mind for some time.

"Hank, that Indian last night was in my power, and he knew it as well as I, but I

spared his life and allowed him to ride away
without a hair of his head harmed. Now,
don't you think he will feel some gratitude
for that?"

Hazletime threw back his head with uproarious laughter. He seemed to have heard
the best joke of a twelvemonth.

"What give you that idee?" he asked,
when he succeeded in mastering his exuberant
mirth.

"Why, the event itself. I know that an
Indian is revengeful by nature, but I have
always believed that he was capable of gratitude for kindness."

"You've read that in story-books, but you
never seed it in life. I won't be quite as
rough as that," added the guide, in the same
breath; "I have seen a redskin that didn't
furgit that a man had saved him from dying
or being shot, but such redskins are as scarce
as hen's teeth. The rule is that they take all
such kindnesses as signs of cowardice, and
despise the one that shows 'em. Let me tell
you something that I know," continued Hazletine, seriously. "Three years ago, when I

was down in Arizona, Jim Huber was the owner of the ranch where I was working. He b'leved in treating Injins kindly. I've seen him give the 'Paches water to drink when they was thirsty, meat to eat, 'bacca to smoke, and even powder and ball for their guns. He kept that up right along, and when he was warned agin it, he said an Injin was human like the rest of us, and he was willing to take his chances. The 'Paches wouldn't furgit what he'd done fur 'em.

"Wal, they didn't. The fust thing we knowed, Geronimo and a dozen of his devils was off their reservation and coming down through them parts like a Kansas cyclone. It happened that me and the boys was several miles off when we heerd the news, and knowing that Huber was alone at the ranch, we rid like all mad fur the place. We got there too late to save him. The ranch was on fire, and he was mangled so we hardly knowed him. But he had died game, and killed two of the 'Paches afore he went under. The three laid aside one another, and the two Injins was the very ones that had set at his table, eat of his food, been given powder and ball, and been treated like brothers."

" Are all red men as bad as that ?"

" I've just said they wasn't. There's lots of 'em that would make an ordinary white man ashamed of himself. But most of 'em are alike. What I'm driving at is to knock out of your head any idee that this Motoza that you let up on last night thinks any more of you for it. It's t'other way. He despises you fur a coward, and if he ever gits the chance he'll prove what I say is true."

This was depressing information for the youths, but they did not think it seeming to express any doubts of the sentiments of one who was so much better informed than they. They hoped that their own experience would be of a different nature.

Having set out with the intention of reaching the ranch that evening, the guide had made the necessary preparations. He rolled up enough cooked pieces of veal to avert the need of starting another fire and looking for more food. So it came about that when the boys began to consult their watches and hint

of it being near meal time, he drew rein at
another stream of water, where the ponies
were allowed to rest and graze while their
masters refreshed themselves. The animals
had been pressed as much as was prudent;
and Hazletine, looking at the sky and their
surroundings, said they were making better
progress than he had counted upon.

The weather remained all that could be
desired, though he assured them that a heavy
rain-storm was impending, and would break
within twenty-four hours—an additional in-
centive for pushing forward.

They were hardly ever out of sight of cattle.
Sometimes they were few in numbers, and
then they suggested the droves of buffaloes,
which, before the animals were extirpated,
numbered hundreds of thousands. Once the
horsemen approached so close that the cattle
were frightened and a partial stampede followed. That Hazletine was among acquaintances was proved by the hails which he received from cowmen, most of whom were so
distant that the wonder was how they recognized one another. The boys studied them

through their spy-glasses, but, of course, all were strangers to them.

When the afternoon was about half gone they came upon a stream that looked formidable. It was a hundred yards in width, with a roiled and rapid current, which, so far as the eye could determine, might be a score of feet in depth. The prospect of having to swim their ponies across was anything but pleasant, but the boys saw that a well-marked trail led down to the bank where they approached it, showing that it had been crossed and recrossed many times.

"There are places in that stream, which flows into the Platte," said the guide, "where it is a hundred feet deep. It has whirlpools and eddies where the best swimmer couldn't save himself, and even a grizzly bear would drown."

"I hope those places are a good way off," said Jack.

"There's one of 'em right over there to the left."

"How are we going to reach the other side?" asked Fred, in dismay.

"Foller me."

As he spoke the guide spurred his animal into the muddy water, with the boys timidly at his heels and closely watching him.

At no time during the fording did the ponies sink above their knees. It was a surprise and vast relief when they rode out on the other side without having been compelled to draw up their feet during the passage.

"And yet," explained their companion, "if you'd gone three yards to the right or left your critters would have had to swim for their lives, and you'd have had the worst soaking you ever knowed. Now fur the ranch!"

CHAPTER VI.

AT THE RANCH.

THE night was well advanced, and the boys, despite their fine physique, felt the effects of the prolonged ride. They had come a goodly distance since morning, the tough little ponies most of the time maintaining a sweeping canter, which placed many miles behind them. Jack and Fred were stiffened, tired and hungry, for no halt was made for supper, it being the intention of the guide to take that meal at the ranch, which he meant to reach before drawing rein.

In the midst of the monotonous gallop of the animals the youths were startled by the sound of a laugh, which suddenly rang out on the still air. It was brief and hearty, such as a man emits who is highly pleased over something said by a companion. There was no moon in the sky, but the starlight was as bright as on the previous evening. Peering ahead in the gloom, nothing was to be seen that explained the singular sound.

"Did you hear that?" asked Jack of Hazletine.

"I s'pose you mean that laugh? Not being deaf, it would have been cur'us if the same hadn't reached my ears."

"What was the meaning of it?"

"It meant, I s'pose, that somebody was pleased."

The lads had to be satisfied with this indefinite answer, but they did not have to wait long for the explanation. Suddenly, from the obscurity ahead, loomed the outlines of a building. It was long, low, and flat, consisting of a single story, like most of the structures in that section of the country.

At the same moment that it was observed, a tiny point of light shone through the gloom, and some one called to them:

"Is that you, Hank?"

"I reckon," was the reply.

At the same moment a tall man, rising from the stool on which he had been seated, came forward. He was smoking a pipe, and the gleam of the fire in the bowl was what had been noted before he became visible.

"These are the younkers we expected," explained Hazletine, "and, if I ain't mistook, they've brought a purty healthy appetite with 'em."

"I've heard of such things afore. Howdy?"

The man, who was known as "Kansas Jim," his full name being James Denham, extended his hand to each boy in turn, and they dismounted.

"I'll look after the animals," he explained. "Go inside, and I reckon Ira can give you some medicine fur that appetite Hank spoke about."

Hazletine led the way to the small covered porch where Ira Garrison, another cattleman, rose to his feet and shook hands with the boys, expressing his pleasure at receiving a visit from them. All three of the arrivals sat down at the front, while Ira passed inside and lighted an oil-lamp. It seemed that he was not absent ten minutes when he called out that the meal was ready—a most welcome announcement to our young friends. The three were quickly seated at the pine table and feasting with keen enjoyment. While they were thus engaged, Ira Garrison sat on a stool a few paces away, smoking his pipe, and was soon joined by Kansas Jim, who brought the saddles and belongings of the ponies that he had turned loose to look after their own wants.

Jack and Fred found their new acquaintances typical cowboys, dressed similarly to Hazletine, though neither wore as much beard as he. Both had long hair, pushed behind their ears, while Jim displayed a luxuriant tawny mustache and goatee, had fine blue eyes, and was thin almost to emaciation. Garrison was short and stockily built, with a powerful physique. His hair, eyes and mustache were as black as coal. He had a fine set of even white teeth, and was so full of jest and humor that it was safe to conclude it was something said by him that had caused Jim to break into laughter.

The structure, as has been said, was a low, flat building, similar to the majority found in that part of the country. It was made wholly of wood, with only a single door at the front, where was a shaded porch, provided with seats, most of which were occupied at times by the cowmen through the day and late into the night.

There were five men employed at the ranch in looking after the immense herd of cattle grazing over the surrounding country and acquiring the plumpness and physical condition which fitted them for the Eastern market. Hank Hazletine was in charge of the four men, and would so remain until the task was finished and the stock disposed of. Barton Coinjock and Morton Blair were absent looking after the animals, whose wanderings in quest of food sometimes took them fifteen or twenty miles from the house. Most of the time, however, the cattle obtained their grazing on the ranch, a half of which belonged to Mr. Dudley, and which extended into the foot-hills of the Wind River Mountains.

It has already been made clear that little was to be apprehended from the hostility of the red men in Wyoming. Rarely is anything of the kind known north of Arizona and New Mexico, and in those Territories it seldom manifests itself since the conquest of the Apaches. There have been fierce collisions of late years between the cowmen and rustlers of the West, and at one time there was considerable bloodshed, but the quarrel seems to have been adjusted.

The reader need hardly be told that in the new States, where grazing has become so important an industry, a perfect system prevails among the cattlemen. Large associations, with their enormous herds of cattle, have their own peculiar brands by which their stock is stamped with their sign of ownership. All these brands are registered, and the cattleman who uses the same, or is found in possession of cattle with the brand of another, is subject to a severe penalty.

Comparatively slight friction, therefore, takes place in those sections. It is a stirring time when the wonderful horsemen are engaged for days in branding the calves that have been added to their herds during the previous months. Sometimes some of the branded cattle wander off while grazing, but if a cattleman from Central Wyoming came upon an animal hundreds of miles north in Montana, bearing his brand, he would promptly cut out the brute from another herd, whose owner would not think of making objection.

It happens now and then that some of the cattle stray off before they are branded. The difficulty of their owners identifying them will be understood. Such cattle are mavericks, and whoever comes upon them loses little time in scorching his brand into their shoulders or hips, after which no one cares to dispute their ownership.

The cowmen whose duty it was to look after the large herd browsing over the thousands of acres composing Bowman's ranch had two annoyances to guard against. It was their duty, as may be said, to keep the animals well in hand. But for this precaution hundreds of them would gradually drift apart until, when the time came for rounding them up, they would be gone beyond recovery. Great loss, therefore, was averted by looking after them.

A more aggravating annoyance, however, brings loss to the owners of the herds. Despite the stringent law, there is always a certain number of desperate men who take perilous chances in stealing cattle and running them off beyond recovery by their owners. This practice is not so prevalent as formerly, for since the brands are registered, and the agents well known at Cheyenne, Helena, and other shipping-points, the thieves find it hard to explain their possession of the carcasses thus marked and escape the arrest and imprisonment provided as a penalty.

One feature of this annoyance comes from the Indians. By far the greater majority of those on the reservations are law-abiding. Under the patient and skilful tutorship of the Government agents they are advancing in civilization, and in a knowledge of the trades and of agriculture. Rarely is there any trouble with them; but it would be strange indeed if, among these people not yet fairly emerged from barbarism, there were not a number sullen because of the change, and who cling to the traditions and practices when the Indian looked upon every white man as his enemy, whom it was his duty to kill upon the first opportunity. The watchfulness of the authorities prevents grave crimes, but no vigilance can keep the dusky thieves from stealthily raiding upon the cattle and property of their white neighbors.

One of the tasks, therefore, of the cowmen of Bowman's ranch was to guard against aboriginal thieves. Since those fellows were sure to have the same trouble as white pilferers in disposing of their stolen stock, they were fond of stampeding the cattle when not under the eyes of their caretakers. About all that resulted from this amusement was extra exasperation and work on the part of the cowmen.

A more serious mischief was that of killing the animals. Having satisfied themselves that they were safe from detection, three or four Indians would entertain themselves for an hour or two in shooting down cattle in pure wantonness, and then making off before they were seen. True, this brought the dusky scamps no gain, but it served as a partial outlet for their enmity of the white man, and that sufficed.

That this peculiar feature of ranch life sometimes assumed grave phases was proved by several narrations made by the cowmen to the boys on their first night at the ranch. Less than a year previous, Kansas Jim shot from his horse an Indian whom he caught killing his cattle; and, not many months previous, the five cowmen, under the leadership of Hank Hazletine, had a running fight for half an afternoon with a dozen Bannocks, engaged in the same sport. At that time Barton Coinjock and Kansas Jim were severely wounded, but three of the marauders were slain, and the mischief nearly ended for a time.

But Jack and Fred were tired, and, though interested in the reminiscences of the cowboys, they longed for rest. The house consisted of four rooms, one being generally reserved for visitors or to serve as a spare apartment. This contained a wooden bedstead and some simple furniture, for luxuries are not popular on cattle-ranches. Surely no bed ever felt more luxurious, however, than the blankets upon which the wearied youths flung themselves, sinking almost immediately into deep, dreamless sleep. There were no wolves or dog Indians to guard against now, and their sense of security was as strong as if in their own beds at home.

The night was well past, when both lads were awakened by the sound of rain pattering upon the roof, which, although they were on the ground floor, was but a brief space above their heads. The storm foretold by Hank Hazletine had come.

There are few sounds more soothing at night than the falling of rain-drops upon the shingles over one's head, but in the present instance the music was anything but welcome to Jack and Fred. It meant that there could be no hunting on the morrow, and probably not for several days. Their time in Wyoming was so limited that they begrudged an hour of enforced idleness.

"But what's the use of kicking?" asked

Fred, after they had fully discussed the situation; "it can't be helped."

Nevertheless, they condoled with each other for some time, until, lulled by the gentle patter, they floated off once more into the land of Nod, from which they did not emerge until morning.

The first doleful fact that impressed them was that it was still raining. A peep through the single front window with which their room was provided showed the dull leaden sky, with its infinite reservoir, from which the drops were descending in streams that bid fair to last for days and weeks. The air was chilly, and the wood fire burning in the adjoining room was grateful.

The boys were surprised by a characteristic fact. At some time previous to their emerging from their sleeping-room Jim and Ira had departed to take their turn in looking after the cattle, while Bart and Mort, as they were called, had come in to spend the day and night at the building. When they saw the boys they greeted them pleasantly and conversed for some time. Blair showed himself a man of education, and it came out afterward that he was a college graduate, who, having been threatened with pulmonary trouble, had gone to Arizona and engaged in the cattle business. The experiment wrought a cure, and he was now one of the sturdiest of the five men, not afraid to face the more rigorous climate of the North and to expose himself to all sorts of weather. It was a surprise, indeed, to Jack Dudley and Fred Greenwood, in the course of the day, when the conversation happened to drift to the subject of higher mathematics, to find this cowboy could give them instruction in the most abstruse problems they had ever attempted to solve. Thus, although they would have preferred to be away on a hunt, they found the time less monotonous than anticipated.

"This will let up afore night," said Hank, much to the delight of his young visitors, "and to-morrow will be clear."

"I hope it will last several days," ventured Fred.

"So it will," remarked the cowman, with that air of assurance which showed he was more reliable than the Government in his forecasts of the weather.

Hazletine examined the Winchester repeating-rifles of the boys with great care. He pronounced them excellent weapons, as were the Smith & Wesson revolvers with which they were furnished.

"Your outfit is all right," he said, "but it remains to be seed whether you know how to handle 'em."

"We cannot claim to be skilful," was the modest remark of Jack, "but we have had some experience at home, though when we hunted there it was mostly with shot-guns."

"The main thing, younker, is not to git rattled. Now, if you happen to see old Ephraim sailing for you, all you have to do is to make your aim sure and let him have it between the eyes, or just back of the foreleg; or, if you don't have the chance to do that, plug him in the chest, where there's a chance of reaching his heart."

By "old Ephraim" the hunter referred to the grizzly bear, as the boys knew.

"I have heard that it generally takes several shots to kill a grizzly."

"That's 'cause the bullets are not put in the right place. You see, old Ephraim don't take any trouble to give you a better show than he has to, and you must look out fur yourself."

"There are other kinds of bears in Wyoming?"

"Rather—several of 'em. For instance, there's the cinnamon, which, in my 'pinion, is about as bad as Ephraim. I've fit both kinds, and the one that left that big scar down the side of my cheek and chawed a piece out of my thigh was a cinnamon, while I never got a scratch that 'mounted to anything from Ephraim."

"What about the black bear?"

"He's less dangerous than any of 'em. A black bear ain't much more than a big dog. Last fall I killed one with my revolver."

"What other kinds of game are we likely to meet?"

"Wal, it would be hard to name 'em all. There's the deer and antelope, of course, which you find in all parts of the West. Then there's the mountain lion, that is fond of living on beef."

" I never saw one of the creatures."

" Have you ever seen the Eastern panther?" asked Garrison.

" No; though they used to be plentiful in the northern part of the State of New York."

" Well, the mountain lion is the same animal. Our climate and conditions have made some changes in his appearance and habits, but there is no doubt the two are identical."

" There's one kind of game that I wish we could meet," resumed Hazletine, " but they've got so scarce that I haven't seen one fur three years. That's the big-horn sheep."

" He seems to be disappearing from certain sections, like the buffalo from the country," remarked Garrison.

" There's plenty of 'em in the mountains of Arizona and old Mexico, and I've no doubt there's thousands of 'em in the Wind River and other parts of the Rockies, but it's mighty hard to find 'em. Then there's the black wolf."

"Is he fiercer than the gray one?"

"He's ten times worse. Whenever he meets the gray wolf he tears him to smithereens. You never seen a wolf of any kind that wasn't as hungry as you younkers was yesterday."

"He couldn't be any hungrier," said Fred, with a laugh.

"I have knowed one of them critters to foller a steamboat down the upper Missouri fur two days and nights, howling and watching fur a chance to git something to eat."

"The buffaloes have disappeared."

"The right name of the animal is the bison," suggested Garrison; "they have been slaughtered in pure wantonness. It is a crime, the way in which they have been extirpated."

"There are a few of 'em left, deep among the mountains," said Hazletine, "where no one has happened to find 'em, but it won't be long afore they'll all be wiped out. Do you know," he added, indignantly, "that last year our boys found a herd of eighteen buffaloes some miles back in the mountains. Wal, sir, we was that tickled that we made

8

up our minds to watch 'em and see that they wasn't interfered with. We kept track of 'em purty well till their number had growed to twenty-four. Then one afternoon a party of gentlemen hunters, as they called themselves, from the States, stumbled onto 'em. Wal, as true as I'm a settin' here, they s'rounded that herd and never stopped shooting till they killed every one of 'em!"

The cowman was so angry that he smoked savagely at his pipe for a minute in silence. His friends shared his feelings, and Kansas Jim remarked:

"Hank and me hunted two days fur them folks, and if we'd have got the chance to draw bead on 'em not all of 'em would have got home. Why, the rapscallions just shot the whole twenty-four, and left 'em laying on the ground. They didn't even take their hides. If there ever was such a thing as murder that was."

"Yes," assented Garrison; "and although the Government is doing all it can to protect the few in Yellowstone Park, somebody is continually shooting into the herd. The bison will soon be an extinct animal."

"It's too bad, but I don't see that we can help it," observed Hazletine, rousing himself; "there's plenty of other game left, and it'll last longer than any of us, but it don't make the killing of the buffaloes any better. We're likely to find a good many animals that I haven't told you 'bout and that I don't think of."

"How is it, Hank, that you don't keep any dogs?"

"'Cause they're no use. The hunters from the East seem to think they must have a dozen or more sniffing at their heels, but I don't like 'em. We had a big hound a couple of years ago that I took with me on a hunt. The first critter we scared up was a cinnamon bear, and that dog hadn't any more sense than to go straight for him. Wal," grinned Hank, "we haven't had any dog since that time."

CHAPTER VII.

THE FIRST GAME.

IT was an ideal day for hunting among the mountains. The sun shone from an unclouded sky, and the air had just enough crispness to make exercise enjoyable. In short, it was a perfect copy of that day which saw the V. W. W. start from Fort Steele on their long ride northward to Bowman's ranch.

The other cowmen would have been glad to join in the hunt, but they could not be spared from duty. Thus it came about that, as in the first instance, Hank Hazletine was the guide and only companion of Jack Dudley and Fred Greenwood on that which was destined to prove the most memorable hunt of their lives.

The three had ridden briskly through a part of the foot-hills until they reached the more elevated portion, when the hunter led the way up a winding trail until, early in the afternoon, they arrived at what may be called the limit of "horse navigation," which is to say their ponies could give them no more help, since the way was too broken for them to climb further.

Accordingly the three dismounted and removed all the trappings of the animals. Hazletine was so familiar with the country that he came to this favored spot without mistake or hesitation. It was a broad, irregular inclosure, in the form of a grassy plateau, where grass grew abundantly, and was walled in on nearly every side by immense rocks and boulders. A tiny stream of icy water wound along one side, disappearing at a corner among the rocks, which were so craggy and eccentric in their formation that a cavity or partial cavern was found, in which the party placed their bridles, saddles and blankets, and which was capable of giving them shelter against the most furiously driving rain-storm.

"Surely we couldn't have found a better spot if we had hunted for a month," said

Jack, admiringly surveying their surroundings.

"This is to be our headquarters," explained Hazletine, "during the few days or the week that we spend in hunting here."

"You mean that we are to spend each night in this place?"

The guide nodded his head.

"I don't know of any better arrangement," said Fred; "we can gather enough wood to keep a fire going, and, if rain should set in, shall have as good shelter as if in the house on the ranch."

"That's it; and you mustn't furgit one thing," added Hazletine; "we fetched along just 'nough stuff fur dinner. We haven't anything left fur supper. None of the cattle git this fur into the mountains, so we can't count on them. Therefore, we've the ch'ice atween shooting game or starving to death."

"That's enough to make us all do our best, but we cannot suffer so long as we have you for our companion."

"But you ain't going to have me fur your companion."

" The boys stared at their friend in astonishment. He explained :

" There ain't much show fur three persons
to find game as long as they stick together.
The right way is fur 'em all to part and each
keep it up on his own hook. A chap isn't
in half the danger of being seen by the deer
or sheep, or whatever it may be he's after; and
he has the chance, too, to show what stuff he's
made of."

" Then you intend to leave us ?"

" You've hit it the first time. I'll start out
on my own bus'ness, meaning to be back here
while the night's young."

Observing significant looks passing between the boys, the man hastened to add :

" Now, don't you folks make the mistake
of thinking I'll get your supper fur you, fur
I don't mean to do nothing of the kind. I
don't intend to do any hunting, but to git
away from you so as to let you have the
chance. I don't say that if a big horn or a
antelope or buck walks up in front of me and
asks me to take a shy at him that I won't pop
him over, though some folks that I know

wouldn't do the same if the buck happened
to be a two-legged one; but such things don't
often happen; and, if you don't fetch in any
game, them appetites of your'n are likely to
bother you as much as they did t'other day
when we was riding from the fort."

"Do you wish Fred and me to part company?"

Hank's eyes twinkled and a quizzical expression lit up that part of his countenance
which was visible.

"'Twouldn't be safe."

"Why not?"

"You'd each take the other fur a wild
donkey and plug him afore you found out
the mistake, which the same wouldn't be such
a mistake after all."

The boys could well afford to laugh at the
pleasantry of the man who, it was evident,
felt a partiality for them. He added, more
seriously:

"You'd have more show to shoot game if
you parted, but I'd not advise you to do it
till after you've hunted for some days together. It's mighty easy for younkers like

you to git lost in these mountains. You must keep your bearings, so it won't be any trouble fur you to find your way back to this spot when it's dark. If you happen to catch sight of any game, try to not let it see you till you git a fair shot at it; and there ain't much good in wounding a critter in these parts, fur it's sure to git away from you."

After some further instructions, Hank bade his young friends good-by and left them. He strode off in the direction of the trail over which they had come to reach this interesting spot in the mountains, and disappeared without once looking back to see what they were doing.

It was odd thus to be left alone in this wild region, and the chums looked in each other's face with smiles. It certainly was a curious experience to be set down in one of the greatest mountain spurs of the West, and to be told that now they must take care of themselves. It was like being cast into deep water and ordered to choose between swimming and drowning.

"It's just as well," said Jack, "or he

wouldn't have done it. Surely the ´V. W. W. ought to be able to take care of ourselves, with our repeaters and pistols. There's nothing to be feared from wild animals, or he would have warned us."

"It strikes me that the most important thing to do is to keep our bearings, for if we should happen to lose our way it would go hard with us."

"We took care to bring spy-glasses, as well as everything else that we thought we were likely to need, but forgot about a compass, which may be worth all the rest."

"Well, we must be careful not to stray too far until we become familiar with the country. Let's not delay our start."

The plateau where their ponies were cropping the grass was several acres in extent, nearly half of it sloping abruptly; but the grass was abundant enough to furnish the animals with all they could need, no matter how long they stayed, since it had plenty of opportunity to renew itself.

Side by side the boys moved across the space, the ponies not raising their heads to look at them, as they passed near. Instead of following the course taken by their guide they bore to the right, but at the same time proceeded nearly westward, which led them deeper into the mountains. Remembering the caution of their friend they studied the landmarks around them, in the hope of not losing their way when it should become time to return to camp.

When fairly clear of the plateau, where they must have been at a considerable elevation above the sea, they found the way so rough that travelling became a task. There was nothing in the nature of a path or trail to follow, and they were compelled to pass around boulders and rocks, sometimes turning back and retracing their steps, and making long detours, so as to flank impassable chasms. All this tended to confuse their knowledge of the points of the compass, but they did not forget to note everything that could serve as a guide, and were confident of finding their way whenever it should become necessary to return.

Most of the time Jack Dudley was in the

lead, for it was not easy to walk beside each other. He was perhaps a half-dozen paces in advance of Fred, when he abruptly stopped with an exclamation of affright.

" What is it ?" asked his friend, hardly less startled.

" Look at that !"

He pointed downward, almost at his feet. Still unaware of what he meant, Fred stepped guardedly forward to his side.

There was good cause, indeed, for the alarm of the elder, for he had checked himself on the edge of a ravine or canyon fully a thousand feet deep. One step further and he would have dropped into eternity.

The peculiar formation of the canyon accounted for this peril. The chasm was barely a dozen feet wide, but the other side was depressed, so that it was not noticed by the youth until on the edge of the danger. The walls were of solid rock, showing the numerous strata of sandstone and other formations, worn so unevenly that it looked possible for a person to use them as stairs in climbing the sides. Pausing on the edge and peering cautiously down the dizzy steep, the youths could see a stream of water, winding its course far down at the bottom, where the roughness of its bed churned it into foam, and gave it the appearance of a white ribbon that had been strung along the course. The murmur was so soft and faint that at times they were not sure they heard it, and when it reached their ears the voice of the distant ocean was suggested.

A striking feature of this phenomenon was the exceeding narrowness of the canyon. It has been stated that directly opposite to where the boys had halted it was scarcely a dozen feet wide, and there were places in sight with the width still less, though most of it was greater. The ages that it had taken this stream to erode such a bed for itself was beyond imagination.

"Jack," said his companion, with that elasticity of spirits natural to one of his years, "if you had pitched down there, how in the world could I have pulled you up to the top again?"

"Why would you wish to do that?"

"Well, you would have been pretty well bruised and would have needed help."

"Possibly; but I wonder whether there are many such pit-holes in this part of the world. It resembles the fissures in the mountains of ice which I have read that the Arctic explorers sometimes find."

However, since the youths were on one side of the canyon, naturally they were seized with the belief that it was necessary immediately to place themselves on the other side. Why it was so they would have found hard to explain, but they were unanimous on the point; and, since there was but the single method of crossing the chasm, they set out to find it.

"It looks narrower over there to the left," said Jack, turning in that direction.

He did not have to go far when he paused, where the width was barely six feet—not enough to afford much of a leap for sturdy lads of their years.

"That's easy," added Jack, measuring it with his eye.

"You must remember one thing, Jack. There's something in the air of this part of the world which makes a mile look no more than a few hundred yards. Suppose that that other bank is fifty feet off!"

It was an alarming thought, and Jack recoiled as if again on the edge of the brink. But he was quick to see the absurdity of the idea.

"If that is so, then the canyon must be several miles deep. But we would better make sure."

It was easy to do this. Hunting around until a chip from one of the boulders was found, Jack tossed it across the abyss. It fell as he expected, proving that, wonderfully deceptive as is the atmosphere of the West, it cannot mislead in instances like that which confronted them.

"That makes it right. I am not afraid to make the leap; are you?"

"Not a bit; but wait."

Near them lay a stone, so large that it required their united strength to move it. By hard work they rolled it to the edge of the canyon and tumbled it over, carefully watching its descent. A curious thing followed. At

first it shot straight downward for a hundred
feet, when it impinged against a projecting
point of the mountain wall, knocked the fragments in every direction, as if it were a ball
fired from a thousand-pounder, and bounded
against the opposite side, further down, scat-
tering fragments again. By this time it had
achieved an almost inconceivable momentum,
and was shooting downward at a terrific rate.

In the depths of this narrow canyon, where
the sunlight never penetrated for more than a
few minutes at a time, it was always twilight.
At the bottom it was almost dark, so that the
stream would hardly have been visible but
for its yeasty foam. At some point near the
base, when the flinty stone was speeding forward like a meteor, it abraded a harder portion than before. Instantly a stream of fire
shot out, such as sometimes flashes from a
murky cloud in the sky, and, as if it were an
echo of the impact, the splash and thunder-
ous thump were heard by the boys at the top.

It was a tempting theme for the imagination, but they were too practical to linger.
Having agreed that the canyon could be readily

jumped, they did not hesitate. Running a few steps, Jack Dudley cleared the passage and landed on the other side, with several feet to spare. He did not take the trouble to toss his rifle in advance, but kept it in his hand.

"I had a queer feeling," he said, as Fred joined him, "when I was right over the middle of the canyon, and knew, if I had made any miscalculation, I should never stop until pretty well down toward the centre of the earth."

"It doesn't take long to do a deal of thinking at such time, but what bothered me was whether I was going to make as good a jump as you. I believe I beat you by two or three inches."

"You wouldn't have done it if I had tried. But, Fred, since we are on this side of that split in the mountain, we have got to jump it again to get back to camp."

"And we must manage to do it before dark, for it isn't safe to take chances where there is so much variance in the width."

"Fact of it is," remarked Jack, expressing

9

that which had been clear to both from the first, "there was no need of our jumping it at all. But we are here, and must make the best of it. It's time we found some game."

And Jack looked sharply around, as if he expected to see a fat deer or big horn step forward and sacrifice himself for their good.

But they were more fortunate than they were warranted in expecting. While surveying the rocks and heights which seemed to wall them in, Fred exclaimed:

"There's our game!"

He pointed to a cliff fully two hundred yards distant, and of half that height. On this projecting ledge stood a noble buck, with antlers and head raised, while he seemed to be gazing over the wild expanse of country below him. They knew he was a fine animal, though the distance made him appear diminutive.

"I wonder if he sees us?" said Jack in a whisper, as if afraid of being overheard.

"If he does, he knows we are too far off to harm him."

The next instant the boys had unslung

" On the projecting ledge stood a noble buck."

their glasses and leveled them at the fellow, who formed a striking picture, as he stood out in bold relief, with his spreading antlers, his fine head, and his brown, sinewy limbs. The next remark by Jack may not have been romantic, but it was characteristic:

"What a fine meal he will make for us!"

"Provided we can secure him. We must get a good deal nearer."

"Our rifles will carry a bullet that far."

"No doubt; but if we hit him he would be only slightly wounded and would make off. We must go closer."

This necessity was self-evident, but the task was certain to be a difficult one. As they approached the animal they were likely to expose themselves to his keen gaze, when he would disappear on the instant.

"Remember what Hank said. There is twice the chance for one that there is for two. I'll stay here, Fred, while you go on. If I see him move I'll try it, and you must do the same. Between us, we may bring him down."

The plan was acted upon. It was agreed that Fred should steal as near to the buck as possible, in the hope of securing him, while Jack should hold himself in readiness to make a shot, with precious little prospect of success.

If the game would maintain his position it looked as if there was a good prospect of the younger lad getting within shooting distance, for the way was so rugged, and offered so many opportunities for screening his approach, that he did not believe he would be detected if he used proper care. Meanwhile Jack took position behind the nearest boulder, where he could keep an eye on the animal and it was impossible for the latter to see him.

Fred was lost to sight almost immediately. He grew so anxious as the interval decreased that he trembled, and it was hard to fight off an attack of what is called "buck fever," and which is fatal to the best hunter; but by and by his nerves settled, and he became as cool and self-possessed as Hank Hazletine himself would have been under the circumstances.

It seemed improbable that the buck would wait where he was, even if not alarmed, for the time necessary to afford a good shot for his enemy. It was some whim that had led him out upon the top of the towering bluff, where he was in view of the young hunters. It is not to be supposed that his kind appreciate such a thing as beauty in a landscape or scene spread before them, and yet the action of the buck almost indicated something of that nature; for he stood motionless, minute after minute, as if absorbed, and suggesting a statue carved from the rock itself.

Foot by foot Fred Greenwood stole forward, crouching behind boulders, creeping beside immense rocks which shut him from the gaze of the watchful animal, until with a rapidly beating heart he whispered:

"I'm near enough to try a shot."

He was making ready, when he observed a well-screened point a few rods in advance, which impressed him as the right place. Once there, he could ask no better opportunity to test his skill. Was it safe to wait a minute or two longer? Yes, he would make the attempt.

With infinite care, and holding his nerves in superb control, he worked his way to the spot without alarming the buck.

CHAPTER VIII.

LOOK BEFORE YOU LEAP.

CROUCHING behind the friendly boulder, Fred Greenwood rested the barrel of his Winchester upon it and took careful aim at the buck, which seemed scarcely to have moved from the moment he was seen by the youths. That he maintained his pose thus long was certainly remarkable, and the fact was due to a cause suspected by neither of the boys.

That the antelope has the bump of curiosity developed to a most amazing degree is well known. It is this peculiarity which has proved fatal to the animals in numberless instances. The curiosity of the *cervus* species, while much less, sometimes manifests itself in an extraordinary fashion. Fred Greenwood managed his approach with so much skill that he was not noticed; but his comrade, further away, was seen by the vigilant animal, when Jack, becoming impatient over the delay, began the attempt to follow him. The sight of the young hunter startled the buck. He was on the point of whirling about and making off, but waited to learn something more definite. The caution of Jack rendered this difficult, and it was because of the animal's hesitation that Fred succeeded in reaching the spot from which to try a shot.

The lad sighted at the front of the game and his finger was pressing the trigger, when, perhaps because of a sudden sight of Jack, the buck turned about to flee. It was at this juncture that Fred fired.

The result was better than he expected. It is almost impossible to kill a deer instantly, instances being known of one running a number of rods with a bullet through his heart; but in this instance the buck, gathering his forelegs under him, as if to leap a high obstruction, bounded straight up in air and dropped back so close to the edge of the cliff that he toppled over and came tumbling downward like a log of wood.

The point where he fell was some distance away and out of sight of the young hunter, who, with a delighted exclamation, rose to his feet and began scrambling toward his prize. But for his excitement Fred would have noted a singular thing. When the report of his rifle rang out in the stillness, the echo from the face of the cliff sounded as sharp and loud as the crack of his own weapon. The explanation of this speedily became manifest.

Although the way was rough, the distance was so short that it took Fred only a brief time to reach the inanimate body of the buck.

"Hank couldn't have beaten that shot himself! I must have driven the bullet through his heart, which I shouldn't have done if he hadn't started to flee at the instant I pulled trigger——"

At that moment an Indian, rifle in hand, stepped into view from among the rocks, and with a grin on his face came toward the youth. Fred was not dreaming of anything of the kind, and looked at the red man in astonishment.

"Eh! howdy, brother? That my buck,"

said the Indian, with his painted face still bisected by a tremendous smile.

The lad flared up on the instant.

"How do you make that out? I just shot him."

"No; me shoot him—he mine."

Fred's gorge continued to rise.

"You are not speaking the truth. I fired at him a few minutes ago and saw him spring in air and fall over the cliff."

"Where you hit him?"

Ready to prove the truth of his own words, the youth stooped over the carcass, which was lying on its left side. A crimson orifice was seen just back of the foreleg, which showed where the tiny messenger of death had entered.

"That's where I struck him! What have you to say to *that*?"

"I shoot at the same time as brother. That where my bullet go in. Dere where it come out."

Reflection convinced Fred of the unpleasant fact that this Indian was speaking the truth. The relative position of the lad and the dead buck had been such that it was impossible for his bullet to take the course of the one that had slain the animal. The decisive shot, therefore, was not his.

" But I know mine struck him somewhere," was Fred's desperate exclamation; "could it have taken the same course as yours?"

The tantalizing smile came back to the face of the red man, who shook his head.

"My brother's bullet strike dere—hurt antler bad."

The Indian thrust the toe of his moccasin against the buck's antlers. It was plain that one of the prongs had been chipped off, as if by the impact of a glancing bullet. Fred could no longer deny the mortifying fact that his shot had no more to do with the death of the animal than if it had been a pebble tossed up the cliff by hand.

The discovery did not add to his temper, and he was in an unreasonable mood.

"You hadn't any business to fire at the buck when I did! I had picked him out for my game and it was a mean act on your part. We both struck him, and I shall claim one-

half of him, for I'm hungry, and it will soon
be supper-time."

A dangerous light shone in the black eyes
of the Indian. Evidently he had no liking
for the race of the young man, and his resent-
ment was roused by his words and manner.

"He mine; me take him; you thief!"

"It occurred to Fred Greenwood at this
moment that it would be unwise as well as
perilous to quarrel with this denizen of the
wilderness. He was in middle life, active,
powerful, wiry and unscrupulous. The youth
was no match for him in a personal encounter; besides which he noticed that the fellow
carried a Winchester like his own, not to
mention the formidable knife at his waist.

Still the lad was too proud to yield the
point without protest. Besides, he was growing anxious about that supper which hung
suspended in the balance.

"It's only fair that you should give me a
part of the body; you can't eat a tenth part
of it. You must divide."

"He mine—me take all—white dog have
none—me kill him."

"You will, eh? I shall have something to say about that."

It was Jack Dudley who uttered these words as he strode into view from the direction taken a few minutes before by his comrade.

The Indian had detected the approach of Jack before he spoke and before Fred knew of his coming. He raised his head like a flash, and the dark, threatening expression vanished, succeeded by the grin that was there when he first appeared to the younger lad.

"Howdy, brother?" he said, extending his hand, which was taken rather gingerly by the surprised youth, who recognized him as Motoza, the vagrant Sioux, with whom he had had the singular experience some nights before, when encamped in the grove on the prairie.

"Why, I didn't suspect it was *you*," added Jack, hardly knowing how to address him.

Motoza would have lacked ordinary perception had he failed to see that the boys were friends. What impulse led him to do

what he did it would be hard to explain, but
without making any response to the remark
of Jack he drew his knife, stooped over the
carcass, and dextrously cut two large pieces
from the haunches. Straightening up, he
handed one to Jack and the other to Fred,
with the words:

"Take, brothers."

"Thank you very much," replied Fred, accepting the "peace offering," while his friend
made similar acknowledgment.

"Brothers want more?"

"That is plenty. We are obliged, and
hope you will pardon our hasty words."

With the chronic grin on his painted face
Motoza stood silent, as if the business was
closed between them.

"That gives us our supper, Fred, and we
may as well go back to camp. Good-by,
Motoza."

The Sioux slightly nodded, but did not
speak. Each boy, carrying his food, turned
his back upon him and moved away in the
direction of the camp. When they had gone
a slight distance, Jack looked back and saw

the Indian bent over the carcass of the buck and busy with his knife in securing a meal for himself. A few minutes later the parties were out of sight of each other.

At the first water they reached the lads carefully washed and dressed the venison and resumed their return to camp.

"What do you make of it, Jack?" asked Fred.

"I don't know enough about Indians to judge them correctly, but I think their nature must be similar to our own. Motoza formed a respect for me because of the manner in which I handled him the other night."

"That is my belief; and it is not only respect, but friendship. He likes you, and will never do you harm."

"What about *you?*"

"I am not so clear there. He and I were quarrelling when you came up. I thought it was I who killed the buck, but he proved it was himself, and that I had no claim to him. But I had set my heart on making a supper off venison to-night, and did not like the thought of giving it up. He was ugly, and if you hadn't come up just when you did there would have been trouble, with the chances against me."

"It was a mistake on your part."

"I fear it was. It may be, however, that Motoza feels better disposed toward me since he has learned we are friends."

"That is my belief. But it is rather curious that we should run across him again, so many miles from the spot where we last met; but, Fred, we must keep our bearings."

They were in a wild section of the mountains, which they had not seen before, but by carefully noting the position of the sun in the sky and observing a towering, snow-covered peak that had been fixed upon as a landmark, they agreed as to the right direction. They were confirmed in their belief shortly after by coming to the edge of the canyon which they had leaped on their outward trip; but the width was fully twenty feet, with no diminishing, so far as they could see, to the right or left.

"I hardly think it will do to make the venture here," remarked Jack, with a shake of his head.

"No; for not only is it too wide, but the other side is several feet higher than this."

They cautiously approached the edge and peered down into the frightful depth. There was the same foamy stream, apparently a half-mile below, dashing over the rocky bottom, and sending up the faint roar that impressed them when the canyon was first seen. It was, in short, a reproduction on a reduced scale of the magnificent Grand Canyon of the Yellow-stone, which is a source of admiring wonder to thousands of tourists.

Something away down in the bottom caught the attention of Fred, and, at his suggestion, they laid aside their rifles and venison and crept forward on their faces until their heads projected over the edge of the dizzying depth.

"Do you see him?" asked Fred.

"Yes; who would have thought of such a thing?"

At many points in the yeasty foam black masses of rocks rose so high above the roaring stream that the water whirled and eddyed around them. It was mostly these obstructions that kept the current in a state of turmoil, and made it show distinctly in the twilight gloom of the canyon. On one of the dripping rocks was a man, standing so like a statue that in the indistinct light Fred Greenwood took him for some fantastic formation of stone, worn by the eroding action of the angry waters, but the suggestion of a living person was so striking that the two called their spy-glasses into use.

The result was astounding. Instead of being an Indian, as they had believed at first, it was a white man. Furthermore, the instruments proved beyond question that he was their old friend, Hank Hazletine.

"What in the name of wonder is he doing down there?" exclaimed the amazed Jack.

"Standing on a rock," was the reply. "He finds some amusement in that, or he wouldn't do it."

"He must have entered at the mouth of the canyon, which cannot be far off."

"That may be so. The sides are so broken and rough that he could use them for stairs in going down or coming up."

"Whew!" exclaimed Jack, with a shudder;

"the thought scares me. I wouldn't undertake it for the world! Suppose, when you
had picked your steps half-way down, you
couldn't find a place to rest your hands or
feet; or, in climbing up, you should be stopped
within a yard or two of the top?"

" It would be the end of the chapter for us;
but Hank knows the country so well that he
is in no danger of making such a mistake;
but none for us."

In the hope of attracting the notice of their
friend the boys shouted to him, but the roar
of the waters was in the ears of the hunter,
who would not have heard the boom of a can-
non fired on the cliffs above. He did not
look up or give any heed to their hail. Fred
thought of throwing down a piece of rock,
but it was too dangerous. It was liable to be
so deflected from its course as to kill the un-
suspicious hunter, who had assumed great
risk as it was.

" Do you see that?" asked Jack.

The question was caused by the action of
Hank, who made a leap that carried him to
the top of the boulder nearest him. Then

he sprang to a second and a third, when, to the astonishment of the watchers, he disappeared.

The reason was apparent. After his last leap he had passed under a projecting ledge, from which, of course, he would emerge whenever he chose to do so. But, though the boys watched for a considerable time, he did not appear; and, realizing that the afternoon was drawing to a close, they rose to their feet, with the purpose of pushing on to camp.

But to do that they must find a place where the canyon could be crossed, and they set out on their hunt, which proved less difficult than was anticipated. Not far off a portion of the rocks on their side projected like a tongue so far over the ravine that it was barely two yards from its extremity to the other bank. Moreover, the sides of the canyon were on a level, so that a more favorable spot for crossing could not have been desired.

An examination of this formation showed that twenty feet below them the canyon was as wide as at the point from which they had watched their friend. The ledge, therefore, arched over, and was in the nature of a partial bridge, whose thickness would have sustained a great many tons.

They peered downward in quest of Hank, but the gorge had taken an abrupt turn since they saw him and he was not in sight.

The task before them seemed so simple that the two gave it scarcely a thought, but it brought them an experience which, in some respects, was the most terrifying of their lives.

While the banks were substantially on the same level, the opposite one was fringed with a species of stunted bush, two or three feet high, quite dense, and bearing a species of red berry such as is found on the fragrant wintergreen. Hazletine had cautioned the lads against eating any vegetable whatever in this section, since many are violently poisonous and have caused the death of more than one thoughtless tenderfoot.

Fred Greenwood made ready for the first jump. As in the former instance, the distance was so slight that it was not necessary to toss any of their impedimenta in advance of their own passage. It was easy to jump with the Winchester in one hand and the goodly piece of meat in the other. Since Fred had beaten his friend some time before, Jack quietly resolved to turn the tables by doing his best, and he was confident of far surpassing him, especially as Fred had no suspicion of his intention.

"Go ahead," said Jack; "night isn't far off, and it will be dark by the time we reach camp."

Fred took only a couple of paces for a start, when he bounded across the chasm with the ease of a chamois. Jack had sauntered a rod back, as if with no special purpose in mind, when his object was to secure the impetus that would land him far in advance of his comrade. Standing thus, he complacently watched Fred, as his body rose in air, gracefully curved over, and landed at a safe distance beyond the edge of the canyon.

It was while Jack Dudley was standing thus that he fancied he saw a disturbance in the bushes where Fred was about to alight. It was so slight that he did not think it meant anything; and, without noticing it further, he started on a series of quick, short steps, which were to give him the necessary momentum to win the victory over his friend. At that instant Fred landed and emitted a cry of terror and warning.

"Look out, Jack! Don't jump! Stop! stop!"

But, though Jack heard the cry, it was too late to heed it. He was so near the edge of the canyon that had he checked himself he would have gone spinning to death down the abyss. The leap must be made, and, gathering his muscles, he rose in the air, with his legs gathered under him, and with the certainty that the jump would far surpass the one that he had just witnessed.

In that critical moment, when his body rose and seemed suspended over the gorge, Jack's attention was fixed upon the strange actions of Fred. The instant he landed he darted to one side, and with his rifle struck at something in the bushes which Jack could not see. As he did so he recoiled, and was in the act of advancing and striking again, when Jack landed upon the ground beyond.

As he did so he heard a vicious, locust-like whir, whose meaning he recognized. An immense rattlesnake was in the bushes, and Fred had descended almost upon it. But for the tremendous effort of Jack he would have dropped squarely upon the velvety body, with consequences too frightful to be thought of; but his great leap carried him over it, while the attack of Fred upon the reptile, in the effort to save his companion, diverted the attention of the rattlesnake for an instant.

Jack saw the flat, pitted head, the gleaming coil, the distended jaws, while the slightly elevated tail vibrated so rapidly with the warning which, once heard, can never be forgotten, that it looked hazy and mist-like. Before Fred, at imminent risk to himself, could bring down his clubbed gun with crushing force, Jack felt a sharp sting in his ankle, and called out, in the extremity of terror:

"*I'm bitten!*"

He was not only terrified but angered, and whirling about, he brought down his gun with spiteful violence on the writhing body.

The reptile struck again, but it was already wounded to that extent that its blow was erratic, and, though it came near reaching the hand of Jack, it missed by a safe margin.

CHAPTER IX.

NIGHT IN THE MOUNTAINS.

ONE of the singular facts connected with the *crotalus* species is the ease with which it is killed. The writer once ended the career of a huge specimen with a single blow of a whip-lash. The first impact of Fred Greenwood's rifle-barrel upon the hideous reptile coiled in the scrub bushes inflicted a fatal wound, though the serpent continued blindly striking for a minute or two longer, and responded viciously to the attack of the scared and angry Jack Dudley, who struck it several times after it had ceased to struggle and all danger was past. A person's first impulse, after being bitten by a snake, is to kill it, after which he looks after the wound he may have received.

But Fred had heard the dreadful exclamation of his comrade and caught him by his arm as he was about to bring down his last blow upon the reptile.

"O Jack, are you sure he bit you?" he asked in a tremulous voice.

"Yes; I felt the sting in my left ankle, like the prick of a needle."

Dropping upon the ground, he hastily unfastened and turned down his legging. There, sure enough, was a tiny red spot, with a single drop of blood oozing from it.

"The rattlesnake has two fangs," said Fred; "but there is only one wound here."

"It wasn't a direct blow, I suppose," said the white-faced Jack, who had good reason to be terrified over the occurrence, for the rattlesnake, although ranking below the cobra in the virulence of its venom, is the most deadly serpent in America, and the veteran hunter fears it more than the most savage of wild animals.

Fred stooped down and examined the wound closely. A thrilling suspicion was becoming certainty in his mind.

"When did you feel that bite?" he asked.

"At the moment I landed on my feet. What a dreadful poison it is! I can feel it all through my body; and don't you see that my ankle has begun to swell?"

Fred continued to study the wound, pressing his finger around it and bending close to the limb. Had the hurt been caused by the fang of a serpent he would have tried to suck out the venom. Suddenly he looked up with glowing face.

"Now, Jack, my dear fellow, don't be frightened; you haven't been bitten at all."

"What do you mean?"

"At the moment you landed on your feet I was beating the life out of the snake, and he was giving his whole attention to me. He did not try to bite you till you turned about and began striking at him."

"But what made that wound?" asked Jack.

"I suspect the cause."

He drew up the legging and examined the part that covered the spot in the ankle which had received the blow.

"There! I knew it! That's what did it!"

He had plucked out a small, needle-pointed thorn. The bushes abounded with similar prongs, one of which had been torn off and pierced the legging of Jack when he was crashing through the tops of the bushes.

"Sure there isn't any mistake about that?" asked the youth, feeling as if a mountain were lifted from his shoulders.

"There can't be."

"Wait a minute!"

With one bound the happy fellow came to his feet, and throwing his arms about his comrade, hugged him into temporary breathlessness.

"Thank the Lord! Richard's himself again! The V. W. W. are born to good fortune."

And joining hands, the two danced with delight. Many in the situation of Fred Greenwood would have laughed at Jack and "guyed" him over his blunder, but the incident was too dreadful and the terror of his friend too intense for Fred to wish to amuse himself at his expense. However, he could not help indulging just a trifle. Suddenly pausing in his antics he looked down at the feet of Jack.

"I suppose in a few minutes your ankle will be so swelled that the buckles will fly off the legging. By this time, too, you must feel the poison in your head."

By way of answer, Jack, who, like Fred, had laid aside his Winchester and venison, seized his friend and tried to lay him on his back. They had had many a wrestling bout at home and there was little difference in their skill. Fred was always ready for a test, and he responded with such vigor that before Jack suspected he received an unquestioned fall, since both shoulders and hips were on the ground at the same time, with his conqueror holding him motionless.

"It was hardly fair," remarked Fred, allowing him to rise to his feet.

"Why not?" asked Jack, also coming up.

"The venom of the rattlesnake so weakened you that you are not yourself."

"I'll show you whether I am or not!"

At it they went again, and this time Jack was the victor, after which they brushed off their clothing and agreed to leave the deciding bout for a more convenient season. Night was rapidly closing in.

"That exercise has added to my appetite," remarked Jack, as they gathered up their belongings and moved off.

"It would have done the same for me, if the thing were possible."

Mindful of the danger of going astray, they carefully studied the landmarks, so far as they could see them. Their main reliance was the lofty peak that was visible for so great a distance, but with that help they saw it growing dark, while they were in a region totally strange to them.

"My gracious!" said Fred, as they came to a halt; "in the face of all that Hank told us, we have lost our way!"

"It has that look," replied Jack, removing his hat and drawing his handkerchief across his moist forehead; "but I don't see that it is such a serious thing, after all. We can spend the night here as well as anywhere."

"What will Hank think, when he goes to camp to meet us?"

"I reckon he'll not be disappointed; besides, we can't be far from the place, and can look it up to-morrow."

"I don't suppose it will hurt us to build a fire among these rocks and spend the night;

but the air is pretty cool and we shall miss our blankets."

"Old hunters like ourselves must become used to such things," complacently observed Jack, who began preparations at the same moment for carrying out his own proposal. It was no trouble to find enough brush and wood to serve them, and they had brought such a goodly supply of matches from the ranch in their rubber safes that they soon had a vigorous fire going, over which they broiled their venison.

The meal of itself would not have been enjoyable at their home, for it was too "new," lacking a certain tenderness that forms one of its chief attractions. Besides, it was unavoidably scorched in the preparation; but the mixed pepper and salt sprinkled over it improved the flavor. But the great thing was their insatiate appetites, for it is a homely truth that there is no sauce like hunger. So it came about that they not only made a nourishing meal, but had enough left to serve them in the morning.

It was fully dark when the repast was finished. The fire had been started against the face of a boulder, and only a small quantity of wood remained—not sufficient to last half through the night. With the going down of the sun the air became colder. It seemed at times as if a breath of wind from the snowy peaks reached them, and it caused an involuntary shiver. The prospect of remaining where they were through the dismal hours of darkness was anything but cheering.

"Jack," suddenly said Fred in a guarded undertone, "there's some wild animal near us."

"How can you know that?"

"I heard him moving about."

"In what direction?"

"Just beyond the ridge there. Hark! Didn't you hear it?"

"You are right," whispered Jack; "let's find out what it is."

Gun in hand, they moved stealthily up the slight ridge near by. It was only a few feet in height. Their experience had taught them that danger was likely to break upon them at any time, and they did not mean to be caught unprepared. Neither spoke as they cautiously climbed the ridge, like a couple of Indian scouts on the alert for the first appearance of peril.

But they reached the crest of the slight elevation without having heard anything more of that which had alarmed them. The next moment, however, both caught the dim outlines of a large animal moving slowly from them. Before they were certain of its identity the creature neighed, as if frightened by the stealthy approach of the youths.

" It's a horse!" exclaimed Fred, who, suspecting the whole truth, moved over the ridge and called, in a coaxing voice:

" Dick! Come here, Dick!"

The animal stopped, looked inquiringly around, and then came forward with a pleased whinny. He was Fred's pony, and, brief as their acquaintance had been, recognized his voice. Fred stroked his nose and patted his neck, and the horse showed his pleasure at receiving the endearments.

When the youths made their halt and cooked their supper they were on the edge of the grassy plateau for which they were hunting, and whose features they would have been quick to recognize were the sun shining. Soon after, Jack's pony came out of the gloom as if to claim attention, and he received it.

"We are more fortunate than I dared hope," said Jack; "here we are at home, after all. I wonder whether Hank is ahead of us?"

This was unlikely, since, if he had reached the spot fixed upon as their headquarters, he would have kindled a fire, whereas it was dark in every direction. The partial cavern was on the other side of the plateau, and the boys walked rapidly to it, the route being clear, now that they had located themselves.

They appreciated the wisdom of Hank, who had made them help gather enough firewood to last through the night. He said (what proved to be the fact) that they were not likely to return till late, when it would be hard to collect the right kind of fuel.

In a brief while a second fire was under way. It was started in front of the cavern, which was of so slight extent that it received and held much of the warmth. Seated within the opening, with their heavy blankets wrapped about them, the boys were thoroughly comfortable. They had met with enough stirring adventure and had had sufficient rough experience to make the rest highly acceptable. They naturally wondered when nine o'clock passed without bringing Hank Hazletine.

"Maybe he has lost his way in the canyon," suggested Fred, giving expression to a fancy which was not serious.

"You mean that he has forgotten where the stairs lead up to the top?"

"I guess that's what I mean, though I never thought of it before. If that is the fact, he may have to pick his way for two or three hundred miles to the mouth of the canyon and then walk back to us."

"That will delay his arrival."

"Yes. He can hardly be expected before morning."

"Let me see," said Jack, becoming more serious; "Hank warned us that no matter where we went into camp, we must keep one person on duty as sentinel."

"Suppose we are separated, and there is only one of us in camp?"

"Then, I presume, he must sit up and watch over himself. But what's the use of one of us keeping guard here?"

"Why not?"

"We are in this cavern-like arrangement, where no one can come upon us from the rear, while the fire will ward off danger from the front."

"Suppose that danger comes in the form of an Indian; what would he care for half a dozen fires?"

"But there are no unfriendly Indians in these parts."

"You are thinking of Motoza. We have agreed that he is friendly, but sometimes I suspect we are making a mistake about him."

The boys would have been glad to convince themselves that it was safe to dispense with guard duty, for a night of undisturbed rest was exceedingly tempting, but no one who starts out with the set purpose of deceiving himself can do so. The result of it all was that the two decided that they must stand guard between them until the sun rose.

On such occasions the sentinel whose turn comes first has the preferable task, since every one will admit that it is easier to keep awake before midnight than afterward. The division was made more equitable by arranging that Jack Dudley should serve until two o'clock, and Fred Greenwood for the remainder of the morning. Before the hour of ten the younger lay down on the flinty floor, with his heavy blanket gathered around him, and sank into slumber. They had matched pennies for the first turn, else the elder would not have claimed it.

Jack found his duty similar in many respects to that of his first night on the prairie, but the surroundings and circumstances were in wide contrast. In the former instance they had the companionship of the cowman and veteran hunter, while now they could not know whether he was within a half-dozen miles of them. Jack, however, did not believe that anything in the nature of danger impended, and that to a great extent he was taking upon himself an unnecessary hardship.

So far as he could judge, the only possible thing to fear was wild animals. There were always some of them prowling through this region, but at that season of the year the wolves and other brutes were not pressed by hunger, and no matter how fierce the creature, he would not attempt to pass the mouth of the cavern so long as the fire was burning. Jack flung a number of sticks on the blaze and then passed outside, where he was beyond the circle of light. Standing thus, in the gloom of the night, he felt that the experience of that hour was worth the journey across the continent.

There was an impressive grandeur in the solitude that he had never felt before. On every side towered the immense peaks of one of the loftiest spurs of the grandest mountain chain of America. The crests resembled piles of blackness, with the stars gleaming behind them, while he, an insignificant atom, stood with gun by his side in one of the tiny hollows, as if to guard against attack from the sleeping monsters.

As is always the case, the stillness of the vast solitude seemed unlike silence, for a low, deep murmur was ever brooding in the air, varied now and then by the soft voice of some waterfall, borne across the vasty depths by an eddy in the gentle wind. Once the bark of a wolf sounded so sharp and clear that the youth started and looked to one side, expecting to see the animal steal forward from the gloom, but a moment's reflection told him the brute was a mile or more distant. Then, some time later, a mournful, wailing cry rose and fell from some remote point. He suspected that that, too, came from the throat of a wolf, but he was not sure.

Just a touch of homesickness came over Jack Dudley, and he felt lonely for the first time since leaving home. As he looked up at the clear sky he wondered whether his father and mother were well and asleep; whether they were dreaming of him; whether they missed him from that loved home and longed for the day when he should return to them.

"Suppose something happens that will prevent my ever seeing them?" he said to himself, while the tears filled his eyes. " I thought when I believed that rattlesnake had bitten me to-day that death was sure; and I was near it, though I was unharmed. We are in more danger here than I expected; but we are in danger every hour, no matter where we are. I hope nothing will befall Fred or me."

And standing alone in the midst of that wild, rugged scene, he silently lifted his heart to the only One who could protect and save them from the hundreds of perils that beset them.

His eye was fixed on the stupendous mountain beyond the plateau, at whose base wound the canyon, when he observed a growing light on its crest. The twinkling stars beyond grew dimmer, and the white blanket of snow that had lain there for centuries rapidly came out in bolder relief, until it sparkled and gleamed much as he had seen it do when the sun was shining. Then a curved yellow rim emerged from behind the mountain, its climbing of the sky so rapid that the progress was readily noted. In a brief while the whole form of the round full moon appeared clear of the peak, and its silvery rays began filling the gorges and chasms below.

The scene was picturesque and beautiful beyond description. As the moon climbed higher, the lower peaks, one after the other, leaped into view, while the hollows between became blacker and more awesome from contrast. Most of these were so deep that the illumination made them appear stronger by the contrast. As the orb ascended it seemed to shrink in size and to climb more slowly; but the shifting of the wonderful panorama, progressing as it did in complete silence, was impressive to the last degree.

It was as if the angels of the sky were noiselessly casting their fleecy veils of light over and into the awful depths below, and driving away the crouching monster of blackness that was thus roused from his slumber and forced to flee. Grand as was the scene, it was soothing in its effect upon the awed lad, who, leaning against the rock behind him, the stock of his rifle resting at his feet, surveyed it all with feelings that drew him nearer to heaven, and gave him a more vivid knowledge of the greatness and majesty of the Author of all that he saw and felt.

Standing thus, with his emotions stirred to their profoundest depths, Jack Dudley took no note of the passage of time. Midnight came and passed, and still he held his post, wondering, admiring and worshipping, as must puny man when brought face to face with such exhibitions of Omnipotence.

It was an unromantic ending to this experience that, forgetful of the consequences of what he did, he finally became sensible of the irksomeness of his standing position, and sat down, with his back to the rock, that he might enjoy it all without fatigue of body.

Need it be said what followed? He had not been seated ten minutes when his senses left him and he became as unconscious as Fred Greenwood, asleep in the cavern, on the other side of the smouldering fire. The hours passed until the light of the moon paled before the rosy hues of the rising sun, and still the boys slumbered and knew naught of what was passing around them.

CHAPTER X.

THE SIGNAL-FIRES.

JACK DUDLEY was awakened by the sound of laughter. Opening his eyes, he stared about him confusedly, unable for some moments to recall his situation. Fred Greenwood stood in front of him, shaking so much with mirth that he could scarcely stand.

"O faithful sentinel!" he said; "how well thou hast kept thy trust!"

"I don't see anything to laugh at," replied Jack, rising to his feet and rubbing his eyes; "you would have done the same if you had been in my place."

"Perhaps I should, and then the laugh would have been on me. But we have cause to be thankful that, while no harm has come to us, we have had a good night's rest. I suppose you dropped into slumber almost as soon as I did."

"No, I didn't," persisted the elder; "I stood here a long time, but made the mistake of sitting down for a few minutes, just before it was time to call you. I ought to have known better, and shall never do the like again."

"Well, we have been fortunate and it has taught us both a lesson. Let's attend to our toilet and have breakfast."

They laved their faces and hands in the cold stream of clear water running near them, combed their hair, stretched and limbered arms and legs by a series of gymnastics to which they were accustomed, and then, returning to the mouth of the cavern, found, by raking over the ashes, that enough live embers remained to broil the venison more acceptably than any meal that had been prepared since coming to the region.

By that time Jack had recovered his usual good nature, and was as ready to jest as his companion over his dereliction of duty.

"I don't know what time it was when I fell asleep," he said, "but it must have been past midnight. The moon had risen over that high mountain yonder, and I was admiring the wonderful picture its rays made as they shot out over the lower peaks and lit up the chasms between. I never saw anything so beautiful."

"You ought to have called me to share the pleasure with you."

"I have no doubt it was time to do so, but I knew you preferred to sleep rather than look upon Niagara Falls or the Yellowstone."

"If so, I am not the only younker, as Hazletine says, who has such a preference. That reminds me, Jack, that it's mighty lucky we are not vegetarians."

"Why?"

"What should we do for our meals? So long as we stay in these mountains we must live on game. This seasoning that Hank was thoughtful enough to give us makes it palatable, but coffee, bread and a few vegetables would help a good deal."

"It doesn't make much difference, so long as we are blessed, or rather tortured, with such appetites as we have had ever since we struck Wyoming."

From where they sat at the mouth of the cavern they saw all three of their ponies cropping the succulent grass. It was evident that nothing could add to their enjoyment of this outing.

Naturally the boys speculated over the absence of their guide.

"He must have expected to spend the night with us. And, Fred, perhaps it will be just as well, when he does come, that we don't tell him how I passed the time when trying to act the sentinel."

"I surely shall not, unless he questions us so closely that we cannot help letting him know the truth."

"He will have a small opinion of us."

"Why of ' us ?' "

"Because you would have done the same as I."

"That has not yet been proven."

"Well, say ' myself,' if that suits better."

"It is a very good amendment. I wonder whether anything can have befallen him ?"

"He is too much of a veteran to make such blunders as we."

"That is true, and yet the most skilful hunter in the world is liable to accident. What's frightened the ponies?"

One of the animals had raised his head, with the grass dripping like green water from his jaws, and was looking off to the side of the plateau as if he scented danger of some kind. He was near the further boundary, thus being considerably removed from the boys, who grasped their Winchesters and rose to their feet.

"It's Hank's horse," said Jack, in an undertone; "the others do not seem to be interested in what disturbs him."

"And there comes Hank himself!" was the delighted exclamation of Fred, as they saw their old friend step into view from behind the rocks and walk with his peculiar silent stride toward them.

The movement of the beard under the broad sombrero showed that the guide was smiling, and doubtless he was as pleased as the boys over the meeting. He advanced with the same lengthy step and extended his hand with his hearty "Howdy?" to each in turn.

"Glad to see you, younkers; you seem to have got along as well without me as if I'd been with you."

"Nothing has come amiss; but, Hank, we're glad indeed to see you."

"Where did you git your breakfast?" he asked, glancing at the signs of the meal of which they had partaken.

"Oh, I thought it best yesterday afternoon to shoot a buck," said Fred, airily; "for the main thing for us to do in this part of the world is to look out that we don't starve to death."

"You shot a buck, eh? How was it?"

Thereupon the younger lad gave the particulars of the incident. Hank listened attentively, and when he learned of the part played by Motoza, the vagrant Sioux, his interest deepened.

"So that scamp is in the mountains? I s'pected it; he claimed to have shot the buck and wouldn't divide till Jack took a hand. Why did you let him have any of it?"

"Because he had the right. I thought it was my shot that killed the game, but the bul-

let only grazed one of his antlers; it was
Motoza who killed the buck, and he was entitled to him. Have you been to breakfast?"

"Yes," replied the veteran, whose manner
showed that he was displeased with the story
he had just heard.

"Hank," said Jack, "why did Motoza give
us any of the venison?"

"I don't know," was the unexpected reply;
"I'd give a good deal to know."

"Do you suppose he was frightened when
he found there were two instead of one to
face?"

"It looks that way, but I can't believe it.
The Sioux is a scamp mean enough to do anything; but he has grit, and I don't believe
that two young tenderfeet like you could
scare him."

"Perhaps he felt a respect and friendship
for Jack because of what took place in the
grove on the prairie," suggested Fred.

The boys expected their friend to ridicule
this idea, but he did not. On the contrary,
he admitted that it was the most reasonable
explanation that presented itself; and because

12

of this admission, both of the lads were confirmed in their faith that the right cause had been named.

"One of you stood guard last night while the other slept?"

The question was so abrupt that Jack's face flushed. Fred was silent, but his comrade thought the best course was to make a clean breast of it, and he did so. Hank won the gratitude of the boys by not uttering a word of reproof or showing any displeasure. More than that, he made the astounding comment:

"I'm glad you slept most of the night."

The two looked at him in astonishment.

"If the Sioux meant you harm, you gave him the best chance in the world. He carries as good a repeating Winchester as yours, and there was nothing to keep him from stealing up in the night and shooting you both; or, if he liked the knife better, it would have been the easiest thing in the world for him to wipe you out when your eyes was closed."

This was a view of the matter that had not presented itself to the youths, for the reason, as will be remembered, that they had accepted the friendship of Motoza as a fact.

"But he could have followed and picked us off when we were on our way here," suggested Jack.

"Yes, he's had all the chances he wanted."

"Then it's safe to set Motoza down as a friend?"

But Hank shook his head.

"The safest thing to do when an Indian is afore the house is to set him down as an enemy waiting for a chance to lift your scalp. That confounded Sioux is one of the cunningest imps that ever stole a white man's pony or helped to stampede a drove of cattle. Everything that he's done since we come into the mountains looks as if he was a friend to us all. I can't help saying that, but it mustn't be furgot that the whole bus'ness may be meant to close our eyes, and that he's got some deviltry in mind back of it all, that neither of you younkers has thought about."

"Have *you* thought of it?"

The hunter would not reply to this direct question except to say:

"We'll have to wait and see."

And so Jack and Fred were left as much in doubt as before; but, it may be added, with their belief in the friendship of the Sioux unshaken. They reasoned that their guide was so accustomed to seeing the worst side of the red men that he found it hard to believe any good of them. As for themselves, they would feel no further anxiety over the enmity of Motoza, for had he not shown the best possible proof that could be asked of his good-will?

Inasmuch as Hank had given them a series of surprises by his questions and remarks, Jack Dudley now turned the tables on him by saying:

"Yesterday afternoon, when we looked down into that deep canyon over yonder, we shouted to you at the bottom, but suppose the noise of the water prevented your hearing us. At any rate, you gave us no attention."

The hunter was astonished, as he showed by his start and inquiring look.

"So you seen me, did you?"

"We did, and wondered what you were doing there."

Hank laughed in his silent way, as if it were all a joke, but did not offer any explanation. Evidently he had some business down there, but, like most of his kind, was not inclined to make known his secrets when the necessity did not exist.

"What a tremendous climb that was! And it must have been dangerous to pick your way down the side of the canyon."

"I s'pose it would have been if I'd done it, but I didn't."

"Then the canyon cannot be as extended as we thought?"

"That depends on how long you thought it was. As near as I can find out, it is between sixty and seventy miles."

Not wishing to persist in speaking in riddles, Hank added:

"Howsumever, though it's as long as I said, there's a break not fur away, where the banks ain't more than a few feet above the stream. The break isn't large, but it don't have to be. You obsarved that the stream runs into the mountains. It seems to be making a dive fur t'other side, as if it meant to make fur the Pacific, but it gives it up and comes back after a while, and finds its way into the Wind River, and so on to the Big Horn and the Missouri."

"Then you came up the canyon from the break and went back again?"

"I didn't say that. I come up to where you seed me, but instead of going back I climbed the side to the top."

"Gracious, what a task! It **must be a** thousand feet."

"It isn't much less, but the sides of **the** canyon are so rough that it's just like so many steps. I've done it often, and ain't the only one. Bart and Mort tried both ways and like the climb better, though Kansas Jim would never take it. Don't furgit one thing, younkers. When you have a job like that afore you it's a good deal easier to climb up than it is to climb down. If you should find yourself at the bottom of the canyon and hit the right spot, you'll larn that the work is easier going up than you think, but it's too resky going down for any one to try."

The boys hoped their friend would tell
them why he had entered the gorge, when
the act at best was exhausting and accompanied by more or less peril, but he ignored
their curiosity, and they did not feel warranted in questioning him. When he
thought it well he would tell them, and they
could afford to wait until then.

The day was as perfect in its way as its pre-
decessor. The blue sky showed only a few
fleecy clouds at wide intervals, and the sun
shone with a strength that made its warmth
perceptible even in that elevated region.
The boys began to feel impatient to be moving. A good many days yet remained to
them, but they were all too few to satisfy
their longing for the inspiriting life they
had entered upon with so much zest.

As the three stood, the backs of Jack and
Fred were toward the cavern, in which the
fire had been burning, while the hunter faced
them. He now turned and looked off over
the wild, precipitous mountains by which
they were surrounded. The youths, who
were observing him, saw him fix his eyes on

a point to the right, at which he gazed so long and steadily that it was evident he had discovered something of more than usual interest. Following the same direction they looked keenly, but were unable to detect anything out of the ordinary.

Despite his own fixity of gaze, Hank noted what they were doing, and turning abruptly toward them, asked:

"Do you obsarve anything 'tic'lar?"

"Nothing more than what we have seen," replied Jack. "There are the mountain peaks, most of them reaching above the snow-line; the dark masses below; the scrubby pines, with more abundant vegetation, still further down."

"Do you see that crag that juts out from the side of the lower part of that peak?" asked Hank, extending his hand in the direction indicated.

Thus aided, both boys looked at the exact spot. It was below the snow-line, where only a few of the rocks showed, because of the numerous pines which grew luxuriantly; but, keen as was their eyesight, they were unable to detect the first sign of moving thing or life.

"Try your glasses on it," said Hank.

The boys brought the instruments round in front and levelled them at the point of interest. As they did so they made a discovery. From the very centre of the clump of wood rose a thin, shadowy line of vapor, which was dissolved in the clear air before it ascended more than a few feet above the tree-tops.

"So you observe it at last," said the hunter, after they had told what they saw. "Wal, now study it closer, and tell me if you notice anything queer 'bout the same."

Wondering what he could mean, they did as he requested. A minute later Fred said:

"The smoke does not ascend steadily; first it shows plainly, then there is none, and then it shows again."

"Seems to keep it up, eh?"

"Yes, like the puffs from the smoke-stack of a locomotive, only they are a great deal slower," explained Jack; "but the smoke soon dissolves in the clear air."

"Not soon enough, though, to keep you from obsarving what we've been talking about?"

"No; it is too plain to be mistaken."

"Did you ever see the smoke of a camp-fire act like that?"

"Never; have you?"

"Many a time; that's an Injin signal-fire."

This was interesting, but caused nothing in the nature of fear on the part of the boys. It was Fred who remarked:

"The Indians must be signaling to some one."

"Exactly."

"It can't be to *us?*"

"Not much; it's to another party of Injins, and that other party is calling back to 'em. See whether you can find t'other signal."

The boys moved the points of their glasses back and forth and up and down, but it was not until their guide again pointed out the right spot that they located the second signal. Indeed the vapor was so fine and feathery that it was wonderful how Hank himself had been so quick to note it.

The points were of about the same elevation, and separated by a distance of some two miles. Peak and valley, gorge and canyon, rock and boulder in profusion lay between. No doubt could remain that two parties of Indians were telegraphing messages back and forth, and that they were understood by each party.

As yet the boys failed to see that the matter was of any special concern to them, though it was interesting to know that they were not the only ones who were hunting in that section.

"I suppose," said Jack, "that the parties are from the reservation and are signaling to each other about the game."

"That may be," replied Hank, after some hesitation, "but I ain't quite sure *we* ain't the game they're signaling 'bout."

"They wouldn't dare disturb us!" exclaimed Fred.

"Not in the open; but don't furgit what I obsarved to you some time ago that an Injin, when he feels purty sartin of not being found out, ain't to be trusted. Now, younkers, I may be all wrong, but if I am, nothing won't be lost by acting as if I was right; whereas if I'm right and we don't act that way, the mischief will be to pay."

"How shall we make sure?"

"By keeping our eyes open; when we're hunting fur game, look out that some of the redskins ain't hunting fur us. I think that confounded Motoza has a finger in this pie."

Without explaining further, the hunter rested the stock of his gun on the ground and leaned upon it in profound meditation. He paid no attention to his companions, but continued gazing in the direction of the first signal-fire he had noticed, and was evidently turning over some scheme in his mind.

Had he been alone he would have given no further attention to the signs, which might mean nothing or a good deal, for he felt able to take care of himself, no matter in what situation he was placed; but he considered that to a large extent the safety of the two boys, who were totally without experience in these solitudes, rested upon him. He must take no chances that were avoidable.

"Younkers," he suddenly said, rousing

himself, "I must larn more 'bout this bus'ness; I'm off; don't go so fur from this place that you can't git back to-night; I'll be here and have some news fur you."

And with this parting he strode across the plateau on his way deeper into the mountains.

CHAPTER XI.

A KING OF THE FOREST.

THE boys remained standing at the mouth of the cavern until the guide disappeared on the other side of the little plateau. Then they looked at each other and smiled.

"Well, it appears that we are to have another day to ourselves," said Jack; "and we can't gain anything by waiting, so let's be off."

Nothing could be more satisfactory to Fred, and the two took nearly the same course as their friend, who passed from sight but a short time before. They had no intention, however, of following him, for that would have been displeasing to the veteran, who, had he desired their company, would have asked for it.

Without any definite object in mind, they took substantially the route of the previous afternoon. Sooner than they anticipated, they found themselves on the margin of the canyon that had been the scene of so stirring an experience, but the point where they reached it was deeper in the mountains.

"Jack, we can't be very far from that break that Hank spoke of; let's hunt it up."

"I am willing; but before we do so we'll peep over the side, to see whether he or anyone else is there."

No change was to be noted in the appearance of the tiny stream at the enormous depth, but neither friend nor stranger was in sight. They did not expect to see any one, and began moving along the side of the stupendous fissure in their search for the place where Hank had entered it. From what he said it could not be far off, but they were disappointed before reaching the right point. A gradual descent of the sides was notable, and continued until the depth of the canyon was decreased one-half, while the roar became more audible.

"We can't be far from the break," said Jack; "that is, if this descent continues."

They found, however, a few minutes later, that it did not continue, but began to increase, until they were fully as elevated above the bottom of the gorge as at the point where they had leaped it. The width also varied continually, sometimes being only three or four feet, while in others it expanded to nearly ten times that extent. They did not pause to look over the margin again, for their aim was to reach the place referred to by their friend.

At the moment when they began to wonder whether a mistake had not been made they came upon the break. Both banks sloped downward so abruptly that it would have been laborious for the two to work their way to the bottom, or from the bottom to the top, though the masses of boulders, with the tough pines growing almost the whole distance, offered secure foothold.

The picture was an interesting one. At the point where the stream issued from the canyon, its width was about twenty yards. It flowed swiftly, but quickly slackened its pace, since its expansion was fully a hundred feet. This flowed for probably double that distance, when the high banks again appeared, and what may be called the regular canyon was resumed.

Jack and Fred sat down to survey the curious picture. They noticed that the canyon seemed to be dotted at intervals with rocks, some of which rose to a considerable height above the current. Many were near one side or the other, while others were in the middle of the swift stream, which dashed against them with a violence that threw the spray and foam high in air. It was easy to believe that Hank Hazletine had made his way up the canyon by leaping from rock to rock, with little more result than the wetting of his shoes.

"It might be done in the daytime," said Jack, "but I should not want to try it at night."

"The water must be very deep in many places; and flows so fast that the strongest swimmer couldn't help himself. I should prefer to climb the wall, as Hank did."

"But that would be dangerous in the darkness."

"The best thing we can do is to do neither," observed Fred, with a laugh. " I have a good deal of curiosity to know what led Hank to pick his way up the canyon, but I haven't enough to lead me to follow him——"

Jack Dudley suddenly griped the arm of his friend and drew him back from the boulder on which they had been sitting. Fred nearly lost his balance, and did not know what to make of the proceeding until both checked themselves at a safe distance and cautiously peeped forth. Then the cause of Jack's excitement became apparent.

From the pines on the other side of the stream, and near the middle of the depressed portion, three Indians stepped into view. The first anxiety of the youths was to learn whether Motoza was one of them; but he was not. All were strangers.

They were dressed much the same as the vagrant Sioux, and, like him, their faces were painted, and their coarse black hair dangled loosely about their shoulders. They were armed with rifles; but two of the weapons seemed to be the long, old-fashioned muzzle-

loaders, while the third carried a Winchester.
Although they emerged from the pines in Indian file, they spread apart and walked beside
one another to the edge of the broad stream,
where they stopped, as if that were the end
of their journey.

Their gestures showed they were talking
energetically, though of course not the
slightest murmur reached the youths, who
took care to screen themselves from view
while cautiously peeping forth. Even after
the warning words of their guide they felt no
special alarm, for they believed the red men
were from the reservation near by, and would
not harm any one. If they attempted it,
Jack and Fred felt they had the advantage
of position, sheltered behind the rocks, far
above their enemies, down upon whom they
could fire with their Winchesters, should the
necessity arise.

It was quite certain that the three belonged
to one of the hunting parties whose signal-
smoke the boys had seen earlier in the day.
Their action was curious. They did not
look up the bank, so that the boys might

have been more careless without being discovered; but it was apparent that two of them
were arguing with the third, who was more excited than either of his companions. Finally
he turned away and made as if to pass up
the canyon, after the manner of Hank Hazletine. He leaped out upon one of the rocks,
then bounded as lightly to another, and then
to a third, which took him within the canyon.
The others watched him without protest or
action.

Evidently the Indian who had started off
so hurriedly was more impulsive than his
companions, for after his third leap he remained standing on the rock; and, although
it would have been easy for him to spring to
the next leading up the canyon, he refrained
from doing do. Instead, he looked around,
and then deliberately rejoined his friends, who
showed no surprise over his reverse movement. They spoke only a few words to one
another, when they moved back in Indian
file toward the growth of pines, among which
they passed from sight and were seen no
more.

"That was a queer performance," remarked Jack; "it looked to me as if that first fellow wanted his companions to go up the canyon with him, and when they refused he started off by himself."

"Only to change his mind."

"There can be no doubt of that; but it strikes me as strange that there should be something up there to attract them as well as Hank."

"Some day Hank will tell us about it. Do you observe, young man, that the forenoon is well along and we haven't had a sight of any game?"

With no thought of the Indians whom they had just seen, the boys began retracing their steps. Inasmuch as it was on the other side of the gorge that they had gained the shot at the buck, the feeling was strong that they should pass it again and push their hunt in that direction.

It did not require long to find a spot where the fissure was easily leaped. In fact, the exploit was becoming quite an everyday thing with them.

"We are not far from the spot where we killed that rattler yesterday," said Fred, recognizing several landmarks. "I wonder whether there are any more near us——"

At that instant Fred uttered a gasp and leaped several feet from the ground, while his companion was hardly a second behind him. Both had heard the well-remembered whir at the same moment, and bounded away several steps before pausing to look back.

Remarkable as it might seem, a second specimen of the *crotalus*, fully as large as the other, lay on the flat surface of a rock only a few inches above the ground. Evidently it was sunning itself when thus disturbed by the approach of the young hunters, at sight of whom it threw itself into coil. The boys were not in danger, for the warning was sounded while they were still a number of paces distant.

Feeling safe, they stood still and surveyed the hideous thing. They agreed that it was larger than the other, and seemed to be darker in color. But for the fact that the reptiles were on opposite sides of the canyon, it might be believed they were mates. The head and tail were elevated, the latter vibrating with the swift, hazy appearance at the end of the rattles which they had noted before.

Jack repeated the oft-quoted expression : "The heel of the woman shall bruise the serpent's head," and added : " I suppose nine persons out of every ten, when they see any kind of a snake, are seized with an impulse to kill it."

" Even though many are harmless and useful."

" I think the best use you can put a rattle-snake to is to blow him into smithereens, which is what I am going to do."

As he spoke, Jack brought his Winchester to a level and sighted carefully at the pitted head of the serpent. He was deliberate, and did not press the trigger until sure his aim was accurate to a hair.

Fred kept his eye on that head. At the instant the sharp crack of the rifle rang out the frightful object vanished, and the long body broke into fierce writhings. Jack had clipped off the head as neatly as if with the blow of a scimitar, the bullet shattering the neck just below, and at its narrowest portion.

"That's as well as I could have done myself," commented Fred, as his friend lowered his weapon and watched the struggles of his victim, which quickly ceased, for, as has been said, the *crotalus* species is easily killed, and when one of them has been decapitated he cannot keep up appearances very long.

When it became certain the reptile was dead the boys drew near for a closer inspection. They counted the rattles, which were seventeen in number, proving the reptile of extraordinary size.

"We didn't think to count those of the other," said Fred, "but I am sure it was not so large as this."

"No; but I wonder whether we are going to stumble over them at every step?"

"This is only the second one; we may not see another for a week."

"I hope we shall not; but so long as they are kind enough to give us notice of their intentions we ought to be able to avoid their bites."

It looked as if their experience of the previous day was to be repeated, for within a hundred yards from the spot an animal was discovered on a rock, a considerable distance above them. Fred was the first to see it, and exclaimed :

"There's another buck, Jack! It's your turn."

But before Jack could bring his weapon to a level the animal saw them and was off like a flash. In fact they had no more than a glimpse of it—barely enough to see that it had no antlers, and probably was not a deer at all.

"It isn't going to be as easy work as we thought," said Fred ; "I shouldn't be surprised if we fail to get a shot to-day."

"Well, we shall have the fun of tramping ourselves tired. It seems to me that when any sort of game shows itself it comes out in plain sight and is not scared up by us. Let's sit down a while and watch things around us."

This singular proposal was acted upon. After picking their way some distance further among the rocks they chose a seat, and then looked searchingly here and there at the different elevations and prominent points, in the hope of catching sight of some game which would give them a shot before dashing off with headlong haste.

"Right over that part of the mountain peak yonder," said Jack, pointing at the place, "I saw the moon rise last night. I have watched it come out of the ocean many a time, but never saw anything so beautiful before."

He described as best he could the impressive scene, while Fred listened, and for the first time felt regret that he had not been awakened that he, too, might have enjoyed the view.

When he had studied the mountain peak for some minutes, he raised his glass and surveyed it steadily for a while longer.

"I thought so," he remarked; "turn your glass, Jack, in that direction."

Jack did as requested, and saw to what his comrade referred. Perched on the highest portion was an immense gray-headed eagle.

Sailing thither from the depths of space, he had paused for a while, with the grand view spread out before him, and what a view it must have been !

It was easy to identify the bird with the aid of their glasses, which were kept pointed for some time at him.

"I wonder whether he sees us?" said Fred.

"There can be no doubt of it, for their eyes detect the smallest object on a landscape. He is probably studying us with as much interest as we are watching him."

"Our rifles couldn't carry a ball half-way to him."

"And what if they could? Would you wish to harm the emblem of our country ?"

"No; unless he attacked us, which I don't think is likely. Halloo!"

Just then the immense bird spread his wings and began skimming through the air with majestic grace. More than that, he was coming in the direction of the boys.

"I believe he means to make a meal off of us!" exclaimed Fred; "we would better be ready for him."

"There's nothing to be frightened at. If he intends to attack us we have only to wait until he is near, when we can puncture him."

If the king of birds held any such intention he changed his mind. Swooping far across the intervening space, seemingly aiming straight at them, he suddenly changed his course, and, ascending high in the sky, swept around in a wide circle and finally disappeared over the peak where first seen.

The boys sat for a while in silence, gazing away in the distance, where the noble bird had vanished, half-expecting it to reappear and probably press its attack; but it had taken its flight for good and was seen no more.

"I wonder whether we would have done any better if we had brought a dog with us?" said Jack, beginning to feel a trifle discouraged over their failure to secure a shot at any game.

"I proposed bringing my dog, you remember, when we left home, but you thought we could do better out here. Hank and the rest of them don't seem to place much value on the animals in hunting. Did you hear that?"

From some point not very far off came the report of a rifle, though whether it was the weapon of Hank Hazletine or one of the Indians that had been discharged, neither could guess.

"Somebody else is in luck, and I don't see why we should not——"

Before Fred could finish his sentence both heard the rustling of bushes behind them. They turned on the instant, and saw a sight which held them transfixed, for never had they expected to view anything of the kind.

They had read and heard much of grizzly bears. They knew they grew to an enormous size, and are the most formidable animals found in the great West, but had they been told that there were such monsters as the one before them they could not have believed it had it been related by Hazletine himself.

To Jack and Fred he seemed fully four times the size of the largest black bear they had ever seen in any zoological garden. Had his legs been longer, Fred Greenwood would have pronounced him the equal of Jumbo himself.

Where this Colossus among beasts had come from it was impossible to say, but the terrifying fact was self-evident that he was advancing to attack the boys!

He must have caught sight of them as they sat on the rock with their backs toward him, and, angered at the intrusion, he was sweeping down upon them like a cyclone, furious and determined to crush them out of existence.

The gait of the animal was awkward, but speedier even than the youths suspected. He swung along with a swaying motion, and his claws, striking the flinty rocks as he passed over them, rattled like iron nails. His vast mouth was open, his long red tongue lolling out, and his white teeth gleaming. As if no element of terror was to be omitted he uttered a deep, cavernous growl at every step or two, while his comparatively small black eyes seemed to glow with a savage light, altogether foreign to the species.

All this was taken in at the first glance of the boys, who, petrified for one moment, realized in the next their fearful peril.

"There's no time to shoot!" exclaimed Jack; "we must run!"

"But he can run faster than we!" replied Fred, who stood his ground long enough to bring his Winchester to his shoulder and let fly straight at the front of the beast. That he struck the bear was certain, but it served only to add to his towering rage, and he plunged forward without halt.

Jack had made no attempt to fire, but was running at headlong speed. Fred was eager to thrust another cartridge into the chamber of his Winchester from the magazine, but to do so would detain him until old Ephraim was upon him, and even then it was not likely the bullet would stay or affect his attack.

Accordingly, instead of firing a second shot he whirled about and dashed after Jack, who was thus placed about a rod in advance. Although the ground was not favorable for running, it may be safely said that neither Jack Dudley nor Fred Greenwood ever gave such an exhibition of speed. They held fast to their rifles, for it looked as if the weapons were to be their final reliance.

Fred glanced over his shoulder to learn how he was making out in the race. With an awful sinking he saw that the grizzly was gaining fast upon him. Still he dared not pause long enough to fire, but redoubled his energies, only to catch his foot in a running vine and plunge forward on his face.

CHAPTER XII.

THE TUG OF WAR.

JACK DUDLEY, being some paces in advance of Fred Greenwood, and alarmed for him because of his greater peril, had slightly slackened his speed, for he was not the one to seek safety at the expense of his comrade. The instant he saw him fall he stopped short, and, wheeling about, fired at the grizzly, and pumping a second cartridge into the chamber of his Winchester, let fly again, both shots striking the beast, who was so close that a miss was impossible.

It need not be said that Fred, having pitched forward on his hands and knees, did not remain thus. No hunter, even if a youth, gives up so long as there is a fighting chance for life. He instantly leaped to his feet, and a couple of bounds placed him beyond reach, for the moment, of his terrible enemy.

The bear seemed to understand who had

14

wounded him last, and, although closer to
Fred than to his companion, he swerved to
the left and headed for Jack Dudley. The
latter did not stay on the order of his going,
but made off at his highest speed. Brief as
was the halt, it wrought a complete change
of situation. Whereas Fred had been in the
greatest danger, Jack was now thus placed,
because the grizzly was closer to him. Not
only that, but, ignoring the younger lad, he
gave his whole attention to Jack.

Events were going with such a rush that
the boys were almost overwhelmed before they
could help themselves. Fred supposed the
bear was at his heels until, having run a
couple of rods, he glanced over his shoulder
and saw the imminent peril of Jack. Then,
with a thrill of alarm, he in his turn checked
his flight, and bringing his Winchester to a
level drove a bullet into the immense head .
of the brute, which by that time had received
a respectable amount of lead in his carcass.

But "old Ephraim" seemed to have determined to dispose of the fugitives in the reverse
order of their ages; that is to say, having

changed his attentions to Jack Dudley, he did not mean to be diverted therefrom, even though the younger lad was showing disagreeable interest in him.

This peculiar turn of affairs gave Fred his favorable chance; and, standing motionless, he continued his miniature bombardment as fast as he could shove the cartridges into the chamber of his weapon, aim, and fire. Surely the bullets, all of which found a lodgment somewhere in the anatomy of the monster, must have produced an effect, but they could not divert him from his main purpose. He bore down upon the apparently doomed Jack Dudley as if he would not be denied.

This fact caused Fred to be thrown partly to the rear, so that the remarkable combat took the form of the grizzly pursuing one of the boys, while the other boy was pursuing the grizzly. The position of Fred, however, thus became unfavorable, for he was unable to aim at any vulnerable portion of the creature. He continued firing into his body, but the bullets produced no perceptible effect in this fight for life.

Meanwhile the situation of Jack Dudley became perilous to the last degree. To stop and fire insured his certain seizure by the grizzly, who would require but a moment to tear the life from him. Jack saw him so near, indeed, that he did that which no person would do except in the last extremity. He flung away his rifle, that it might not impede his flight, and concentrated all his energies into the one effort of running.

He had no time to look where he was going. He could only strive with the desperation of despair to preserve the distance between him and his pursuer, in the faint hope that something would intervene to save him. Fred was not only firing his gun as fast as he could, but he shouted to the bear, in the hope of diverting his attention from Jack, who could not keep up the unequal flight much longer.

The terrified fugitive leaped over boulders, dashed around interposing rocks, and bounded across open spaces, hardly daring to look over his shoulder, for he knew from the sounds of pursuit that the animal was at his heels. It seemed every moment as if the prodigious paw of the grizzly would smite him to the earth, when no human power could save him.

Suddenly the fugitive, while dashing forward in this blind, headlong fashion, found himself confronted by the canyon with which he and Fred had already had a memorable experience. It yawned at right angles to the course he was following, its width so great that it was impossible for him to leap it at that point. But he knew there must be some such place, and he continued his flight along the side of the chasm, hunting for a spot that would permit him to reach the other bank.

He did not stop to think how this could benefit him, for it was to be supposed that if the grizzly could outrun he could also outleap him, and the moment the fugitive landed on the further bank the brute would do the same, without losing an inch of the advantage already gained. In fact, Jack Dudley had no time to think of anything except to run with all the vigor which nature had given him.

All at once he saw a spot where the feat looked possible. There was no time for him to turn off to gain the momentum, but, measuring the interval with his eye, he gathered his muscles and leaped outward. The jump was diagonal, and made under most difficult circumstances.

Who shall describe the awful thrill that shot through Jack Dudley when, at the moment of leaving the rocky edge of the rocky wall, he was sure he was about to fail in his last effort? The other margin of the canyon wall appeared to recede, and he uttered a despairing cry, certain that the next instant he would go spinning down the frightful abyss.

It is at such critical times that the question of life and death is often decided by incidents so trifling that they are unnoticed. Had Jack Dudley retained his Winchester in his grasp he would have been lost. It would not have been alone the weight of the weapon, but its interference with the free use of his hands. As it was, the latter were untrammeled, and, though his feet missed a firm hold, he instinctively clutched the craggy projections, and, with a supreme effort, drew himself over the margin and beyond all danger of falling back into the canyon.

And where, all this time, was old Ephraim?

The remark just made concerning the effect of trifles was shown as strikingly in his case as in that of the fugitive. Despite his enormous weight and awkwardness of action, the grizzly without special exertion could have made the leap that had just been exhibited before his eyes had he been in his usual condition, but it has been shown that he had been struck by several bullets. Though most of these inflicted little more than flesh wounds, which under the circumstances were trifling, yet others did effective work. This was especially the case with those that found a lodgment in his head, which, big and tough as it was, lacked the power of turning aside a rifle-ball, as the indurated back of an alligator often does.

It is to be supposed that the enraged grizzly did not comprehend the possible weakening of his colossal power through the effect of these pellets, and it is quite likely that even with such weakening he would have accomplished the leap of the canyon, but for the interference of an incident which cannot be considered in any other light than providential.

Fred Greenwood's anguish was for his companion, whom it seemed impossible to help, despite the desperate effort he was making to do so. He saw the grizzly lumbering after Jack, giving no heed to the shots he sent after him, but steadily gaining upon the fugitive, whose fate hung in the passing of the seconds. Fred knew what it meant when his friend abruptly changed his course and began skirting the canyon in his frantic hunt for a narrower place. The bear was so close upon him for several paces that the terrified Fred stopped short, ceased shooting, and held his breath, expecting the great beast to strike down his comrade. The younger lad could do no more, and, staring at the two, he asked in agony that heaven would not desert his friend.

Suddenly Jack Dudley rose like a bird in air. At the instant the monster was upon him he made the leap, landing on the further edge, as has been told, and quickly scrambling upon solid foundation. Had he been ten seconds later nothing could have saved him, for the grizzly showed no more hesitation than he in making the jump.

At the instant Fred read the brute's intention he brought his rifle to his shoulder. Unsuspected by himself, the last cartridge in the magazine of his Winchester was in the chamber of the weapon, so that, if it failed to help, the service of the younger lad was at an end for the time, for it would be all over before he could bring into use any cartridges from his belt.

To make the leap to which we have referred the grizzly changed his position. Until that moment he had been running straight away from Fred, but now, of necessity, he turned partly toward him. Recalling the words of Hank Hazletine, Fred aimed at a point just back of the foreleg, as it reached forward. The ball sped true to its aim, and entering, perhaps, the most vulnerable point of the body, did more than all the other bullets that had found a lodging-place in the grizzly, for it inflicted a mortal wound.

It was this fact that destroyed the effort of

the bear at the crisis of its inception. The
attempt already put forth carried him well
beyond the side of the canyon, but it failed to
land him firmly on the other margin. His
forepaws went over the top, precisely as the
hands of Jack Dudley had done, and began a
furious scratching of the flinty surface, while
the hind feet clawed with equal fierceness the
inner side of the wall. The brute was striv-
ing to save himself, and it is to be presumed
would have done so but for the cause named.

That last shot told the story. The shot
had seriously weakened the bear, and his
mighty strength was fast oozing away. His
struggles grew less vigorous, though they
continued up to the last moment. Jack Dudley had become aware of what was going on,
and, stopping in his flight, shouted:

"Shoot him, Fred, before he can climb
out!"

Fred attempted to do so, but discovered he
had no more cartridges at command. Since
the bear at best could not harm the younger,
he ran forward to the side of the canyon, just
behind the beast. Jack had paused, so that

both were looking at the grizzly, whose huge head and massive shoulders protruded above the edge of the canyon. While they looked the head dropped from sight, followed by the forefeet, whose claws scratched over the flinty surface as they slipped backward.

Knowing what had occurred, Jack and Fred ran to the edge and looked down. They were in time to see the mountainous bulk tumbling into the vast chasm. The body maintained a horizontal posture, as in life, until it struck a projecting point which sent it bounding against the other side, where the impact added to the tendency of the first blow, and the body turned over and over, like an immense log rolling down hill. Despite the gloom of the abyss the sun was shining so brightly, and was in such a favorable position, that everything was seen with distinctness.

Peering downward, the awed and grateful boys saw the black mass suddenly strike the foamy waters and send the spray flying in all directions. It disappeared for a moment and then popped up like a rubber-ball, and went dancing down the current toward the break in the walls which they had visited a brief while before.

Still silent and watching, they observed it dancing up and down with the violence of the stream until its motion was arrested by striking an obstruction, which held it motionless. There it stayed for the remaining minutes spent in peering into the abyss.

Jack and Fred looked up and across the canyon at the same instant. They were directly opposite, and hardly twelve feet apart. The elder took off his hat and called:

"Are you ready?"

"Yes," said Fred, removing his head-gear.

"All together!"

And then they swung their hats and hurrahed with the vim which, all things considered, was justified by events. They were happy and grateful, and neither forgot to thank, with all the fervency of his nature, the One who had delivered them in safety from the very jaws of death. No matter what other dangers might come to them, there could be none narrower or more striking than that through which they had just passed.

"Do you intend to stay on that side of the canyon?" asked Fred.

"I don't know that there is any choice between our places, but if you feel lonely I'll come over to your help."

"I thought you might want to pick up the gun you threw away."

Jack looked at each of his hands in turn and laughed.

"Do you know I had forgotten all about that? I don't remember having thrown it aside."

"I saw you do it, and it was a lucky thing you did."

The two walked beside the canyon until they came to a straight place, where Jack easily made the leap and joined his friend. Then they set out to recover the Winchester, which, as matters stood, was almost beyond value to them.

"I can't recall the spot where I dropped it," remarked Jack, allowing his companion to take the lead.

"I do; you and I were doing such tall running then, and for some minutes afterward, that we covered more ground than would be supposed. That's the spot, just ahead."

He indicated an open space, thirty or forty feet in width, lying between a ridge of boulders, over which it was astonishing how the fugitive had managed to make such good progress.

"We shall find it right there——"

Fred checked his words, for at that moment they came upon the spot he had in mind and both swept their gaze over it. Their dismay may be imagined when they saw nothing of the Winchester.

"You must be mistaken as to the place," said Jack.

"I can't be; it was just after you had leaped down from that low boulder that you gave your right arm a swing and away the gun went."

"Did you notice where it landed?"

"I can put my hand on the very spot."

"Do so."

Fred led the way a few paces and said:

"It was there, and nowhere else."

Jack bent over and carefully studied the earth.

"My gracious! you are right; that dent in the ground was made by the stock of my gun, and it couldn't have gone its own length further."

The space was clear for several yards, and they would have discerned a small coin lying anywhere on it, but nothing suggesting a weapon was in sight.

A momentary consternation took possession of them. Only one conclusion was possible: some person had taken the Winchester.

"Do you suppose it was Hank, who wanted to have some fun with us?" asked Fred.

Jack shook his head.

"At any other time I might believe it, but Hank isn't one to look for fun when the lives of two persons are in danger. It wasn't he."

"Who, then, could it be?"

Again Jack shook his head.

"You know there are a number of Indians hunting in this neighborhood. Some of them may have been near us, and, hearing our cries and the reports of our guns, started to find out what it meant. Coming upon my Winchester, they carried it off."

This was the most reasonable explanation they could think of, but it did not lessen their disappointment at the loss of the indispensable weapon.

"I won't stand it!" exclaimed Jack, whose indignation was rising; "the man who took that gun must give it back!"

It was impossible to know in what direction to look for the pilferer, but the youth's long strides led him toward the break in the walls of the canyon where they had seen the three Indians earlier in the forenoon. Whether it was reasonable to expect to find them, or rather the thief, there, would be hard to say, but Jack did find the one for whom he was looking.

Half the intervening distance was passed, when he turned his head and said in an excited undertone to his companion:

"He's just ahead, and as sure as I live the thief is Motoza!"

Before Fred, slightly at the rear, could gain sight of the Indian, Jack broke into a lope and called:

"Hold on there, Motoza! You have something that belongs to me."

The dusky vagrant was alone and walking at a moderate pace from the youth. Although he did not look around until hailed he must have known he was followed, but he stopped short and wheeled about with a wondering expression on his painted face.

There could be no mistake by Jack Dudley, for Motoza was carrying two Winchesters, one in either hand, and a glance enabled the youth to recognize his own property.

"Howdy, brother?" asked Motoza, with the old grin on his face.

Jack was too angry to be tactful. He continued his rapid strides, and as he drew near reached out his hand.

"Never mind how I do; give me my rifle."

But with the fingers of Jack almost on the weapon, Motoza shifted his hand backward, so that the gun was held behind his body. He did not stir, but continued grinning.

"What do you mean?" demanded Jack, his face flushed, and his anger greater than before; "didn't you hear me ask for my gun?"

"Whooh! brother frow way gun—me pick him up—he mine."

15

"I threw it down so as to have a better chance of getting away from the grizzly bear; I intended to pick it up again. I know you are a great thief, Motoza, but you can't steal that Winchester from me; hand it over!"

And Jack extended his hand again; but the Sioux persisted in keeping the weapon behind him, though his own was in front, where the lad might have been tempted to snatch it from his grasp.

The youth was fast losing his self-command. He had learned the character of this vagrant from Hazletine, and it was plain that he meant to retain the valuable weapon, while Jack was equally determined he should not.

"I tell you for the last time to give me my gun! *Do you hear?*"

The demand was made in a loud voice and accompanied by a threatening step toward the Indian, who showed no fear. The grin, however, had left his face, and he recoiled a step with such a tigerish expression on his ugly countenance that his assailant ought to have been warned of his danger. Motoza, the Sioux, was ready to commit murder for the sake of retaining that which did not belong to him.

"Stop!" commanded Fred Greenwood, whom both seemed to have forgotten in the flurry of the moment.

The younger was standing a little to the rear and to one side, but his Winchester, it will be remembered, was in his hand, and was now pointed at the dusky scamp.

"Motoza, if you want to preserve that sweet countenance of yours, hand that gun to my friend before I let daylight through you!"

CHAPTER XIII.

A STRANGE OCCURRENCE.

ONCE more Motoza had allowed an American youth to get the drop on him, for he could not mistake the meaning of that command, nor the deeper eloquence of the pose of Fred Greenwood with his rifle at a dead level. The Sioux must have despised himself for his forgetfulness.

But he had already proven the readiness with which he accepted a situation, no matter how unwelcome. The hand that held the weapon of Jack Dudley whipped round to the front with a deft movement, which, however, was not quicker than the return of the grin to his countenance.

"Motoza friend—he not want gun of brother," he remarked.

"You wouldn't get it if you *did* want it," said Jack, not to be mollified by this sudden change of front. Instead of accepting the hypocritical proffer, the youth was imprudent enough to add, as he felt his Winchester once more in his grasp:

"You are the meanest thief in the country, Motoza, and this must be the last time you try your hand on us."

"Off with you!" added Fred, beginning to tire with the constraint of his position; "goodby, Motoza, and I hope we shall not meet again."

At the moment of obeying, the Sioux glanced at the lad who had thus turned the tables on him. The expression of his face was frightful. Ferocious hate, thirst for revenge and flaming anger shone through the coat of paint and were concentrated on the younger of the youths. Fred saw it and cared not, but Jack was so alarmed that he almost wished his comrade would fire his weapon and thus shut out the fruition of the horrible threat that gleamed through that look.

It lasted, however, but an instant. Much in the same manner as in the grove, when caught at a disadvantage by Jack Dudley, the Sioux walked off and was quickly lost to view.

Neither of the boys spoke for several minutes. Then Jack asked, in an awed voice:

"Did you see his face when he turned toward you just before walking away?"

"Yes; and I have seen handsomer ones."

"You may make light of it, Fred, but I was much nearer than you, and that expression will haunt me for many a day and night to come."

To the astonishment of the elder, Fred began laughing, as if he found it all very amusing. Jack, in surprise, asked the cause of his mirth.

"If Motoza had only known the truth! There isn't a cartridge either in the magazine or the chamber of my rifle, which reminds me."

And still laughing, the younger proceeded to fill the magazine from his belt and to put his Winchester in condition for immediate use.

"We have been told many times, Jack, that the first thing to do after firing a gun is

to reload, and I see how much more important it is here than at home."

When Jack came to examine his weapon
he found a half-dozen cartridges remaining
in the magazine, and he, too, placed the
weapon in the best form for use. They
changed their position, returning to the spot
where the crisis had taken place with the
grizzly, for both felt some misgiving concerning the Sioux, who could not be far off.

"Jack, what about the feelings of Motoza
now ?"

"It begins to look as if Hank was right.
I am sure the Indian doesn't hold much
friendship for either of us. He is bad clean
through."

"He may have some regard for *you*, but
there wasn't much tender affection in the last
lingering look he gave *me*."

Jack shuddered.

"I never saw anything like it. If he had
had the power he would have killed you with
that look. I feel like urging Hank, when we
next see him, to make a change of quarters."

"Why ?"

"That we may find some section where we are not likely to meet Motoza again. I don't understand why so many Indians are off the reservation. There must be a number of them that are friends of Motoza, and they will try some other trick on us."

"He has tried one or two already," replied Fred, much less impressed with the danger than his friend.

"True, we have had remarkably good fortune, but it can't last. Motoza will learn to be more cunning next time."

"If you feel that way, Jack, the best thing for us to do is to go home."

"Your words are hardly worthy of you, Fred," replied Jack, hurt at the slur.

"I ask your pardon. I know it is your friendship for me that speaks, but I cannot feel the fear that disturbs you. Suppose we drop the question till we see Hank. We will let him know everything that has taken place and rely upon him."

This was a wise conclusion, but the fact remained that there was no expectation of seeing their guide until night, which was a number of hours distant, and, since the Indians were in the vicinity, there was plenty of time for a great many things to happen. It would seem, indeed, that the advantage was almost entirely on the side of Motoza, for, with his superior woodcraft, he could keep track of the movements of the boys without their discovering or suspecting his presence. Altogether, it looked as if a meeting with their guide could not take place too soon.

From a point perhaps a mile away came the faint report of a rifle, followed in the same second by another report. The fact suggested more than one startling supposition, but the youths were in no mood to speculate thereon, for it will be admitted that the incidents of the forenoon were sufficient to engage their thoughts.

It was a hard fact, however, that when they looked at their watches and found that it was noon, the most interesting subject that presented itself was as to how they could secure the meal which they felt was overdue.

"Let's make a hunt in a different direction," said Fred. "It is best to keep away from the neighborhood of those Indians, so far as we can locate them from the shots we occasionally hear, for the game isn't likely to stay where they are."

"Off yonder to the north appears to be a valley," remarked Jack, after the two had studied their surroundings for some minutes through their glasses. "I can't tell how extensive it is, for it is shut out by that mountain peak on the right, but I suppose one place is as good as another."

. Having agreed as to their course, they wasted no time. It was a long and severe tramp to the locality, for again the peculiar purity of the atmosphere misled them, and what they took to be one mile proved to be fully double that length. Finally the hungry lads reached a ridge from whose top they could look down in the valley that had first caught their attention, but which for the last hour had been excluded from their sight by the intervening obstacles.

"Now, we can't tell whether any game is below waiting for us," said Jack, "but we can't lose anything by acting as if there is."

It was a wise precaution, as speedily became apparent. As carefully as a couple of Indians they picked their way up the slope, and just before reaching the crest sank upon their knees, and, crawling a little further, peeped over the top as if they expected to discover a hostile camp within a hundred yards.

The prospect caused an involuntary exclamation of pleasure from both. The valley was two or three hundred yards in width, and, after winding past, curved out of sight behind the mountain range already referred to. It was one emerald mass of rich grass, in which ten thousand cattle could have found abundant pasturage. No trees appeared anywhere except at the furthest bend in the valley, where a small grove stood near the middle, and seemed to surround a spring of water, which, flowing in the other direction, was not within sight of the young hunters.

What lent additional beauty to this landscape was the singular uniformity of the valley. The slope was gentle on each side, without any abrupt declivities, and there was hardly any variation in its width. The dark-green color of the incline and bottom of the valley gave the whole scene a softness that would have charmed an artist.

The young men admired the picturesque prospect, the like of which they had never before viewed, and yet it must be confessed that one feature of the landscape appealed more strongly to them than all the rest. Perhaps a half-mile away six or eight antelope were cropping the grass, unconscious of the approach of danger. They were near the small clump of trees alluded to, and may have lately drank from the water flowing therefrom. They were in a bunch, all their heads down, and had evidently taken no alarm from the occasional distant reports of guns.

"I say, Jack, there's a splendid dinner!" whispered Fred, excitedly.

"What good will it do us, so long as it is *there?* I should like to have it *here.*"

"It ought to be easy to pick off one of those creatures; Hank told us they make fine eating."

"That is all true, but it is also true that the

antelope is one of the most timid of creatures, and the best hunter finds it hard work to get within reach of them."

"You know how curious they are? The men at the ranch told the other night about lying down in the grass in the middle of a prairie and holding up a stick with a handkerchief at the end of it. Timid as was the antelope, it would gradually draw near to find out what the thing meant, and pay for its curiosity with its life."

Such incidents are quite common in the West, but neither of the boys felt it safe to rely upon the stratagem. They feared that at the first attempt the antelope would take fright and make off beyond recovery, and Fred Greenwood's proposition was adopted.

"There doesn't seem to be any wind blowing, but if we try to steal down the side of the valley we are sure to frighten them off. Now, if you will stay here, Jack, I'll pick my way round to the other side, so that the herd will be between us. Then I'll do my best to get near enough for a shot; if I fail, they will run for this point and come within range of you. Between us two, one is certain to get a shot at them."

"It's putting a big lot of work on you, Fred," said the chivalrous Jack.

"It won't be half as hard to bear as the hunger I'll feel in the course of an hour or two if we don't get one of them."

The plan was so simple that no explanation was necessary. Jack Dudley had only to remain extended on the ground where he was, with his Winchester ready, and keep an eye on the little herd, which could not observe him unless he was unusually careless. He could easily judge of Fred's success or failure by watching the animals, and it would seem that success was almost certain for one of the young hunters. The only thing to be feared was that Fred would betray himself before reaching the other side of the game that was so tempting to both.

The comrades looked at their watches at the moment of separating, and found it was precisely one o'clock. Fred gave himself an hour to reach a point from which to start on his return, though it was possible that double that time would be required. Before the interval had expired Jack had his glass to his eyes, and was studying the valley below.

As the antelope cropped the rich grass they occasionally took a step in the direction of the watcher; but the largest one, evidently the leader, changed his course so as to work back toward the little grove of trees, the others following. Now and then the leader raised his head and looked around, as if suspecting danger, though his fears were not confirmed. At longer intervals other members of the herd did the same, but it was evident that they neither saw nor scented anything amiss.

Jack's constant fear was that Fred would betray himself through some accident. His course would bring him nearer the game and the risk was considerable; but as the minutes passed without anything of that nature taking place, his hope increased.

"More than likely Fred himself will get the shot instead of me. It makes no difference, so that we don't lose our supper; for," he added, dismally, "the dinner is already gone."

When another half-hour had passed, he was sure his chum was on the other side of the herd.

"There must be a break pretty soon. Suppose that instead of coming toward me," added Jack, giving expression to a dread that had not occurred to him until then, "they dash off into the mountains on either side. Then we shall be doomed to starvation!"

He thought that with the aid of his glass he would be able to follow Fred as he stole down the side of the valley, since the position of the spectator was much more elevated than that of the antelope. It would require sharp scrutiny even with the aid of the instrument to do this, and, look as keenly as he might, he could discover nothing that suggested anything of that nature.

When three o'clock went by without any evidence of alarm among the animals browsing in the middle of the valley, Jack Dudley began to wonder what it could mean.

"Fred was sure that a single hour was enough to place himself on the further side of them, and double that time has passed. He ought to be well down the slope, but I can see nothing of him."

One fact, however, was apparent: the antelope were steadily though slowly working toward the ridge on which the young man lay. At the rate they were advancing it would not be long before it would be safe to try a shot.

This progress could not be laid to any alarm coming from the other side. If the animals received fright they would be off with the speed of the wind, instead of inching along in the fashion they were now following.

"It begins to look as if I am to secure the meal, after all," thought Jack, forgetting his slight uneasiness for his friend in his growing excitement.

The following minute gave proof of the timidity of the American antelope. With all the care possible, the youth extended his gun in front of him over the slope, but the herd took the alarm on the instant, though it seemed impossible that they should have seen or heard anything. The leader raised his head, and whirling to one side, started at a swift gallop toward the other end of the valley, the rest of the animals being hardly a second behind him.

The peculiar panic and stampede of the creatures gave Jack Dudley the best possible target, though the shot was a long one. He did not aim at the leader, but at a smaller animal that immediately followed him. The bullet pierced the heart of the antelope, which made a frenzied leap high in air, staggered a few paces, and dropped to the ground without a particle of life.

"Hurrah!" exclaimed the delighted Jack, springing up and dashing down the side of the valley toward his prize; "I beat you, after all, Fred!"

Not doubting that his comrade would speedily appear, Jack gave no further thought to him, but continued running until he reached the prize. He had learned the art so rapidly that it took but a few minutes to cut all he could need for himself and friend. Then he hurried to the little grove near by, washed and dressed the food, which seemed to be juicy and tender, and started a fire for the purpose of broiling it.

He had not paused in his work up to this point, but now he stopped with the first real thrill of alarm for his friend.

"Four o'clock!" he exclaimed to himself; "what can have become of him?"

He walked to the edge of the trees and looked out, anxiously peering in different directions, but nothing was seen of his friend. Knowing Fred's waggish nature, Jack hoped that he was indulging in some jest, but he could not quite convince himself that such was the fact. The hunger of Fred would have prevented his postponing the meal one moment longer than was necessary.

When an abundance of food was browned and crisped and ready the appetite of Jack Dudley was less than it was two hours before, the cause being his growing alarm over the unaccountable absence of Fred.

"I can't understand it," he repeated for the twentieth time; "some accident must have befallen him. Can it be Motoza has had anything to do with it?"

It was the first time that Jack had expressed this fear in words, but it was by no means the first time he had felt it. Rather curiously, from the moment his friend passed out of sight, several hours before, the vague misgiving began to shape itself in his mind. He fought it off and succeeded in repressing it for a time, but he could do so no longer.

"Fred didn't seem to give any meaning to that awful look of the Sioux when he started to walk away, but I saw what it meant, though I never dreamed the blow would fall so soon."

His heart was depressed almost beyond bearing, and the anguish was deepened by the fact that he could see no way of helping his friend. The only thing possible was to follow as nearly as he could the course taken by Fred, but there was no certainty of that. He knew he had turned to the right when he left the crest of the ridge, after which there had been no glimpse of him.

"But he made for a point over yonder," reflected Jack, "and there I'll search for him."

This was exceedingly indefinite, but it was better than standing idle. The antelope had long since vanished, and there was no need of care in his progress—rather otherwise, since he desired to attract the notice of his friend. Jack broke into a loping trot, emitting the familiar signal so often used by both, calling his name, and even firing his rifle in air ; but there came back no response, and his fears deepened.

Jack was in the mood to be unjust.

" I don't understand Hank Hazletine's action. He sets out to take us on a hunt among the mountains, and then goes off and leaves us alone. Why doesn't he stay with us? If he had done that, this never could have happened. Fred and I can generally take care of ourselves, but we are not used to this plagued country, which I wish neither he nor I had ever set foot in."

CHAPTER XIV.

MISSING.

THE minute quickly arrived when Jack
Dudley could no longer doubt that a
great misfortune had befallen his comrade,
Fred Greenwood.

In the anguish of anxiety Jack's imagination pictured many mishaps that might account for the disappearance. He must have
heard the report of the elder's Winchester,
and, since Fred's attention was centred upon
the herd of antelope, he could not fail to
know that his friend had secured one of them
for their evening meal. The only thing to
prevent his hastening to join Jack must have
been his inability to do so. There was the
remote possibility that his accident had been
of a nature that involved no one else—such,
for instance, as sudden illness, though Jack
had never known anything like that to over-
take his friend.

All that the youth could do was to attempt to follow the route that Fred had taken when he set out to place himself on the other side of the game. It was guesswork to trace his footsteps, but the elder youth made the effort. When he had progressed half the distance, however, he paused, convinced that his labor was utterly useless. He called to Fred, repeated their familiar signals and fired several charges in air, with no more response than at first.

"He has been either killed or carried off by a party of Indians," was the conclusion that forced itself upon him.

And with this conviction came the certainty that it was out of the power of Jack Dudley to do anything for his friend. He might tramp back and forth for nights and days, but with no success, for Fred Greenwood was gone—whither?

Had Jack been skilled in woodcraft, possibly he might have discovered some signs along the valley that would have enlightened him, but he was untrained in the ways of red men and was not equal to the task. A dog that knew how to track a person would have been of immeasurable value, but such a canine was not to be had.

One memory clung tormentingly to the searcher. It was the demoniac face of Motoza, the Sioux, when Fred Greenwood compelled him to return the Winchester of Jack. There could be but one interpretation of that expression, and it boded the worst for the missing youth.

"Motoza feels no affection for me, but his hatred of Fred is so intense that he is bent on revenging himself; yet I did not think he would strike so soon."

The afternoon was drawing to a close, and Jack was fully two miles from camp. If he wished to reach their rendezvous before night he had no time to waste. The problem was now in the shape that Hank Hazletine's help was indispensable. If anyone could assist Fred Greenwood, the guide was the man.

"He promised to meet us this evening, and if I wait I shall lose my way."

Accordingly the lad faced in the direction of the plateau and pressed forward with en-

ergy. In his haste he kept the former landmarks in view, and his previous experience
had given him a certain familiarity with the
region which prevented his going astray.
Once more he leaped the canyon, without
pausing longer than to glance into its depths
as he swung over it. He saw nothing of the
bulky carcass of the grizzly bear that had
fallen a victim to the marksmanship of himself and friend, and just as night was shut-
ting in he reached the edge of the small
plateau where the ponies were contentedly
grazing.

In one respect better fortune than he anticipated awaited him. Instead of being
compelled to pass the intolerable hours in
waiting for the coming of the guide, he saw
he had already reached the spot. A fire was
burning at the mouth of the cavern, and the
sinewy figure of the veteran was observed as
he moved to and fro before it. Detecting the
approach of Jack, he stood erect and silently
watched him as he drew near.

A person as agitated as Jack Dudley finds
it hard to conceal his feelings. Something in

the action and the expression of his white face as he came near enough to be seen distinctly gave the hunter the knowledge that matters had gone amiss with the boy. True to his word, Hank had brought no food back to camp. He had eaten his evening meal before going thither, leaving his young friends to provide for their own wants.

"Where's the younker?" was his question, before Jack halted.

"O Hank! I do not know what has happened; I fear we shall never see Fred again!"

And, unable to restrain his grief that had been pent up so long, Jack broke down and sobbed like a child. The veteran showed a delicacy that would hardly have been expected from him. He knew it would do Jack good to yield to his sorrow for a brief while, for he would soon become cooler and more self-possessed. Accordingly the hunter remained silent until the youth mastered his emotions, when he laid his hand tenderly on his shoulder and said:

"Now, set down here beside me and let me know all about it."

Jack appreciated his consideration, and taking the seat to which he was invited, he told, in a choking voice, the story of the incident beside the little valley, when Fred Greenwood, in high spirits, walked away and vanished as if the earth had opened and swallowed him. Jack did not break down again, for he was resolved to be manly and brave. He would not think of his young friend as wholly lost, nor allow himself to consider the awful possibility of returning home with the message that Fred would never be seen again. Jack felt it was time for action, not for lamentation.

Hazletine was grave and thoughtful, but the youth had hardly finished his narrative when he said:

"You haven't told me all."

"I do not think of anything I have omitted."

"Your story begins with the first sight of the antelope; what happened afore that?"

"A good deal; I did not think you would care to hear it."

"I want every word."

So it was that Jack began with their departure in the morning from camp, and made clear every occurrence down to the start for the valley where the great misfortune overtook them. He realized, while describing the meeting with Motoza, the important bearing that it had upon the disappearance of Fred Greenwood.

When the story was completed the guide emitted a low whistle, followed by an exclamation of so vigorous a character that it startled Jack. Hank sprang excitedly to his feet and strode back and forth until able to control his feelings. Then with a voice and expression of scornful contempt, he asked:

"What do you think of Motoza's love for you and Fred?"

"I admit that you were right and we were wrong about him; I feared for Fred, not for myself, and you see he has not tried to harm *me*."

"That ain't 'cause he loves you like the brother he calls hisself, but 'cause he hates Fred more'n he does you. If he hadn't had such a good chance to grab the other younker, he would have grabbed you."

"Then you have no doubt that Motoza is the cause of it all?"

"No more doubt than that you're a setting on that stone there."

"I can't understand it; Fred is not the one to let a single Indian make him prisoner, when one is as well armed as the other."

"Who said there was only one of the imps?"

The abrupt question meant a good deal. It had already been proven that a number of other Indians were in the vicinity; but Jack had not thought of associating them with the vagrant Sioux in his hostility to the young hunters, although there was scarcely a doubt that Motoza had had one helper or more in his designs against Fred Greenwood. This put a new face on the matter, and Hazletine discussed the question more freely.

"There must be a half-dozen varmints or so in the mountains; they've sneaked off the reservation and are hunting here without permission from the folks that have 'em in charge. It ain't likely they started out with any other idee than to have a little frolic of their own, meaning to go back when they was through; but, as I remarked afore, when an Injin sees a good chance to raise the mischief with just as good a chance of not being found out, he's pretty sartin to do it. Wal, things took such a queer shape when you younkers and Motoza seen each other that all the ugliness in him has come out, and that's what's urging him now."

"It seems to me, Hank, that if he meant to punish Fred for humiliating him, the method was simple."

"How?"

"By shooting him from ambush; he could do it without being seen, and I can think of no way by which the guilt could be brought home to him."

"You're off there. Motoza knows that you and me are in these parts, and that we're the friends of the younker; what had took place afore, with what I'd swear to, would hang Motoza, and he knows it."

This declaration was not quite clear to Jack, but it sounded as if the guide was willing to so modify his testimony in court as to insure the conviction of the Sioux in case he followed the plan named by the youth.

The veteran would have considered it right, under the circumstances, to do such a thing.

"Since the fear of our testimony restrained him, why did he not seek to remove *us* in the same manner, when he has had more than one opportunity?"

"And there you're off again. Motoza wouldn't have had any trouble in wiping out two young tenderfeet like you, but he'd likely run agin a snag when he tried it on *me!*"

The hunter shut his lips and shook his head with eloquent earnestness.

"S'pose he'd done such a thing," he added, angrily; "don't you see that when the Government larned, as it would be sure to larn, that three persons had been killed near the reservation by some of the Injins, there would be the biggest kind of excitement? It would put its best officers at work, and never let up till everything was brought to light. You see that, Motoza not being the only Injin in these parts when the thing was done, the officers would have some of the other varmints to work on, and they'd got the whole story from 'em, which would mean the hanging of the Sioux."

Jack saw the force of his friend's words. Even in this wild region, where one would naturally suppose he was beyond reach of the law, the man who committed a grave crime faced a serious risk. Certainly there was much less danger in "removing" one person than three.

"As it is, Motoza has placed himself in a bad position, but it would have been tenfold worse had he shot you and me."

Hank nodded his head, but qualified his assent:

"He could have picked you off, but not *me*, and he knows that he would have had me on his trail without waiting for the officers to help."

"But he must face the same thing as it is."

"Don't you see that he had to make the ch'ice atween doing nothing at all or tackling the younker? The Sioux is such an imp and is so crazy for revenge that he made up his mind to chance it the least he could, and he went for the tenderfoot that he hates the most."

Jack tremblingly asked the question that had been in his mind for some minutes.

" Do you think he shot Fred?"

The guide slowly turned his head and looked fixedly at the youth before replying:

" Wouldn't you've heerd his gun?"

The question sent a thrill of hope through the heart of Jack, but it was quickly succeeded by the dull torture that was there before. True, he would have heard the report of a rifle if fired anywhere near him during the afternoon, but a treacherous Sioux like Motoza was too cunning to expose himself in that manner, and would have resorted to a different method.

" He could have slain poor Fred in some other way, but do you believe he has done so?"

" Younker," replied the sympathetic guide, " I ain't the one to trifle with your feelings, fur you don't feel much worse than me, but I own up that I don't know anything more 'bout this bus'ness than you. I mean by

17

that," he hastened to explain, "that I can't figger out in my mind what that varmint has done till I pick up more knowledge than you've been able to give me, and I can't do that afore to-morrow morning."

This sounded reasonable, but it was trying beyond imagination, for it indicated that the long night must be spent in idleness, without the raising of a finger to help the one who perhaps was in the most imminent need of such assistance. There was no help, however, for it, and Jack accepted the decision of his friend without a murmur.

The two sat at the mouth of the cavern, talking in low tones, until the night was well advanced, when Hank said, with a voice that sounded wonderfully low and tender for him:

"Now go in and lay down, younker, fur there'll be plenty of work fur you to do to-morrer, and there's no saying when you'll git the chance to sleep agin."

"Call me when it is my turn to go on guard."

"All right; and don't show yourself till I *do* call you."

Jack walked into the cavern, first pausing to fling some wood on the fire. Mingled with his feeling of despair was a dread of being alone in the gloom. He did not believe he would sleep a wink through the night, for never were his emotions wrought to a more keenly torturing point. It was almost impossible to remain still, but he forced himself to lie down, with his heavy blanket gathered around him.

It would be distressing to dwell upon the anguish and grief of the youth, as he lay wide awake, his brain alert and his blood at fever-heat. At times it all seemed so like a dream that he turned his head to make sure Fred Greenwood, his loved chum and comrade, was not lying at his side. But no, it was all a dreadful reality, and he groaned in spirit.

As the minutes passed he appeared to grow more wakeful, until he was in as full possession of his faculties as when fleeing from the grizzly bear. And it was while lying thus, wondering what the hour could be, that he became aware that Hank Hazletine was standing at the mouth of the cavern, on the other side of the smouldering fire. The light was reflected so clearly from his bearded face that it was seen distinctly, while the position of Jack, muffled in his blanket, threw his own countenance in shadow, which prevented the guide seeing it clearly.

Something prompted Jack to lie still and feign sleep, while he kept his gaze on the man, who was looking fixedly at him. Suddenly Hank pronounced his name in a low voice, repeating the call in a louder tone. He wished to learn whether his young friend was unconscious, and, since Jack made no reply, must have concluded he was sleeping.

The guide next threw more wood on the blaze, which burned up so brightly that the reflection reached far out on the grassy plateau. Then, with a single glance at the prostrate figure, the hunter turned away, his footsteps as noiseless as if he were stepping on velvet.

Jack was mystified by the proceeding, but, suspecting its meaning, he arose from his hard couch and passed outside. The moon had not yet risen, but the bright stars were in the sky, and shining with the brilliancy that he had noticed and admired on the previous evening. He looked around for Hazletine, and, not seeing him, imitated his action by pronouncing his name, but, as he suspected, he was not within hearing.

"He has gone off to make some investigations between now and morning. I am glad of it, for he may learn something which he desires to know, and which he would never find out by staying here. I wish I could have gone with him, but no doubt he will do better alone."

It was demonstrated, therefore, that the guide had violated the very rule which he had impressed more than once upon his young friends, for he had left Jack Dudley sound asleep, as he believed, without any one standing sentinel over him. But it was because the circumstances were so exceptional and extraordinary that it justified such suspension of the rules.

Jack did not hesitate to make himself as comfortable as the situation would permit.

He folded his blanket on the ground, and sat with his back against the very rock where he had fallen asleep the night before.

"No danger of my doing it again," he reflected; "and it wouldn't make any difference if I did, since Hank believes I am dreaming."

Jack supposed he threw the wood on the flame to keep away the possible danger from wild animals that might be prowling in the neighborhood; though, because of the reasons named, there was little to be apprehended from them. The youth was so alive to the situation that he heard a cough from one of the ponies lying on the ground near the further side of the plateau, and beyond sight. Twice the watcher fancied he detected a shadowy figure stealing here and there in the gloom, and he grasped his rifle, ready for instant use; but it must have been a mistake on his part, for nothing materialized, and, curious as it may seem, he finally sank into a fitful slumber, which lasted a long time without interruption.

CHAPTER XV.

TOZER.

MEANWHILE Hank Hazletine was busy. He had formed several theories to account for the disappearance of the youth, of whom he had grown extremely fond, brief as was their acquaintance, but the data upon which he based these theories were so vague and meagre that he could do nothing until more definite knowledge was obtained.

When first talking with Jack Dudley, the hunter expected to retain his place near the cavern until morning, for it would seem that there was little hope of doing anything until the sun shone, but reflection convinced him that there was a possibility of accomplishing something during the long interval that must intervene. Still it is not probable he would have made the attempt had not something invited it.

Standing in the gloom on the outside of the cavern, he saw a point of light against the side of the nearest mountain peak, less than half a mile distant. It could not be a star, for his familiarity with the country told him the background must prevent an orb showing at that height above the horizon. It came from a fire burning at the place, and that fire had been kindled by Indians.

Hank's decision was to visit the camp, in the hope of picking up some information about the missing boy. It has been shown that he was so convinced that no danger threatened Jack Dudley that he did not hesitate to leave him alone, believing him asleep. As a precaution, however, he flung additional fuel on the fire, with a view of keeping away any wild animals that might be in the vicinity. Had Jack answered to his name when called by the guide he would have been invited to accompany him for a portion at least of the way on the reconnaissance, as it might be termed—a most welcome relief. Thus, trifling as was the deception, it operated unfavorably for our young friend.

The progress of the veteran through and over the rough country was a very different proceeding from that of the two boys. He seemed never to hesitate or be in doubt as to the shortest and easiest course, and his advance, therefore, was much the same as if he were striding across the grassy plateau near camp. As he went forward his shifting position frequently shut out the beacon-light, but he made no mistake at any point in his walk. It was a striking proof of his woodcraft that when he reached the canyon it was at a spot where it was so narrow that he appeared merely to lengthen his step when he placed himself on the other side. Progressing in this manner, it did not take him long to reach the immediate vicinity of the camp.

The blaze had been kindled among a clump of cedars which were a continuation of a growth that extended with more or less vigor for miles among the mountains, gradually disappearing as the snow-line was reached. Hazletine recalled the particular spot so clearly that he knew precisely what to do.

It was not very late in the evening, else there

would have been one of the Indians on guard.
As it was, the three were lolling in lazy atti-
tudes, smoking their long-stemmed pipes and
talking in a disjointed fashion. If they had
eaten anything in camp, there were no evi-
dences of it.

Having reached a point from which he
could survey the party without being observed, the hunter proceeded to do so. His
first feeling was of disappointment, for Motoza
was not one of the three bucks, who appeared
to be in middle life, and were dressed and
painted similarly to that individual. In fact,
the trio were the ones seen by the youths
earlier in the day, at the point where the
break in the canyon occurred.

Hazletine had set out with the belief that
the vagrant Sioux was the one chiefly concerned in the disappearance of Fred Greenwood. His absence from camp confirmed
that belief, while the indifferent manner of
the three, and the apparent lack of subjects
of discussion among them, indicated that they
knew nothing of the abduction or death, as it
might be, of the missing one. Had they

known of it, the guide was confident it would have been betrayed by their manner, since they could have no suspicion that they were under surveillance at that time, and therefore would act their natural selves.

What would have been the course of Hazletine had he seen Motoza, not doubting, as he did, the guilt of the miscreant? He would have walked directly forward to the camp and warned the Sioux that if he harmed a hair of the youth's head his life should pay therefor.

Since Motoza was not in the situation thus to be warned, the hunter did the next best thing. With no attempt to veil the sound of his footsteps, he strode into the circle of light thrown out by the Indian camp-fire. The bucks looked up curiously at him, but betrayed no emotion beyond a few grunts. They did not invite him to be seated or to join them in smoking, and had they done so, neither invitation would have been accepted.

Hank knew nothing of the lingo of the red men, but it was presumed they had a fair understanding of English, taking which for granted, he proceeded to carry out his self-

imposed mission. He told the bucks they had
no business off their reservation, although it
was a matter of indifference to him. He knew
there were others in the mountains, and Motoza
was among them. It was concerning this
scoundrel, as Hank characterized him, that he
had something to say. A white youth, while
hunting that afternoon not far off, with his
companion, had disappeared. Hazletine had
looked into the matter far enough to discover
that he had been stolen by Motoza. The white
man was hunting for Motoza, but in the brief
time at his disposal had not been able to find
him, though he was confident of doing so on
the morrow.

Meanwhile, the white man wanted these
three, or any one of them, if they should meet
the aforementioned scoundrel, to repeat what
he had said about him. If any harm had befallen the missing boy, Hazletine would take
it upon himself to hunt down Motoza and
"execute" him himself, without waiting for
the United States authorities to do it. Such
a summary course would save expense and
make the white man feel better.

If Motoza should return the stolen boy within twenty-four hours, and it was found he was unharmed, the whole matter would be treated as a joke, and no punishment would be visited upon Motoza, provided he didn't do it again.

This was the substance of Hank Hazletine's communication to the three bucks, to whom he repeated and discussed it until there was no fear of a misunderstanding, after which the visitor strode out of camp, without so much as bidding the trio good-night. His whole manner was that of contempt, for, had it been otherwise, he would not have dared to turn his back upon them, when they could have shot him down with impunity.

The cowman had accomplished something, though less than he hoped. While he failed to gain definite knowledge of the missing youth, he had brought a message which was certain to be delivered to the right party before the next set of sun. But Hank knew the men with whom he was dealing, and could not feel assured that any ultimate good would result until nearer the end.

"I wish I knowed whether them imps know anything about that younker; they don't act as if they did, and yet they may be as deep in the bus'ness as Motoza."

The last remark suggested a possibility which the cowman shrank from considering. It was that the Sioux was wholly innocent, and that all the mischief had been done through unsuspected parties. It has been shown that other Indians, not yet encountered, were in the vicinity, and it was not absolutely certain that they were not the criminals. The thought, however, opened the illimitable fields of speculation, and the hunter was wise in determining to hold to his original belief until assured it was an error.

Before he was half-way back to camp the moon appeared above the mountain peak behind him, and the rugged scenery was lit up by the rays that streamed on every side. He paused where he could observe the gleam of his own camp-fire at the mouth of the cavern, while, by turning his head, he saw the twinkle of the one he had left behind. All between lay as silent as the tomb.

"I bluffed it pretty heavy," he reflected, "and I guess it'll work with them bucks; I ain't so sartin of Motoza, fur if he has had anything to do with the taking off of that younker he's covered up his tracks pretty well and it'll be hard work to run him down, but *I'll do it!*" he savagely exclaimed, as he resumed his strides toward his own camp.

As he drew near he caught sight of the unconscious figure of Jack Dudley, sitting with his back against the rock. The moon revealed him clearly, and the cowman approached him with noiseless step.

"Poor fellow! he come out here to watch, thinking he couldn't sleep, and now he's good for nothing till sunup."

Hank leaned over and tenderly adjusted the blanket around the figure of the handsome youth, as his mother might have done had she been present. Then passing within the cavern, he lay down and slept until the night was ended.

The presence of the lad on the outside of the cavern showed that he knew of the departure of the guide. Hank, therefore, explained his reason for leaving him, and told him all that had occurred.

"The first thing to do, younker, is to find Motoza; that's what I'm going to do. You can't stand it to be alone with yourself, so you can come with me, though I hain't no idee that you'll be able to give any help."

"I hope I shall; though, if you think there is more chance of success in making the hunt alone, I'll do the same."

Hank was silent a moment, as if considering the matter, but he quickly added:

"Come along. But how about breakfast?"

"I haven't the least appetite."

"I thought so by your looks," he said, sympathizingly. "I'm blamed sorry fur you, and hope your appetite will soon come back to you."

"It will as soon as we find Fred," said Jack, with a faint smile; "but what about yourself?"

"It's all the same; if we had meat here I'd cook and eat it; but I'm willing to go a day or two, if I haven't the time to take any meals."

"That's strange!" broke in Jack; "yonder comes a white man; he must be one of your acquaintances, though I never saw him before."

Hazletine turned round in surprise. A tall white man, dressed as a cowboy, with long dangling yellow hair and a thin mustache and goatee, and with rifle slung over his shoulder, had appeared on the further side of the plateau, and was approaching the couple at a deliberate pace.

"Wal, I'm hanged!" exclaimed Hazletine; "if there isn't Bill Tozer! He's the last man I expected to meet in these parts."

These words did not bring Jack Dudley much enlightenment, but he felt no special curiosity concerning the individual, and silently waited till he came up. The youth judged from the manner of the guide, however, that he was not overly pleased with the new arrival, whose countenance was not attractive. Nevertheless, the two shook hands with seeming cordiality, and the new-comer looked inquiringly at Jack.

"This is a friend of mine, Bill, that I took

18

out on a hunt t'other day with another younker; Jack Dudley, Bill Tozer."

"Glad to know you," said the man heartily; "I see you're a tenderfoot."

"Yes," replied Jack; "less than two weeks ago I had never set foot in Wyoming."

"Wal, now that's funny; you'll like the country after you get used to it."

"Would to heaven I had never seen it!" was the bitter exclamation of the youth, hardly able to keep back his tears.

"Sorry to hear that, my young friend; but cheer up; it'll come out all right."

It struck Jack that this was a singular remark for the man to make, for it sounded as if he knew the cause of Jack's emotion; but before the boy could seek enlightenment the man made a more extraordinary remark:

"You'll excuse us for a few minutes, my young friend; I've some words to say in private to Hank."

"Certainly," replied Jack, turning on his heel and walking beyond earshot. He gave the men no further attention, for he did not suspect the new-comer had anything to impart of interest to him. The boy felt more like resenting this interference with the momentous business he and the guide had on hand.

But Jack was mistaken. Hardly was he a hundred feet from the couple when Hazletine asked:

"What's up, Bill?"

"One of them young tenderfeet is missing, eh?"

"How did you find that out?"

"I reached the camp of Bok-kar-oo last night within a half-hour after you'd gone; he and two other bucks are out on a hunt, which they haven't any business to be, but that's nothing to us. Bok-kar-oo told me what you had told him; it's queer business, isn't it?"

"I should say it was. That Motoza has had a hand in it, and I've set out to find him and settle the account."

"Why are you so sure about Motoza?"

"'Cause I *know* him!" said Hank, savagely; "and I've knowed him fur a good many years; there isn't a worse Injin in Wyoming."

Instead of commenting on this remark, Tozer stood silent a moment, and then made a flirt with his head as a request for Hank to step aside with him. The cowman obeyed, and they seated themselves still further from Jack Dudley.

"What makes you so afeard he'll hear us?" asked Hazletine, impatiently, noting the suspicious glances which the man cast in the direction of the youth.

"For the reason that I don't want him to hear us; I've something to say about him and his friend."

"His father owns half of Bowman's ranch."

Bill Tozer started with an angry exclamation.

"Is that so?" he asked in amazement. "I thought it was the other fellow's father."

"How should you know anything about it anyway?" demanded Hazletine, who made no attempt to conceal his dislike of the man. "I'd like to know where you picked up so much knowledge 'bout these two younkers."

"There's no need of getting huffy about it,

Hank; it seemed to me that I was to be on your heels for the last few days, for I stopped at the ranch and had a talk with the fellows only a short time after you left with the tenderfeet for this hunt. I understood Kansas Jim to say that it was the father of the Greenwood boy that owned half the ranch."

"If Jim told you that, which I don't believe he done, he told you what ain't so."

"But the father of the other boy—the one that's missing—he's rich too, ain't he?"

"I don't know nothing 'bout it; what are you driving at? Bill, you know that my 'pinion of you is 'bout the same as it is of that tramp Motoza, so, if you've got anything to say to me, out with it! I hain't any time to fool away."

"I *have* something to say, Hank, and it's about them young tenderfeet: I've seen Motoza."

"When?"

"This morning."

"Did you give him my message?"

"Every word of it, as I received it from Bok-kar-oo; I made it as strong as I could."

"You couldn't make it any too strong; how did he take it?"

"It didn't seem to worry him much; he says he don't know anything about the missing boy and your threats don't scare him. But, Hank," added Tozer, lowering his voice almost to a whisper and glancing furtively around, "I suspect Motoza was lying."

"I *know* he was, fur he doesn't know how to tell the truth."

"If he's treated right, I believe he'll produce the missing youngster."

Hank Hazletine was keener mentally than most of his friends suspected. He had more acumen than even Bill Tozer suspected. A great light flashed upon the cowman, and the questions and answers which fell from his lips during the next few minutes were intended to hide his real purpose.

"What do you mean by treating Motoza right? If he was treated right he'd be kicking the air this very minute."

"I agree with you," said Tozer, laughing; "but Motoza doesn't, and he's the one who asks to be treated right, as he considers it."

"I've said that if he produces the younker, and we find he hain't been harmed, why we'll call it a joke and drop the whole thing."

Tozer gazed at a distant mountain peak and thoughtfully chewed tobacco for a minute. He was approaching delicate ground and needed all his *finesse*.

"That's fair on your part, and is more than he ought to expect, but I've a suspicion it isn't what he means."

"Do you know what he means, Bill?"

"No; he hasn't told me a word, but I think I can guess it."

"Wal, then, guess."

"Remember it's only a guess, and I may be away off."

Hazletine nodded his head.

"I'm listening."

"I suspect Motoza has the tenderfoot in hiding somewhere, where there's no chance of his getting away or of any of his friends finding him."

"What does the scamp mean by doing that?"

"He must have had an idea that the father

of the Greenwood boy has enough money to pay a good sum to recover him unharmed."

"That's a new scheme! I've heard of such things in the East, but never knowed 'em to be tried in this part of the country."

"Bear in mind," Tozer hastened to add, "that it's all guesswork on my part."

"You've said that afore, but it's powerful good guessing, Bill. It's my 'pinion you ain't a thousand miles from the truth, but you can see this makes a mighty different thing of the bus'ness."

"How so?"

"The younker's father lives in New York; he's got to be reached, and the question laid afore him. How much money will Motoza ask to produce the younker?"

"Certainly not much—something like five thousand dollars, I should say."

"That is rather a healthy pile for you or me, but I don't 'spose it's more than a trifle for them folks in the East."

"Of course not; they'll raise it at once, and be glad to do so."

"But it'll take two weeks at least."

"Not necessarily; you can telegraph from Fort Steele, and two or three days ought to wind up the whole business."

"But you can't telegraph the money."

"Yes, you can; nothing is easier."

Hazletine was silent a minute or two.

"It sounds easy 'nough, the way you put it, but it won't be so powerful easy after all. I s'pose the Sioux will want the money afore he turns over the younker?"

"Of course; that's business."

"How can we know he'll give up the younker after he gits the money?"

"In a matter of this kind, a point must be reached where one party has to trust the other, and Motoza wouldn't dare play you false."

"He wouldn't, eh? Just give him the chance."

"Then we won't let him. I'll guarantee that he shall keep his part of the agreement in spirit and letter."

It was on Hazletine's tongue to ask who should guarantee the honesty of Bill Tozer, but for reasons of his own he kept back the question.

"Wal, now, to git down to bus'ness, as you say; s'pose Doctor Greenwood sends word that he won't or can't raise the money you ask—what then?"

Tozer shrugged his shoulders suggestively.

"Don't forget that I am guessing all the way through. I should say, however, that Doctor Greenwood would never see his boy again."

"I'm afraid he never will, as the matter now stands."

"That depends on the parent. If he is not rich, the father of that young man over yonder is, and he would let him have the money."

"No doubt he'd do that very thing; but s'pose the thing is all fixed and carried out as you've been saying—does Motoza fancy there won't be some accounts to be squared with him afterwards?"

"You know what a cunning fellow he is. He wouldn't go through with the job until he was guaranteed against any punishment for his part in it."

"The father of the younker would give

the pledge, and he'd keep it, too, if he's anything like his son. But what 'bout Hank
Hazletine?"

"He would have to make the same promise
—that is, I presume he would. It might be,
however, that Motoza would feel able to take
care of himself, so far as you are concerned.
But we are talking blindly."

"Is there any other way to talk?"

"You say you were just about starting out
to hunt up Motoza. You won't be able to
find him, for he'll keep out of your sight.
Leave that part of the business to me."

"What'll you do?"

"I'll explain the situation to him, and then
come back and have another talk with you."

"All right; you can't do it any too soon."

CHAPTER XVI.

WATCHING AND WATCHED.

BILL TOZER rose to his feet. The interview was over, and little remained to be said between the two.

"Then, Hank, you'll leave matters with me till I see you again?"

"When will that be?"

The man stood a moment in thought.

"In order that there shall be no mistake, let us agree that I shall call here to-morrow morning—twenty-four hours from now. How does that strike you?"

"That will do."

"I can make it less time than that, if you wish it."

"That suits; it's a go; good-by."

"Good-by," and the visitor turned on his heel and strode across the plateau, disappearing on the further margin, where he had first shown himself.

Hank Hazletine stood looking after him as long as he was in sight. When at last he vanished, an expression of scornful contempt darkened the bearded face of the cowman, and he muttered:

"Bill Tozer, you think you're smart, but *I understand you!*"

In the interview which has just been recorded the visitor believed he had outwitted the guide at every step, and yet exactly the reverse was the fact. Hank Hazletine had pretended a stupidity which was not real. He noted the contradictions in the declarations of Tozer the instant they were made, but gave no evidence of it, his object being to draw out the miscreant, in which purpose he succeeded perfectly.

The whole truth was manifest to the guide. Fred Greenwood had been abducted not by Motoza alone, but by him and Bill Tozer. Beyond a doubt the daring scheme was the invention of the white man, who found a willing partner in the vagrant Sioux, who burned with enmity toward the youth. It was Tozer who made the mistake of supposing that the father of Fred was half-owner of the ranch, and, therefore, presumably a rich man. Tozer had formed the plan of the abduction while at Bowman's ranch, and showed by his promptness that he had not allowed the grass to grow under his feet.

These meditations occupied but a few minutes, when the cowman walked toward Jack, who, seeing him approaching, advanced to meet him. Hazletine felt that the change of conditions made it necessary to talk more freely than heretofore with the boy.

"Hank, it seems to me we are throwing away time," said the youth, a trifle impatiently.

"I'm not so sure of that, younker. I've news fur you."

The guide had a good memory, and he repeated, almost word for word, all that had been said by Tozer and himself. Jack was astounded. His first emotion was of profound gratitude and delight, for the interview seemed to establish that Fred Greenwood was alive, and consequently within reach of recovery.

"He's not dead!" exclaimed the happy lad; "thank Heaven for that! I shall soon see him! It seems too good to be true."

"It isn't best to be sartin of anything in this world," remarked his friend, with a gravity of expression that ought to have chilled the ardor of Jack, but it did not. The tidings were too exhilarating for that.

"Now, younker," added the man, "we've got more time on our hands than we know what to do with. Come over by the fire and set down fur a while. How's that appetite of yours?"

"I am beginning to feel hungry."

"I thought so," observed Hank, with a smile.

"But there's no hurry. I can wait a little while."

"You'll have to."

"Now tell me who this man Tozer is?"

"Wal, he's a reg'lar Motoza, except in blood. I run across him five years ago in Arizona, where he had been in the stage-robbin' bus'ness. Things got so hot he had to git out. I didn't hear anything more of him till I was driving cattle in Montana, when I discovered he was one of the worst rustlers in that part of the world. I'm sartin he has done a good many things fur which he ought to hang, but he's more cunning in his way than the Sioux, and has kept out of the penitentiary when anyone else would have been doing a life-term. Bill is a great gambler, and has made and lost fortunes, but he is always out of money and figgering how to git it ag'in. There isn't anything too mean fur him to do fur money. He doesn't care any more fur the feelings of others than Geronimo."

"It looks as if the plan of abducting Fred and holding him for ransom is his."

"There ain't no doubt of it; he come to the ranch soon after we'd gone and larned all 'bout you tenderfeet from the boys themselves. The thought come to him at once that one of the chances of his lifetime was his. It's queer he made the mistake of believing that it was the father of the other younker as owned part of the ranch, but he got matters twisted in some way. You can see that if it hadn't been fur that blunder of his, it would be *you* that your friend and me would be looking fur."

"I wish it were," was the honest exclamation of Jack Dudley; "but how was it he came to form his partnership with Motoza?"

"You've heard it said the devil takes care of his own; Bill and Motoza are old friends and have been in more than one shady job. I can't know, but I think Bill must have larned or suspicioned that the Sioux warn't fur off and he set out to hunt him up. Anyway they managed to come together, and the job was fixed up atween 'em. Howsumever," said the guide, "there ain't no use of talking and guessing over what *has been*, but we must face what *is*. Now, if Doctor Greenwood has word by telegraph that he must pay five thousand dollars to git his younker back agin, what'll he think?"

"He will think that this has been a pretty expensive outing for Fred," replied Jack, whose buoyancy of spirits prompted his trivial answer.

"Will he pay the money?"

"Yes, and twice as much more, if it is

19

necessary; but won't he be startled and puzzled to know the meaning of it all! He will come right out here himself and bring some of the best detectives in the country."

"And if he does that, he'll never see his boy alive."

Jack looked at Hazletine in alarm and amazement. The cowman saw phases of this extraordinary business that had not presented themselves to the youth, and he now proceeded to impress them upon him. In the first place, the cunning Tozer would make sure of protecting himself and Motoza, though the last was purely a matter of policy and self interest, since he was always ready to sacrifice a comrade. In arranging the ransom or exchange, Tozer would take no chances. The friends of Fred Greenwood would have to remain out of sight and in the background. It would be impossible for any of them to try to checkmate him without his quickly learning it, whereupon he would abandon the job and turn over the boy to the savage will of the Sioux.

"And you know what *that* means," added

the cowman, impressively. "I should tell you
something else, too. It's my belief that if the
money is give to Tozer, and the Sioux is
ordered to surrender the younker, he hates
him that bad that he'll try to bring about his
death and run the chances of hanging for it.
Where two such wretches as him and Tozer
are in a job there's bound to be crooked work,
and I won't never believe you're going to shake
the hand of t'other younker till I see it done
with my own eyes."

The emphasis of this declaration sent a
thrill of alarm through the frame of Jack
Dudley, though it could not wholly destroy
the exhilaration caused by the knowledge that
Fred Greenwood was alive.

It was proof of the kindliness of Hank
Hazletine that he made no mention of a strong
suspicion that had been in his mind from the
first. This was that when Tozer met Motoza
he learned that the Sioux had already slain
his prisoner, for Hank knew of the furious
hate the fellow held toward the youth. Consequently, Tozer had arranged to carry out his
original scheme, and was now seeking to gain

a large sum of money, knowing that it was out of his power ever to fulfill his part of the bargain.

Hazletine, we repeat, strongly believed that this ghastly phase of the business was true, but, inasmuch as there was no certainty of it, he was too considerate to bring additional grief to the heart of Jack Dudley.

But the cowman had formed a resolution which he carefully held back from his companion. An interval of twenty-four hours must pass before the second interview with Tozer, during which, as the latter was given to understand, the negotiation would be left wholly with him. Hank and Jack were to remain quiescent, at least until after the next meeting. But the cowman nursed a very different determination. He intended to employ all the time and the utmost ability he possessed in defeating the atrocious plot of the miscreants. It will be seen that the easiest plan for him was quietly to help forward the negotiations, but his nature forbade such meek submissiveness on his part.

This course, however, was perilous to the

missing boy; for, if Tozer or Motoza saw himself in danger of losing the prize, he would make short work of the prisoner. It was clear that all the skill and woodcraft of which the cowman was master would be needed in the delicate task he had assigned to himself.

"Younker," he said, when the conversation had continued a while longer, "after thinking over this bus'ness, I've made up my mind it's better we should keep apart fur the day."

"Follow your own judgment. I shall try to be back this evening."

"To-morrer morning will be time 'nough. I had my supper last night not fur from here, and if the wild animals haven't visited the spot since, we shall find 'nough to make a square meal."

This was acceptable news, and the result all that could be desired. Hank had cooked a considerable quantity of venison at a romantic place among the rocks, his first intention being to carry enough of it to headquarters to supply his young friends with what they needed. Afterward he changed his mind and decided that it was time they learned to provide for themselves. Upon making his way to the spot he found everything as it had been left the previous evening, and thus much more readily than Jack had dared to expect he secured the needed food.

"Right here we part," said Hank at the conclusion of the meal.

"How am I to spend the time?"

"As your fancy strikes you. As I told you, it will be soon 'nough fur you to git back to camp to-morrer morning, but you must keep your eyes open. It may be that Tozer, having larned that your father is the man he meant to bleed, will try to make a prisoner of you."

Jack Dudley's eyes flashed.

"Let him try it! I should like to be in Fred's company."

"Mebbe you wouldn't be so well suited as you think, but look out fur snares in your path—that's all I've got to say. I'm off."

It was characteristic of the cowman to take his departure in this abrupt manner, his intention being to undertake without delay the difficult task he had set out for himself, but

five minutes later he gave over his purpose,
and, to the surprise of Jack Dudley, came
back to him.

In doing this, Hazletine was wise. His
purpose, as already intimated, was to discover
if possible Motoza and Tozer, but especially
the former. There was little doubt that the
Sioux would communicate with his prisoner
during the day, or, if Fred Greenwood was
not among the living, his unrelenting enemy
was likely to give some evidence of where his
taking off had occurred. Hazletine's belief,
therefore, was that by shadowing the Sioux
he had a good chance of securing the information that would overturn all the calcula-
tions of the abductors.

But this task was tenfold more delicate than
would seem at first, for not only had the cowman to learn the whereabouts of the Sioux, but
he must do it undetected and dog the fellow
without discovery on his part. When it is
remembered that Motoza would be on the
alert against this, one is almost ready to de-
clare the cowman had attempted an impossible thing.

When he left his young friend, however, it was with the firm purpose of doing, or rather trying to push through this purpose. Within a hundred yards of the point where he left Jack the guide had a glimpse of what may be called the shadow of a movement. Something flickered among the rocks a short distance ahead and then vanished before he could identify it.

But he knew what it meant. Some one was watching him. If the watcher was not Motoza or Tozer, he was an ally of theirs. He was holding the cowman under surveillance, ready to report or shoot on the first proof of his real purpose. The truth flashed upon Hank, and pausing in his walk, without any evidence of what he had discovered, he began a hasty examination of his pockets after the manner of a man who suddenly misses some prized article that he believed to be in his garments.

The little farce was cleverly acted. Each receptacle was examined several times, some of the pockets being turned wrong side out, while the face of the cowman, or rather his

eyes, betrayed his excitement. Then he
looked at the ground in front and at the
rear, apparently to learn whether he had
dropped the missing treasure. Failing to
find it, he uttered an angry exclamation and
walked hurriedly back to his companion. No
one observing the performance would have
doubted its meaning.

"I'm going to stay a while with you," he
remarked, seating himself upon the ground
and lighting his pipe.

"It was a sudden change of mind," replied
Jack, glad to have his company.

"Yes; a redskin helped me to make it,"
and he explained the nature of his discovery.
Inasmuch as the guide had turned back because of the same, it was easy to understand
what his original intention was; for had it
not existed, why should the cowman care if
he was kept under surveillance? He would
not be betraying himself any more during an
innocent walk and hunt through the mountains than by sitting on the ground and
smoking his pipe.

The result to a certain extent was a disappointment to Jack himself, for he had quietly resolved upon a venture in the same line. Of necessity he would be governed almost entirely by guesswork, but it was his determination to spend the day, and if possible the night, in trying to gather some trace of his missing friend. And while it must be said that his prospect of success was exceedingly meagre, it should be borne in mind that he would possess one great advantage over the veteran while similarly engaged — neither Tozer nor Motoza would fear anything from what he did, and would give him no attention. He therefore would be left comparatively free to do what he chose. Despite the warnings of Hank, Jack was confident nothing was to be feared from the enmity of the two miscreants while the negotiations were in progress. They were not the men to destroy the hen that was expected to lay the golden egg.

For hours Hazletine and Jack lolled in this primitive camp, the cowman smoking his pipe most of the time, while the two discussed over and over again the various phases of

the momentous business that engaged their
thoughts and to which they yearned to de-
vote their utmost energies. The guide longed
to be off, and as the sun descended the heavens
it was one of the hardest tasks of his life to
restrain his impatience, but he had been
trained in a school where patience is one of
the greatest of all the virtues. Suddenly he
rose to his feet, stretched his arms and
yawned.

"I'd like to borrer that spy-glass of yours
fur a few minutes."

"You are welcome," replied Jack, slipping
the string over his head and passing the instrument to him. The cowman sauntered off,
taking the same direction as before. His first
wish was to learn whether he was still under
surveillance. So far as he could determine
the watcher had grown weary and withdrawn,
though there could be no certainty that he
was not in the neighborhood.

Jack Dudley, without leaving camp, was
able to keep an eye on the movements of his
friend. He saw him make his way to a jut-
ting rock, partly screened by a growth of

cedar. Concealing himself as well as he could, he raised the glass to his eyes and spent several minutes in studying the wild country spread below him. He was looking in the direction of the break in the canyon, beyond which, as will be remembered, was the plateau where the ponies had been left to crop the grass while their masters were engaged elsewhere.

Jack did not attempt to survey the same field, but kept his gaze upon Hazletine. He could see that he directed his attention toward a particular point, as if he had either discovered something or expected to do so. The study continued only a few minues, when he came back and handed the glass to the youth, with the remark:

"I'm going to try it agin. I won't expect to see you till to-morrer morning."

The lad bade him good-by, and he took his departure; but instead of descending the mountain toward the point that had interested him, he followed the opposite course, as if he intended to push through to the other side of the Wind River range. This was so trans-

"He was looking in the direction of the break in the canyon."

parent a subterfuge that it did not deceive Jack.

"He has discovered something," was his conclusion; "he doesn't choose to tell me, and it makes little difference. I wonder whether he believes I intend to idle my time till night and then go back to headquarters and wait for him? If he thinks so, he makes a mistake."

Waiting until sure his friend was beyond sight, Jack carefully picked his way to the rock from which Hank had made the observation that decided his line of action. The better to screen himself the youth lay down on his face, as when peering over the ridge into the valley where the antelope were grazing, and held the glass to his eyes.

Thus looking out, he saw the plateau in the distance, seemingly but a few rods in extent. Only one of the ponies was visible, and he resembled a small dog, standing with head down, in the middle of the grassy plot. Beyond and between were foot-hills, peaks of varying heights, gorges, ravines and hollows, with rocks, boulders and stunted trees scattered in profusion. The picturesqueness of the scene was deepened by a thin, blue column of vapor in the distance, ascending from an invisible camp-fire. The smoke rose steadily, so it was not to be supposed that it was meant for a signal, like those already described.

The most attractive point was the break in the canyon, already described. This was in plain sight, with the expanse of swiftly-flowing water, which soon disappeared between the walls on the opposite side.

Suddenly Jack started. Two Indians were visible, though they were in view for only a few minutes. They came from the base of the incline where the boys had seen three of them the day before, and passed out of sight before the interested observer could decide whether Motoza, the Sioux, was one of them.

"I believe Hank has gone down there," was the conclusion of Jack, "and I shall do the same."

CHAPTER XVII.

INTO AND OUT OF THE CANYON.

JACK DUDLEY'S enforced idleness had become intolerable. He could stay no longer in the place from which Hank Hazletine had departed a half-hour before. It was a waste of time to speculate over the intentions of the veteran, and the youth made no attempt to do so. He had set out to see whether he could act even an insignificant part in the recovery of his loved comrade.

It has been said that the boy had the advantage over the man in that it was not to be supposed any importance would be attached to his actions. At the same time he was liable to "put his foot in it" in more ways than one.

Somehow or other the conviction clung to Jack Dudley that the key to the situation was in the neighborhood of the canyon. There must be hundreds of places among the mountains where a prisoner could be hidden from human eyes, but Hazletine's interest centred in that wild gorge, and Jack was certain he had gone thither.

Then there was the fact of the cowman's visit two days before, concerning which he would have said nothing but for his discovery by the boys. Why Hank should have picked his way up that dangerous place was known only to himself. Jack could form no theory to explain it. But he did not forget the dispute of the three Indians in front of the break and the start which one of them made to follow the footsteps of the white man. There must be some attraction in the canyon for them all.

Jack's dread was that Hazletine, despite his undoubted skill, would frighten Tozer and Motoza by his efforts to defeat their purpose, and drive them into slaying Fred and making off before they could be punished. But the cowman had his own views, and it was too late to dissuade him.

Keeping in mind the warning of his friend to use all possible circumspection in his actions, Jack was so guarded that a full hour had passed when he once more reached the break in the canyon, which had already afforded them more than one interesting experience.

So far as he could judge, he was the only living person within miles. The two Indians that had flitted across his field of vision were gone, and it was impossible to say what had become of Hazletine. Determined, however, to run no unnecessary risk, Jack remained among the trees and rocks on the upper side of the break, where he could not be seen unless some one almost stepped upon him. Not satisfied with his first position, he shifted further to the right, and lay down to wait and watch.

A gradual obscuring of the sky caused him to look at his watch. Could it be possible? The autumn afternoon was almost gone. Night was at hand, whereas he had supposed several hours of daylight remained. Thus valuable time had slipped past and nothing had been done for Fred Greenwood.

From where Jack lay he had a perfect

20

view of the upper gate, as it may be called, of the canyon. The gorge has already been described as narrow at the point where the foamy waters dashed through and expanded into the broad pool, after which they flowed a short way and reunited, to make their next plunge between the mountain walls on their journey to the sea thousands of miles distant. Looking across this break, the boy could penetrate with his eye for a dozen yards into the upper canyon. He saw the dripping rocks upon which the angry buck sprang, only to pause and turn back to join his companions below.

A curious thing happened. Jack was looking in the direction named, when, with startling suddenness, an Indian shot into sight on the furthest rock, beyond which the canyon made a sweeping curve that shut off further view. His appearance was like the upleaping of a Jack-in-the-box at the touch of the spring, but the explanation was evident: he was making his way down the gorge from above, when his leap from one rock to another brought him thus abruptly into view.

This was interesting of itself, but a still more interesting discovery came with the second glance at him. He was Motoza, the Sioux!

It looked as if Hank Hazletine, with all his subtlety and woodcraft, had failed to do that which came of itself to Jack Dudley.

The actions of the Sioux showed he was unusually careful about being seen as he emerged from the canyon into fuller view, for, after leaping to the rock which stood at the door of the gorge, he stood a minute, then leaned forward and peered around the sides as far as he could without losing his balance. He next stood erect and looked keenly across the pool, and apparently at the very spot where the boy lay hiding.

" What a face!" muttered Jack; " I never saw one so ugly, with those daubs of paint; and his eyes shine just like that rattlesnake's we killed. It can't be he sees me," added the youth in alarm, as he cowered still lower; " one would think he could look through a stone."

But nothing less than the Roentgen ray

would have revealed the young man, who was stealthily watching the ferocious buck. The latter must have decided that the coast was clear, for with another bound he landed upon a rock quite a way from the opening of the canyon, and a second leap placed him on the shore where three of his race had been standing when discovered by Jack and Fred.

Motoza did not linger, but moved with a very rapid stride across the open space, where he was in full view of anyone in the vicinity.

"If I were sure you had done any harm to Fred," muttered Jack, never removing his eyes from the repellant countenance, "I believe I could treat you as we did the grizzly bear without a sting of conscience. The idea of your harming a hair of the head of Fred Greenwood, who showed you tenfold more mercy than you deserved—my gracious! he must have seen me."

This involuntary exclamation was caused by the fact that the Sioux was following a bee-line for the spot where Jack lay. Believing a meeting inevitable, the youth placed his hand on his revolver, the preferable weapon in the event of coming to close quarters.

But at the last moment Motoza turned to the left and passed among the rocks within a couple of paces of the youth, who held his breath until he was gone.

For some reasons Jack Dudley would have welcomed a meeting with this miscreant, for he held him in no fear. For one moment he meditated "holding him up," with the threat of death unless he produced Fred Greenwood; but fortunately the youth had time in which to see the wild absurdity of the thing, which could have done no possible good and probably would have brought great harm. So it was that Motoza passed out of sight and the youth was once more left alone.

But Jack's thoughts had taken a new turn. Hazletine had expressed the belief that in the interval between the first and second meeting with Tozer either he or Motoza would hold communication with their prisoner; consequently, if the Sioux could be kept under surveillance without exciting his suspicion, he was likely to give some involuntary and useful information.

"I wonder where Hank is; can it be that he, too, is watching in the neighborhood and has seen Motoza come out as I saw him? If so, the next fellow to pass in review before me will be my esteemed friend."

When, however, a half-hour had gone by without anything being seen of the cowman, Jack was warranted in believing that he was the only one who was aware of the coming and going of the red man.

Following out Hazletine's theory, it would seem that the prison of Fred Greenwood, instead of being among the mountains, was within the gorge. This was a startling conclusion, but the more Jack reflected upon it the more strongly did he believe it.

"At any rate, I mean to find out whether it is so."

But on the verge of setting out he hesitated. There was more than one reason why he should do so. In the first place, it was exceedingly dangerous to attempt to make his way up the canyon even by daylight, and the sun had already disappeared. He was totally unfamiliar with the windings and would be in constant danger of drowning. Moreover, he was liable, in the event of Fred being held a prisoner in the gorge, to place himself with him, or to defeat the negotiations for restoring him to liberty.

And yet, in the face of these and other obstacles, the youth decided to make the foolhardy attempt.

First of all he fastened his Winchester to his back, both he and his comrade having made provision for doing that before leaving Bowman's ranch. Then he thrust his revolver more firmly into its resting-place. This left his hands free, in case a sudden emergency should call for their use, and gave him an opportunity of saving the more important weapon. Then, night being fully come, he stepped into the open space which marked the bank at the break of the canyon. The stars were shining, but it would be a long time before the moon rose.

A quick glance to the right and left revealed nothing to cause alarm, and Jack pressed on until he stood on the spot where the Sioux had landed when making his last leap. There was enough star-gleam to show the black mass of stone, like a crouching monster gathering to spring upon him. It will not be forgotten that the youth was an exceptionally fine athlete, and, pausing but a moment, he easily made the leap that carried him to the rock. In fact the task was easy, and he would not have hesitated to follow in the footsteps of the white man and Indian, could he have had the twilight of mid-day to assist him.

The next bound placed him within the walls of the canyon, where he paused with the question whether it would do to venture further. The rushing waters were on all sides of him, and the cool spray was dashed in his face and over his clothing. It was to be supposed that where this furious current was compressed into such a narrow compass its depth was considerable, and within its grasp the most powerful swimmer would be helpless.

Peering into the gloom, the youth saw the top of the next rock which was used as a

stepping-stone by other visitors. If he were
mistaken it would be bad for him, but, with
only a few minutes' pause, he gathered his
muscles and proved he was right. He was
now fairly within the canyon and still standing on solid support, while there had been no
trouble to maintain his foothold from the moment he made the first leap.

His success thus far gave him renewed
courage.

"What one person has done another can
do," was his thought. "Fred and I agreed
that there is a good deal of risk in this, but
if I had a little more light nothing could be
easier. These rocks seem to be placed at the
right intervals, and so long as I can locate
them I'll go ahead."

The belief of Jack was that somewhere in
the side of the canyon was a cave in which his
comrade was held captive. The sight that the
two boys had obtained of Hank Hazletine,
when he disappeared so suddenly from sight,
lent strength to the theory. If the youth was
right, the time of his attempt to ascend the
gorge, with the exception of the darkness,

could not have been more favorable, for Motoza was absent, and it was hardly to be supposed that his place had been taken by Tozer
or anyone else. What a happy meeting it
would be if the elder could find the younger!

The natural reasoning was that, if one boy
was able to ascend the canyon to where the
other was imprisoned, the latter ought to be
able to leave his prison when the gaoler was
absent. Jack's explanation was probably the
right one—either that Fred did not know
how readily the thing could be done, or Jack
was soon to find himself unable to complete
his journey.

Spurred on by the hope of doing so much
for the one he loved, Jack paused only long
enough to locate the next rock, when he again
leaped with the easy strength and grace that
were natural to him. His success did not render him careless. He was almost in utter
darkness, and was surprised that the way
proved so easy. By leaning forward and
peering into the gloom he could generally
distinguish the most shadowy outlines of the
nearest part of the support, which, had it been

slightly further removed, would have been altogether beyond his reach.

It was unreasonable to expect the favorable conditions to continue, and they did not. The time came very soon when, after one of his leaps, the youth paused to collect himself, and was unable to distinguish the next rock projecting above the roaring current. The canyon just there was wider than usual, and he stooped over and gazed to the right and left in turn, hoping to discover the indispensable support.

"It must be somewhere near," he reflected, "else Hank and the rest of them could have ascended no further; perhaps they did not do so."

He gazed up the walls of darkness, but saw nothing that could help solve the question. If there was a cave near at hand its presence was betrayed by no friendly light. Although the tumult of the current was almost deafening, he shouted the name of Fred and listened for the response which came not.

It was not difficult for Jack Dudley to form the explanation of why he failed to discern the next support. Hitherto his leaps had been comparatively trifling. It would have been no trouble to make them several feet longer. This was a spot where such a jump was necessary, and therefore he could not discern the rock which would have been visible with the help of the sun or moon.

What should he do? Turn back or keep on? It was a most serious question, and he debated it a long time before forming a conclusion.

It is remarkable how readily, at times, we can convince ourselves of the truth of that which we wish to believe. By and by Jack Dudley was sure he made out the dim outlines of the lower point of a huge rock, just where it ought to have been.

"I can't be mistaken, so here goes!"

And go he did, with a vengeance. It was the finest leap yet made, but, unfortunately, the support upon which he so confidently counted had no existence. Instead of landing on solid stone, he dropped into the raging torrent and went spinning down stream like a cork in a whirlpool.

He kept his presence of mind, and did not exhaust his strength by trying to stem the current. His great peril was in being hurled against some of the rocks and killed or having a limb broken. Throwing out his arms just in time he averted this calamity, and feeling himself scraping swiftly past one of the masses of stone that had served him as a support, he desperately griped it and drew himself out of the water.

He was uninjured, but became immediately conscious of a great misfortune. In the flurry his Winchester had become displaced and was irrecoverably gone. It was with an exclamation of relief that he found his revolver in place at his hip.

"This expedition of mine, considered strictly *as* an expedition, is a failure," he grimly muttered, thankful for his own escape, and still convinced that it was not as bad as it might have been with his friend. "It won't do to try it again, and it remains for me to get out of the canyon altogether."

He had landed upon the extreme upper end of the most immense rock of all that had been used to help in the ascent. He remembered it well. The upper portion was depressed and sloping, being three or four feet above the current. Thus it happened that the point to which he was clinging allowed him to be deluged with spray, and he strove to climb to the higher part.

He was thus engaged, conscious of a number of severe bruises, when an object whisked past his shoulder, taking a direction up the gorge. He felt it graze his face, and detected something that can only be described as a deepening of the dense gloom as it shot over his head. It came and vanished like the flitting of a bird's wing.

The youth for the moment was amazed beyond expression, and was at a loss to explain what it could be. Then the truth flashed upon him. Some one else was also going up the canyon, and had leaped from the rock to which Jack was clinging, on his way to the next one. He strove to pierce the darkness, but the effort was useless.

"I would give a good deal to know who he was; I couldn't make out whether it was a white man or an Indian. It may have been Motoza, Tozer, Hank, or a stranger; but whoever he was, he has no use for me."

Half suspecting a third party might put in an appearance, Jack waited on the rock for some minutes, but nothing of the kind occurred, and he prepared to continue his retreat.

The water was almost icy cold, the temperature being perceptibly lower between the walls of the canyon and the clear air outside. With his saturated garments, the youth was chilled and anxious to reach a point where he could start a fire and obtain warmth for his body. He had given over the expectation of seeing any more persons in the gorge and wished to look after his own comfort.

To this haste was to be attributed the second accident that overtook the young man. He had no difficulty in locating the place to land, but he put too much vigor in the effort, so that when he struck the slippery rock his momentum carried him forward, and despite his resistance he took another plunge into the raging current before he could check himself.

The place was preferable to the previous one, for it was almost at the mouth of the canyon. He was guiding himself as best he could, and on the alert to grasp something to check his swift progress, when he debouched into the broad, open pool or miniature lake at the break in the banks, where the current became so sluggish that he swam with ease.

"This is growing monotonous," he muttered, as, after a few strokes, his feet touched bottom and he walked out on dry land. "My rifle is gone, but luckily I have kept my revolver for emergencies——"

He got no further with the remark, for his hand had gone back to his hip with the result of discovering that the smaller weapon had been lost during his last bath. But it was impossible wholly to lose his good spirits.

"Whew! but that puts me in a fine condition to hunt grizzly bears and meet bad Indians; I'm not so anxious to see Motoza as I was."

His teeth were chattering, and to start his blood in circulation he began climbing the sloping bank, at the top of which, as will be remembered, he had remained hidden with Fred Greenwood when looking down upon the three Indians.

It was a laborious task, and he was panting when he reached the summit, where he paused for a few minutes' rest. The prudent course was to return as speedily as he could to the cavern by the plateau and start a fire. His blanket had been left there, and would be of great use in his present condition.

"I wonder, now, if somebody has been there and stolen them?" he muttered, resuming his homeward tramp; "this thing ought not to stop, and it seems to me Hank takes big chances in leaving the blankets and ponies where some of these Indians can steal them."

Jack had still to leap the canyon in order to reach his destination, but the task had become an easy one and caused him no anxiety. All was going well, when his first shock of alarm came with the discovery that a wild animal was following him. His first thought was that it was one of the Indians, but a glimpse, on the edge of a slight clearing, showed that it was a quadruped.

21

Jack paused and looked intently at the creature. He could see it only dimly, but sufficiently so to identify it as a wolf of unusually large size. He suspected it was of the black species, one of those savage brutes to be dreaded tenfold more than the ordinary grey kind.

" I wonder whether he knows I haven't got a firearm about me? Ah, old fellow, if I had my Winchester it wouldn't take me long to settle you."

It was no jesting matter, and Jack kept close watch of him while threading his way to camp, as their headquarters were called. Several times, when he turned quickly, he was startled to observe that the animal had stolen quite close to him, as if to leap upon his shoulders; but he showed his cowardly nature by darting back, only to return the moment the youth turned his face away.

The question with Jack was whether he should stop and kindle a fire, or wait until he reached the cavern. He preferred to do the latter, but it looked unsafe to defer the precaution. The distance, however, was short, and he hurried on until he clambered over to the plateau and was greeted by a whinny from his pony, Dick, who was quick to recognize him. Instead of keeping up the pursuit, or attacking one of the horses, the wolf seemed to conclude it best to turn his attention elsewhere. He slunk off, and was seen no more.

CHAPTER XVIII.

THE QUEST OF THE COWMAN.

IT was Hank Hazletine, the cowman, who leaped over the head of Jack Dudley when he was crouching on the rock in the canyon, and it happened in this way:

It has been intimated that when the veteran left the boy at the temporary camp on the mountain side his intention was to learn the whereabouts of Motoza, the Sioux, hoping thereby to gain knowledge of the missing Fred Greenwood.

This was a task of extreme difficulty, inasmuch as it was certain the vagrant red man would be on his guard against such strategy. The Indian whom Hank saw with the aid of the spy-glass was not he whom he wished to trace, but, suspecting he was in the vicinity, the cowman made his way thither by a roundabout course. He was on the alert for the

fellow, or for his ally, Bill Tozer. Should
either or both of them discover Hank, he
might well assume that it was an accident.
It could hardly be expected of him that he
would remain at the cavern for twenty-four
hours, awaiting the time for Tozer to meet
him. His most natural course would be to
engage in hunting with his youthful companion, and he could reasonably claim to be
thus engaged if a meeting took place.

Should events prove that the plotters were
too watchful to be caught off their guard, then
the second phase of the business was to be
considered; but it remained to be seen
whether such was the fact. The ransom was
to be agreed to when it was apparent that no
other course could save the lad.

Advancing with the care and stealth of a
trained Indian scout, Hazletine remained but
a short time near the break in the canyon,
for suspecting, as did Jack Dudley, that it
was in that neighborhood the key to the situation was to be found, he was exposing himself to discovery. He climbed the same ascent, leaped the canyon, and ensconced him-

self on the further side. His intention was
to peer over the edge into the depths below,
instead of taking the course followed later by
his young friend.

He was acting on this idea, when he came
within a hair of spoiling everything by committing the very blunder against which he
had sought with so much pains to guard. At
his height above the torrent, as will be remembered, no one was disturbed by the roar
of the waters far below. Because of his sus-
ceptibility to sounds, he heard an exclamation
uttered by some one near him. The point
whence it came was a clump of rocks hardly
fifty feet distant, and he fancied he recognized
the voice as Bill Tozer's. To his relief he
could see no one, and it was safe, therefore, to
assume that no one as yet saw him.

The ground was favorable, and by using
the utmost care he secured a position from
which he discovered Tozer and Motoza in
conversation. The white man was sitting on
a boulder, while the Sioux was standing in
front of him, gesticulating as if angry over
something that had been proposed or said.

Tozer was smoking a pipe, and seemed cool and collected, though the exclamation which had betrayed him indicated that it had not been thus from the beginning.

It was an important discovery for Hazletine to make, but it was attended by two exasperating facts: the interview was nearly over, and the words that remained to be spoken were uttered in such moderate tones that he could not hear a syllable. If the couple had been obliging enough to raise their voices, it is probable that the knowledge sought by the eavesdropper would have soon been at his command.

But nothing of that nature took place. Within five minutes after the arrival of the cowman, prepared to act his part as spy, Motoza turned about and walked away in the direction of the canyon, while Tozer took a course which, if continued, would lead him to the plateau.

"I don't think he'll go there, fur he's no reason to look fur me in that place afore tomorrer morning."

But the white man was not the important

factor in the problem. Hank waited for some minutes after he had passed from sight, and then set out to regain sight of Motoza, which task proved more difficult than he expected. The fellow had vanished, and it was impossible to tell whither he had gone. The rocky surface left no trail which even an Apache could follow, and it only remained for the cowman to fall back upon what may be called general principles.

The experience of the cowman was another illustration of how much depends in this world on what is called chance.

Jack Dudley, without any preliminary training in woodcraft, discovered Motoza as he emerged from the canyon, while the veteran of the West, skilled in all the ways of his venturesome life, spent hours in looking for the Sioux without obtaining the first glimpse of him. That he missed him by a margin that could not have been narrower was a fact; but "a miss is as good as a mile," and the autumn afternoon drew to a close without the first glimmer of success on his part. He had gone so far, even, as to visit a distant camp-fire, whose smoke still faintly showed against the clear sky, but failed to see a living person.

He was on the point of giving over his quest, when the unexpected happened. Within a few hundred yards of the break in the canyon he caught sight of Motoza and Tozer holding another consultation. They had evidently just met, and the configuration of the ground enabled Hazletine to steal near enough to catch some of the words spoken by the couple.

The two were standing face to face, and their actions were peculiar. Motoza was in the act of handing his Winchester rifle to Tozer, who, accepting the weapon, turned it over and examined it with interest. Since he could not speak the Sioux he used the English language, of which, as will be remembered, Motoza possessed a fair knowledge.

"You're lucky," he said; "the gun is worth more than yours. So you made a trade with the young man?"

"Yes—me trade," replied the Sioux, his painted face relaxing with the grin that had become almost chronic.

"I don't s'pose he made any objection—that is, he gave you his gun without making a kick?"

The Sioux nodded his head and still grinned, Tozer joining him in the last expression of his feelings.

"How about his revolver?"

"He gib me that," said the scamp, drawing forth the handsome weapon, where Hazletine had not observed it, thrust into the girdle about his waist.

There was no mistaking the meaning of these words and proceedings. All doubt was removed as to the abduction of Fred Greenwood. Motoza was the agent in the outrage, though whether Tozer had taken an active part in the same was yet uncertain. He scanned the smaller firearm, and then, instead of returning it to the Sioux, deliberately shoved it into his hip-pocket.

"I think I'll take charge of that, Motoza."

The buck was about to make angry objection, when the white man explained:

"When I meet Hank to-morrow he'll want some proof that I can turn over the youngster to him. He won't believe I can do so till he sees that proof. I'll show him this revolver, and he'll know it belongs to the youngster. That will be all the proof he'll ask. The rest will come easy; and, Motoza, you and I will be rich."

There was an emphasis in this declaration that was convincing to the dusky partner in crime. He nodded his head and made no further protest. Evidently he was under the influence of his white ally.

At this juncture the couple turned their backs upon the eavesdropper, who had stolen to within a few paces of them. They continued talking, but the change of position prevented his hearing what was said. It was peculiarly exasperating, for, though he had gained considerable information, he still lacked the most important news of all. He had heard no intimation of where the prisoner was held. Could he but learn that, he would have lost no time in attempting his rescue. It must be said, furthermore, that had such knowledge come to him he would not have hesitated to draw bead on the two miscreants in turn, and shoot them down in their tracks. He was thoroughly enraged, and they deserved the fate.

A few minutes after the change of position the couple walked away, side by side, still conversing. Certain discovery would have followed any attempt on the part of the cowman to keep at their heels or nigh enough to overhear their words, so he held his place and saw them pass from sight. He had noted the direction, however, and observed that it led from the canyon and deeper into the mountains.

This was puzzling. It seemed to Hank that one or both would make their way to the prison of the youth, for it was unlikely that he would be left alone through the night. Having no thought of being under surveillance, Motoza and Tozer would take a direct course to the place of confinement, which now seemed to be deeper in the mountains, and at some point of which the cowman had no suspicion.

It was of the highest importance that the couple should not be allowed to pass beyond

sight, and the cowman began a cautious
search for them. But once more he was
doomed to disappointment. In the gathering twilight it was impossible to regain sight
of them, and, convinced of the uselessness of
the attempt, he gave it up.

"It begins to look as if Tozer holds the
winning hand," he angrily muttered; "there
ain't no question that the two have the
younker safe, and I've no idee where to hunt
fur him—but hold on!"

The conviction, or rather suspicion, that
the prison of the youth was within the canyon returned to the hunter with redoubled
force. Why had he not searched there before? If it was a mistake, no harm could
follow; if it was not a mistake — well, he
should see.

Wondering at himself because of his over-
sight, he abandoned all attempt to regain
sight of the couple and headed for the break
in the canyon. He arrived only a brief while
after Jack Dudley attempted and failed to
follow up the gorge, and except for the mishap of the youth the two would have met

within the following few minutes. It has already been shown how narrowly they missed doing so.

The familiarity of the cowman with the canyon averted the mistake made by his young friend. He ascended it with scarcely any hesitation, although in the dense gloom his vision was almost useless. It was because of that that he well-nigh stepped upon the crouching figure without suspecting it. Reaching the stone where Jack had been overwhelmed by failure, the cowman paused for a minute and peered round in the gloom. Not until he had glanced upward and studied the projecting crags over his head as outlined against the starlit sky was he absolutely sure of his location That glance made everything clear.

The next rock upon which it was necessary to leap was within easy reach, and had Jack Dudley known its location he would have fallen into no trouble. It lay to the left, close to the side of the canyon, and really carried one no further up the gorge; but from its surface he readily bounded to one beyond, and continued his leap-frog performance until he had ascended another hundred yards.

He was now close to the point he had in mind. It was there that he had been picking his way when the wondering boys, looking down from the top, saw him. Hazletine would have explained his action to them but for a certain feeling of shame which was not unnatural.

There had been rumors for years among the cattlemen of Southwestern Wyoming of a cavern in the canyon which was studded with gold. Many searches had been made for it, but without success. Hank Hazletine was among those who engaged in the hunt, but neither he nor his friends succeeded in finding the place. The veteran was not quite ready to abandon hope, and when he found himself in the section once more, on the hunt in which he acted as guide for the boys, he determined to make a decisive exploration without letting any one know his secret.

It was on this expedition that he succeeded in finding the cavern, but his trained eye immediately told him the marvellous legend was a myth. It was a romantic and picturesque spot, but there was not a grain of auriferous metal or ore in sight. Hoping that a second cavern was in the vicinity, he extended his search. When he emerged from the gorge, at the point where the break occurred, it was with the certainty that the whole thing was a fable. With a grim smile he dismissed the matter and resolved not to think of it again. He felt that he had acted foolishly, and his reluctance to tell his story to his young friends, therefore, was only natural.

But once more the cowman was on his way to the mysterious cavern, drawn by the hope, rather than the belief, that it was there he would find Fred Greenwood a prisoner and awaiting the completion of the bargain for his release by his abductors.

Determined to make no mistake, he halted under the projecting ledge and spent several minutes in peering around in the gloom. It looked as if he was right; but the darkness was too profound for him to make sure, and even the scrutiny of the ribbon of sky that showed above the narrow opening a thousand feet above his head failed to remove the last vestige of doubt.

Like the boys, Hank carried a rubber safe of matches. Producing this, he struck one of the tiny bits on the corrugated bottom of the little black box, and, shading the flame with his fingers from the moist wind caused by the dashing waters, he glanced at his immediate surroundings. He had strapped his Winchester to his back, and his arms were free.

A thrill of pleasure went through him, for the first scrutiny showed he was right. Directly over his head projected a thin ledge within ready reach. It was what might be termed the doorstep to the cavern. He had come to the exact spot for which he was searching.

Flinging the extinguished match into the waters at his side, he reached upward, and without difficulty drew himself upon the ledge. He was now in front of the cavern which he had visited by daylight, and whose interior was impressed so vividly on his memory that he knew every foot of it.

22

"Is the younker in there?" was the question he asked himself after regaining his feet. To test the matter, he called his name. The fierce torrent roared below and around him, but he was sure his words must have penetrated into the dismal recesses. He repeated the call several times without response.

"It may be the younker is asleep, or, if he hears me, he may take me fur Motoza; and yet that couldn't be, for our voices don't sound alike."

Once more he produced his rubber safe and struck a match, holding the twinkling flame above his head as he slowly moved forward into the cavern. Before the light expired he had another, for he intended to make his search thorough.

The opening in the side of the canyon had a width of ten or twelve feet, was of the same height, and extended back for more than double the distance. Side, floor and roof were of irregular formation, and the craggy stones rough and wet. Had there been any gleaming stalactites or stalagmites in sight, the cause of the legend attaching to the place would have been understood, but there was nothing of that nature. The cavern was simply a rent in the side of the canyon wall, created by some convulsion of nature, and all that was visible was damp limestone.

By the time the visitor had burned three matches his examination of the place was completed and he had made the discovery that he was the only occupant. Fred Greenwood was not there, nor did the cavern show signs of having been visited by person or animal.

But hold! When Hank threw down the last expiring match, he caught a glimpse of something white on the flinty floor. He had not thought of looking for anything, and it was the accidental following of the match with his gaze that revealed the object. Instantly another match was sending out its feeble rays, and he stooped down and picked up that which had arrested his attention.

It was a piece of paper, apparently the blank leaf of a letter. There was no writing or mark on it to indicate its ownership, but had it been the visiting-card of Fred Greenwood, Hank Hazletine could not have been more positive that it belonged to the young man.

It was impossible that Motoza should carry writing-paper with him. The cowman never did so, consequently he could not have dropped it on his late visit. It was equally improbable that Bill Tozer had anything to do with it. He knew that both of the boys had paper and pencils with them, for he had seen them figuring over some problems they were discussing, and with a thrill of conviction he remembered that the paper they used was of precisely the same pattern as the piece he held in his hand.

"The younker has been here, but what the mischief has become of him?" and the mystified cowman looked right and left, on the floor and at the roof, as if he suspected the youth was hiding in one of those places.

An explanation suggested itself. After taking the lad to the cavern, his captor from some cause had changed his mind and transferred him to another place of confinement.

No; there was another theory which would

explain the mystery : it was that Motoza, yielding to his implacable enmity of the youth, had placed him beyond all reach of his friends. The spirit of revenge with an American Indian is tenfold stronger than cupidity. It was not improbable that the miscreant, having committed the unspeakable crime, was concealing it from Tozer, his ally in the dreadful business.

The work of the cowman was finished for the time. He carefully let himself down from the ledge to the rock immediately beneath, and began working his way through the canyon to the opening at the break. His familiarity stood him in as good stead as before, and he reached the place without mishap. Climbing the steep slope to the higher ground, he sat down for a few minutes' thought.

It was well into the night, and it was useless to attempt to do anything more. He was as firmly resolved, however, as before not to be outwitted by the ruffians with whom he was dealing. He would consent to no attempt to pay them a ransom until he knew beyond peradventure that their part of the contract would be fulfilled.

"If they try any crooked work," he muttered, with deadly earnestness, "both of 'em have got to settle with Hank Hazletine."

He gave no thought to Jack Dudley, for he took it for granted that he had been able to look out for himself during the day. Following the route so well known to him, he reached the plateau within an hour after the arrival of the youth, who had started a fire and was doing his best to dry his clothing and gain some warmth for his chilled body.

It need not be said that the cowman was interested in the story told by the youth, and was astonished beyond measure to learn that both had taken the same route, one actually passing the other without either suspecting it. On his part, Hazletine related all that he had passed through, and explained the reason of his ascent of the canyon some time before, when he was observed by the wondering lads.

Meanwhile, where was Fred Greenwood?

CHAPTER XIX.

INTO THE CAVERN.

HANK HAZLETINE and Jack Dudley having failed to find the missing Fred Greenwood, let us try our hand at the task.

Going back to that afternoon when the elder youth from his concealment on the crest of the ridge fired down into the little herd of antelope grazing in the valley in front of him, and secured a supper for the two, it will be remembered that Fred had started along the side of the valley, with a view of placing himself beyond the game and rendering the success of himself and friend certain.

He never dreamed of danger to himself. His attention was fixed upon the pretty animals, and, hungry as he was, he felt a sympathy for them, knowing that in all probability one of the number would be sacrificed. Nevertheless, he put forth the utmost pains to prevent their taking alarm, and there is hardly a doubt that he would have succeeded in his purpose but for the catastrophe which overtook him when half the distance had been passed.

Suddenly, while he was stealing forward in a crouching posture, a low, threatening voice reached his ear. Only the single word, "*Stop!*" was uttered, but it could not have startled the youth more than the whir of a rattlesnake under his feet. Before he could straighten up he turned his head like a flash. Not a rod distant, kneeling upon one knee, was Motoza, the Sioux, with his Winchester aimed at him!

Believing that he would press the trigger of his weapon the next moment, Fred Greenwood was transfixed. He could only look at his enemy and await the end. He was without the power to raise a finger in his own defence.

"Drop gun!" commanded his master. The words showed the lad that he had a few minutes at least to live, but the "drop" was on him and he promptly obeyed.

"Drop little gun!" added the Sioux, who never wavered in keeping his rifle pointed at the chest of the young man.

Fred withdrew his revolver and flung it at his feet. He was now without a single firearm. An infant could not have been more helpless.

As yet he had not spoken a word. He recalled the warning of Jack Dudley, and knew the ferocious hatred this vagrant redskin held toward him. To appeal for mercy would delight the miscreant and not aid the prisoner. He tried another tack.

"What do you want with me, Motoza?"

The question pleased the Sioux, who, partly lowering his rifle, still held it ready for instant use. His ugly countenance was broken by the old grin.

"Huh! You call Motoza tief, eh?"

"That's what I called you, and that's what you are!"

"Huh! Me kill you!"

"*You* can do that easily enough, but you'll never live to brag about it. If the officers don't hang you, Hank Hazletine will make daylight shine through your hide! He is only waiting for an excuse."

"White man dog—me not afraid—me kill *him!*" said the Sioux, with a dangerous glitter in his snake-like eyes.

"You can't do it too soon. But what are you waiting for?"

Motoza had not counted upon such defiance; but if it lessened his contempt it did not diminish his hate nor weaken his purpose.

"You go; me follow; me point rifle if you run; if you call, me shoot!"

"Which way do you wish me to travel?"

The Sioux pointed toward the bend in the valley for which Fred was making when checked in this peremptory manner. To obey was to take him further from his comrade, but he obeyed.

As he moved off, Motoza picked up the two weapons from the ground, thrusting the revolver into the girdle at his waist, while he carried the Winchester in his other hand. Fred heard him a few paces in the rear, as well as the repetition of his threats to fire on the least attempt of the prisoner to regain his freedom or to attract the attention of his friends.

The youth never doubted that he would carry out this threat, and he would have been a zany to draw the explosion of wrath. He walked forward and did his best to obey the orders of his enemy in spirit and letter.

The young man thought intently. The shock of the belief that instant death impended was somewhat softened by the knowledge that the crisis was deferred for a time at least, though it was impossible to guess for how long.

What was the ultimate intention of the Sioux? It seemed probable to Fred that he was afraid to slay him at the spot of capture, since the body would be sure of discovery by his friends, with a good chance of learning the identity of the assassin. What more likely, therefore, than that he was conducting him to some remote place, where his body would never be found?

It was not natural that an active, sturdy youth like Fred Greenwood should submit to be led thus meekly to slaughter, but in what possible way could he help himself? If he wheeled about to assail the buck he was without a single weapon, while the Sioux was doubly armed. A glance over his shoulder showed his enemy almost within arm's reach.

Not the least trying feature of this extraordinary proceeding was that Fred had to hear the report of Jack Dudley's rifle, followed by his shouts, which plainly reached the ears of the one who dared make no reply. He could only continue walking until the bend in the valley was passed, when a change of direction took place.

It was no longer necessary to conceal themselves from observation, for there was no one to be feared. From the facts that afterward came to light there is little doubt that Tozer and Motoza had held a conference previous to the capture and fixed upon a definite line of procedure, for otherwise it is not conceivable that the Sioux would have spared the life of his captive.

With numerous turnings, and with the sounds of Jack Dudley's shouts and firing faintly reaching his ears, young Greenwood

continued marching in front of his captor
long after the sun had set and night closed
in. He had lost all idea of the points of the
compass, but the fact that the tramp continued and that no harm was done him inspired
the prisoner with a degree of hope that was
altogether lacking at the opening of his
strange adventure.

Suddenly a roaring noise struck him, and a
short distance further he reached the break
in the canyon with which he had become
familiar. This enabled him to locate himself,
and he looked around to learn the further
wishes of his master. From the moment of
starting Fred had been on the alert for a chance
to make a break for liberty, but none occurred.
The Sioux was too vigilant to tempt him.

The long immunity from harm had given
the lad a certain self-assurance. As yet he
had formed no suspicion of the real purpose
of the Sioux, but, somehow or other, he believed his own death was not likely to be attempted for a number of hours to come.

"Well, Motoza, here we are! What's the
next step?"

The Indian raised one of the hands grasping a Winchester and pointed toward the canyon.

"Go dere—jump on rock!"

"My gracious! I can't do that!"

"Den me kill!"

As if angered beyond restraint, he made a leap toward the startled youth, who recoiled a step, and, esteeming a death by drowning preferable to the one which threatened him, made haste to reply:

"All right; I'll try it."

But it was necessary that the miscreant should give some instructions to his prisoner. These were simple. He was to leap upon the rock nearest to shore, and then, by the same means, ascend the canyon until ordered to stop. From what has already been related concerning Jack Dudley's experience, it will be seen that the task was difficult and dangerous.

There was no choice, however. He had gained a general knowledge of the canyon and felt almost certain he would be overtaken by accident; but in many respects his experience was so similar to that which was afterward undergone by his comrade that the particulars need not be dwelt upon. He found the work less laborious than he expected. The Sioux by gesture indicated the rocks, when they were not clear to the boy, who found no trouble in making the leaps. In every case he had hardly landed when the buck dropped lightly at his side.

A desperate scheme was half-formed more than once while this singular progress was going on. It was purposely to miss his footing and allow himself to be carried away by the tumultuous torrent. He was restrained by two good reasons. Motoza was likely to seize him before he was swept beyond reach, and if he did not he would inevitably drown. Accordingly, Fred kept at it until finally they reached the ledge up which Hank Hazletine climbed twenty-four hours later.

By this time a suspicion of the partial truth had penetrated the mind of Fred. There must be some cavity in the rocks where his captor meant to hold him for awhile as prisoner. The plan of securing a large ransom in payment for his freedom was not dreamt of by the youth. No one would think of looking in this place for him, and he would be secure for an indefinite period.

Motoza had learned several things from his association with those of Caucasian blood, one of which was that a rubber match-safe is preferable to rubbing two dry sticks together when in need of fire, or using the old-fashioned steel and flint.

He managed with some trouble to make Fred understand he was to climb up the ledge, and he followed so deftly that the prisoner was given no chance to try to prevent him. A minute after they stood side by side, Motoza struck a match, and his captive had a glimpse of the cavern which has already been described.

Here, then, was the end of the journey. This was to be the prison of Fred Greenwood until when? When was he to be released, or was he not to be released at all?

Passing well back in the gloom the two sat down, so far removed from the roar and tumult of the torrent that they could talk without difficulty. Fred was still apprehensive of some sudden violence from the Sioux, and, though in the gloom he could see nothing of him, he was ready to make the best struggle possible.

"Am I to stay here, Motoza?" he asked, raising his voice to a high pitch.

Instead of replying directly, the Indian asked :

"Huh ! you fader hab heap money, eh ?"

This simple question revealed the whole plot and confirmed the statement already made that the scheme for holding Fred Greenwood for ransom by his relatives was arranged before his abduction took place.

It was a great discovery for Fred Greenwood to make. On the instant nearly all his fears vanished and his heart glowed with hope. This being remembered, he can hardly be blamed for drawing matters with rather a long bow.

"Yes," he made haste to say, "my father has money; a hundred times more than I have," all which was true without involving more than a moderate sum.

23

"He gib heap money fur *you*, eh?"

"Of course; I come high."

"He gib thousand—gib ten thousand—hundred thousand—million dollar—eh?"

"Well, that's a pretty good sum; I'm afraid my father wouldn't think I am worth as much as that; but there's no doubt, Motoza, he will pay you a good price; is it your plan to sell me to him?"

The Sioux made no answer to this, though Fred repeated the question. The sullen silence of the Indian brought back the misgivings of the captive. He could not doubt that he had been abducted with a view of being ransomed, but it was impossible to credit Motoza with the whole scheme. He must have allies, and, knowing nothing of Bill Tozer, Fred suspected that a half-dozen vagrant Indians, more or less, were engaged in it, though it seemed singular that no one else had shown himself thus far.

Although the prisoner had been in better spirits than would be suspected, his situation was uncomfortable and he lost hope with the passage of the hours. Motoza refused to hold any further conversation, and was evidently brooding over something of an unpleasant nature. By and by he lit his pipe and silently puffed. He was sitting on the flinty floor, with his back against the side of the cavern and his legs thrust out in front of him.

Now and then, when he drew a little harder on the pipe, the glow in the bowl revealed the tip of his nose, a part of the painted forehead, and the glittering black eyes. It was a gruesome picture, for, even when he was invisible, it seemed to Fred he could see the gleam of those eyes fixed upon him.

"Now, I know he hates me beyond expression," mused the youth, "and nothing would delight him more than to torture me to death. If he agrees to give me my liberty, it will be just like him to kill me as soon as he gets the money which father will gladly pay for my safety."

It will be seen that the trend of Fred's thoughts was similar to those of Hank Hazletine, when considering the same matter. Whatever project might be in the minds of others, the youth would be in danger so long as he was in the power of the wretch whom he had unpardonably insulted.

Naturally, Fred had asked himself more than once whether it was possible for him to make his escape from the cavern. It was out of the question so long as the Sioux was his companion, but if he should leave him alone, even for a short time, the youth was resolved to make the attempt.

These and similar thoughts were chasing one another through his brain when he fell asleep. He was very tired from his long tramp and did not open his eyes until the faint light of morning penetrated his prison. He had not forgotten to wind his watch, and when he looked at it he saw to his astonishment that it was nearly eight o'clock. He had slept for more than ten hours.

The next cause of his surprise was to find he was alone. Motoza had left while he was asleep, though how long previous it was impossible to guess. But the hunger which Fred Greenwood had felt on more than one previous occasion was as naught compared to the ravenous appetite that now had possession of him. It was a long time since he had eaten, and it looked as if it would be a long time before he ate again. There was absolutely nothing in the cavern beside himself. He felt in his pockets in the weak hope of finding a forgotten fish-hook that could be used, though he possessed nothing in the nature of bait; but, inasmuch as he had not brought a hook with him, it would not do to say he succeeded in his search, though he displaced the piece of writing-paper afterward found by his friend.

Forcing all thought of food from him for the time, he asked why, now that his gaoler was absent, he should not pick his way down the canyon and make a break for liberty. At the same time he could not forget that one of the most improbable acts of the Sioux would be to give him any chance at all to escape.

It was more than likely that Motoza had laid the temptation in his way, that it might serve him as a pretext for shooting his prisoner. Fred resolved, therefore, to be careful in all that he did. The necessity of drinking and bathing his face was his excuse for walking out to the border of the ledge and letting himself down to the rock underneath. There he dipped up what water he needed in the palms of his hands, and while doing so scanned every part of the canyon in his field of vision.

He noted the narrow strip of sky far aloft, the tumbling waters above and below where he stood, the black boulders protruding their heads above the torrent which flung itself fiercely against them, the craggy walls of the canyon, but nowhere did he catch sight of the Sioux who had brought him hither. None the less, Fred felt so certain his black eyes were watching him from some hidden point that he did not yield to the temptation to leap to the nearest boulder and start on his flight for liberty. Instead, he grasped the margin of the ledge and drew himself up to his former place.

There, however, he paused with folded arms and surveyed the strange scene more leisurely than before. He was anxious to discover the Sioux if anywhere in sight, but the fellow did not show himself.

The roar of the canyon had been in his ears so long that it seemed like silence, and it had lulled him to sleep hours before. He was still suffering from hunger and longed for the return of his captor, for he thought he would bring food with him.

Providentially the lad had stood in this position but a short time when he looked aloft toward the sky. At the moment of doing so he uttered an exclamation of affright and leaped back into the mouth of the cavern. The next instant a boulder that must have weighed a ton crashed upon the ledge where he had been standing, splintered off a number of pieces, and plunged into the torrent below.

Fred did not try to make himself believe that the falling of this mass of stone was an accident. Motoza or one of his allies had been on the watch above for the appearance of the youth, and when the boulder had been adjusted as well as possible it was tumbled over into the canyon. Had Fred remained on the spot a few moments longer he would have been crushed like an insect under the wheel of a steam-engine.

It was a startling occurrence, and in his weakened condition made him so faint that he withdrew still further into the cavern and sat down, trembling like a leaf. His hunger had vanished and hope almost departed.

"It will not do for me to leave the cavern in the daytime, for he is waiting for me to do so. I can't do it at night without some one to guide me. He means to keep me here until I die of starvation."

Fred had come really to believe this. He knew enough of Indian nature to understand that the race rarely inflict instant death upon an enemy when it is in their power to subject him to torture or slay in some horrible fashion. Motoza had not slain him before because he was unwilling that the one whom he hated so intensely should receive such mercy. It would be a hundredfold sweeter to the Sioux to see his prisoner dying by inches.

"If he has a plan for making father pay a ransom for me it will take a number of days to bring the thing to an end. During all that time I am to be left without a morsel of food; he would deprive me of water, too, if he could."

It was a shocking conclusion to form, but the usually clear-headed boy became convinced he was right.

"Poor Jack must be worried almost to death," he murmured, sitting on the stones and giving rein to his fancies; "he will know that something has gone wrong with me, but he can never know what it was. Hank will lay it to Motoza, for he has said there is nothing too wicked for him to do, but the cowman has no way of finding what has become of me, and he can't make Motoza tell him. He and Jack may hunt for weeks without suspecting where I am."

In this declaration Fred Greenwood, as is known, was not quite correct, though the search of his friends was fruitless.

CHAPTER XX.

A CLIMB FOR LIBERTY.

A YOUTH in the situation of Fred Green-wood cannot reason clearly, even though he be right in his main conclusions. He had settled into the belief that Motoza, the Sioux, had determined to subject him to a lingering death through starvation; and yet if it were he—as undoubtedly it was—who rolled the boulder into the canyon, it indicated a wish to put the most sudden end possible to his existence.

It would be painful to attempt to describe the experience of the lad in the cavern at the side of the canyon. As is often the case, his hunger diminished and was succeeded by a dull indifference, in which the suffering of the mind outweighed that of the body. The dreadful day at last drew to an end, and his situation and condition were much the same as earlier in the forenoon. He had not seen a living person, and had given over all hope of another visit from his merciless enemy.

"He means that I shall perish for want of food, and there is no help for it."

But with the coming of darkness the energy of the boy's nature asserted itself. It was impossible now for the Sioux or his allies to maintain a watch upon the mouth of the cavern, where the lad was observed the moment he showed himself, and Fred determined that as soon as it was fairly dark he would make an attempt that should be crowned with success or that would end his sufferings and wretchedness.

His plan was to let himself down from the ledge to the top of the nearest rock, and then try to reach the break in the canyon as he had ascended it under the guidance of his captor. It was not to be supposed that the vigilant Motoza would leave the way open for him, though his actions pointed to the belief that it was utterly impossible for the prisoner to escape by that means.

Nor in truth was it possible, for in the impenetrable gloom he was certain to miss his foothold sooner or later and be flung into the torrent, with no possibility of the good fortune that attended Jack Dudley, who had a much less distance to traverse.

It was yet early in the evening when Fred came once more and for the last time to the front of the cavern. With that attention to trifling matters which a person sometimes shows in the most trying crises he wound up his watch, examined his clothing to see that everything was right, adjusted his hat so that it was not likely to be displaced, and looked out in the gloom. All that he could see was when he gazed upward and observed a few stars twinkling in the thin streak of sky.

"Two things are certain," he mused: "that Indian does not think it possible for me to make my way out of the canyon; and, if I should succeed, he will be on the watch for me and shoot or try to force me to return. He shall never get me back here, for I will take the risk of drowning, and then——"

A thought flashed through him like an inspiration and fairly took away his breath.

Why not climb the side of the canyon?

He was so overcome by the question, which seemed born of heaven, that he stood dazed and bewildered. Then he became cool again and asked:

"Is it possible?"

He recalled that Hank Hazletine had told him he had done it during the daytime, and it must have been somewhere in this neighborhood. The task would seem easy if the sun were shining, but if it were shining Fred Greenwood would not have been permitted to make the attempt.

He was convinced of another thing: the depth of the canyon had been repeatedly referred to as being a thousand feet, but there were places where it was less than half that extent, and he remembered a depression in the earth, almost directly overhead, which must have lessened the prodigious height found at other points.

Nevertheless, a climb of several hundred feet up the perpendicular side of a canyon or mountain wall is severe work to the most powerful and best trained man, and its formidable nature was proved by the fact that some of the cowmen would not try it by daylight.

Nothing could be clearer than that Motoza had not hesitated to leave his prisoner alone in the cavern for the reason that he was certain he could not effect his escape therefrom. The last means the youth would think of employing was that of climbing the side; therefore, as Fred reasoned, that was the very means to adopt, and the only one that could possibly succeed.

"I'll try it!" was his conclusion, after a few minutes' thought.

Before setting out on the unparalleled task he fervently asked the help of the only One who could extricate him from his peril. Then he summoned his strength and courage to the tremendous work.

His dread now was that Motoza would put in an appearance before he was clear of the mouth of the cavern. Had the lad thought of the daring scheme earlier in the day he would have studied the stupendous stairs upon which all his hopes now rested, but it was too late to think of that.

Reaching upward, he grasped one of the projecting points of rock and drew himself clear of the opening in front of the cavern. Naturally muscular and active, with all his nerves in superb control, the effort was trifling. Within less time than would be supposed he had climbed fully fifty feet without meeting with any difficulty. Then the first thrill of alarm shot through him as one foot slipped and he narrowly missed falling.

He found a good place to rest, and immediately adopted a sensible precaution. Removing both shoes, he tied the strings together and slung them over his shoulder, with the fastening under his chin. This would make it rough for his stockinged feet, but it was worth it all. He was not discommoded by rifle or pistol, and could not have been better prepared for climbing.

He felt as yet no fatigue, and resumed his work as soon as he was ready. If he continued to find projections such as he had found thus far, there was no reason why he should not reach the level ground above in safety. As an evidence of how fate sometimes plays

fast and loose with us, it is certain that Hank
Hazletine entered the cavern while his young
friend was climbing the wall overhead, without either dreaming of the actual situation.

Fred Greenwood, at the beginning of his
climb for liberty, was subjected to a peculiar
peril. He had rested but a moment, when he
was seized with an extraordinary " panicky"
feeling. He was sure that Motoza was standing on the ledge below, peering upward in the
gloom, and holding his rifle ready to fire at
him on the instant he could make his aim
certain.

Like all such emotions, it was opposed to
common sense. According to his belief it
was out of the power of the Sioux to obtain
the most shadowy glimpse of him, and the
youth ought to have felt as secure against being picked off as if in his home, hundreds of
miles away; but the feeling for a time was
uncontrollable, and, yielding to it, he began
frantically climbing, never abating his efforts
until he had gone fully fifty feet higher. By
that time he was all a-tremble, and so weak
that he was forced to pause for rest. Thus

far he had been extremely fortunate in meeting with no difficulty, the projections affording abundant support for hands and feet. Moreover, he had again attained a ledge where he was able to sustain himself with comparative ease.

He paused, panting, trembling and exhausted. Thrusting out his head as far as was safe, he looked downward. Nothing but impenetrable gloom met his eye. He could hear the torrent rushing against the rocks and boulders in its path, and flinging itself against the walls of the canyon, but he could distinguish nothing, and his strong sense now came to his rescue.

"If he is down there he cannot see me; he will not dream I have started to climb the wall, and therefore will not follow. If he does, he must appear below me, and I will kick him loose the minute I see him. How foolish to be afraid!"

In a few minutes his nerves became calmer, but he began to realize the nature of the terrifying task before him. There was no thought of retreat on his part, and he was

24

determined to keep on, so long as the work was possible.

His feet were paining him, and were certain to pain him a good deal more before he reached the top; but healthy, rugged youth has elastic muscles, and in a short time Fred was ready to resume his work. His panic was gone, and he exerted himself with the deliberate care which he should have shown from the first.

As nearly as he could judge he had climbed some twenty paces, when he was startled, upon extending his hand upward, to encounter only the smooth face of the wall. Hitherto there had been more projections than he required, but now the steps appeared to vanish, leaving him without any support.

Could it be he would have to abandon his effort after making so fine a start? Must he pick his way down the side of the canyon, again, to the cavern, and there meekly resume the torture of waiting for death from starvation? Failure was too terrible to be thought of, and he resumed his searching for the indispensable support.

Certainly there was nothing directly above

him that would serve, and he passed his right
hand to one side.   Ah! he caught the sharp
edge, after groping for a few seconds.   Leaning over, he reached out as far as possible and
found the projection extended indefinitely.

"It will do!" he muttered, with a thrill,
and, without pausing to reflect upon the fearful risk of the thing, he swung himself along,
sustained for an instant by his single hand;
but the other was immediately alongside of it,
and it was easy to hold himself like a pen-
dulum swaying over the frightful abyss.   But
there was nothing upon which to rest his feet.
He did not wish anything, and, swinging side-
ways, threw one leg over the ledge beside his
hands, and, half-rolling over, raised himself
securely for the time on his perch.

"Gracious!" he exclaimed, pausing from
the effort; "if I had stopped to think, I
shouldn't have dared to try it.   If this ledge
had been smaller I shouldn't have found
room for my body, and there is no way of
getting back to the stone on which I was
standing.   I *must* go on now, for I cannot go
back."

It was plain sailing for a few minutes. The flinty excrescences were as numerous as ever, and he never paused in his ascent until prudence whispered that it was wise to take another breathing spell. It was a source of infinite comfort to feel that when he thus checked himself he was not compelled to do so for lack of support.

There was no way of determining how far he had climbed, and he based his calculation on hope rather than knowledge. The roar of the canyon was notably fainter, and, when he looked aloft, the ribbon of starlit sky appeared nearer than at first. There could be no doubt that he was making his ascent at the most favorable point, for the height was much less than at most of the other places, and he believed this was the portion where Hank Hazletine had climbed from the bottom to the top of the gorge. Could he have been certain of the latter, all misgiving would have vanished.

Not a trace of his panic remained. If Motoza had returned to the cavern, and, discovering the flight of his prisoner, set out to follow him, there was little prospect of his success, for the fugitive had varied from a direct line, and the Sioux might pass within arm's length without being aware of the fact.

There was one peril to which Fred was exposed, and it was fortunate it never entered his mind. Supposing Motoza was standing on the ledge at the bottom of the canyon and gazing upward, weapon in hand, it was quite probable that he would be able to locate the youth. This would be not because of any superiority of vision, but because of that patch of sky beyond, acting as a background for the climber. With his inky figure thrown in relief against the stars, his enemy could have picked him off as readily as if the sun were shining.

This possibility, we say, did not present itself to Fred Greenwood, and, more providential than all, Motoza was not in the canyon.

The slipping of one foot tore most of the sole from the stocking, and his foot had henceforth no protection against the craggy surface.

"I don't mind the stocking," grimly re-

flected the youth, " for there is another pair
in camp and plenty of them at the ranch,
but how it hurts!"

He would have been altogether lacking in
the pluck he had displayed thus far had he
been deterred by physical suffering from
pushing his efforts to the utmost. He would
have kept on through torture tenfold worse,
and he showed himself no mercy.

Few people who have not been called upon
to undertake such a work can form an idea
of its exhausting nature. It would be hard
to think of anyone better prepared than Fred
Greenwood to stand the terrific draught upon
his strength ; but while a long way from the
top, and while there was no lack of supports
for his hands and feet, and in the face of his
unshakable resolve, he was compelled to doubt
his success. It seemed as if the dizzy height
did not diminish. When he had climbed for
a long time and stopped, panting and suffering,
the stars appeared to be as far away as ever.
He felt as if he ought to have been out of the
ravine long before, but the opening looked to
be as unattainable as at the beginning.

His whole experience was remarkable to
that extent that it can be explained only on
the ground that the intense mental strain
prevented his seeing things as they were. He
had subjected his muscles to such a tension
that he was obliged to pause every few minutes and rest. One of his feet was scarified
and bleeding, and the other only a little better. When he looked upward his heart sank,
for a long distance still interposed between
him and the ground above.

"I must have picked the place where the
canyon is deepest," was his despairing conclusion; "I feel hardly able to hang on, and
would not dare do what I did further below."

He now yielded to a curious whim. Instead
of continually gazing at the sky, that he
might measure the distance remaining to be
traversed, he resolved not to look at it at all
until he had climbed a long way. He hoped
by doing this to discover such a marked de-
crease in the space that it would reanimate
him for the remaining work.

Accordingly he closed his eyes, and, depending on the sense of feeling alone, which in truth was his reliance from the first, he toiled steadily upward. Sometimes he had to grope with his hands for a minute or two before daring to leave the support on which his feet rested, but one of his causes for astonishment and thankfulness was that such aids seemed never to be lacking.

He continued this blind progress until his wearied muscles refused to obey further. He must rest or he would drop to the bottom from exhaustion. He hooked his right arm over the point of a rock, sat upon a favoring projection below, and decided to wait until his strength was fully restored.

He could not resist the temptation to look up and learn how much yet remained to do.

Could he believe his senses? He was within a dozen feet of the top!

He gasped with amazement, grew faint, and then was thrilled with hope. He even broke into a cheer, for the knowledge was like nectar to the traveller perishing of thirst in the desert—it was life itself.

All pain, all suffering, all fatigue were

forgotten in the blissful knowledge. He bent to his work with redoubled vigor. If the supports continued, his stupendous task was virtually ended.

And they did continue. Not once did the eagerly-feeling hands fail to grasp a projection of some form which could be made to serve his purpose. Up, up he went, until the clear, cool air fanned his temples, when, with a last effort, he drew himself from the canyon, and, plunging forward on his face, fainted dead away.

He lay in a semi-conscious condition for nearly an hour. Then, when his senses slowly returned, he raised himself to a sitting position and looked around. It was too early for the moon, and the gloom prevented his seeing more than a few paces in any direction.

But how the pain racked him! It seemed as if every bone was aching and every muscle sore. The feet had been wholly worn from each stocking, and his own feet were torn and bleeding. He had preserved his shoes, but when he came to put them on he groaned with anguish. His feet were so swollen that it was torture to cover them, and he could not tie the strings; but they must be protected, and he did not rise until they were thus armored.

He was without any weapons, but the torment of his wounds drove that fact from his mind. All that he wanted now was to get away from the spot where he could not help believing he was still in danger of recapture. But when he stood erect and the agony shot through his frame, he asked himself whether it was possible to travel to the plateau without help; and yet the effort must be made.

He had a general knowledge of his situation, and, bracing himself for the effort, he began the work. It was torture from the first, but after taking a few steps his system partly accommodated itself to the requirement and he progressed better than he anticipated. He was still on the wrong side of the canyon, which it was necessary to leave before rejoining his friends. He was wise enough to distrust his own capacity after the fearful strain, and did not make the attempt until he found a place where the width was hardly

one-half of the extent leaped by him and
Jack Dudley. As it was, the jump, into which
he put all his vigor, landed him just clear of
the edge, a fact which did much to lessen the
sharp suffering caused by alighting on his
feet.

He yearned to sit down and rest, but was
restrained by the certainty that it would make
his anguish more intense when he resumed
his tramp toward camp. Furthermore, as he
believed himself nearing safety, his impatience deepened and kept him at work when
he should have ceased.

As he painfully trudged along, his thoughts
reverted to his climb up the side of the canyon and he shuddered; for, now that it was
over, he could not comprehend how he dared
ever make the effort. Not for the world
would he repeat it, even by daylight.

"Heaven brought me safely through," was
his grateful thought.

But as he drew near the plateau his mus-
ings turned thither. He had counted upon
finding Jack Dudley and the guide there; but
they might be miles away, and he would not

see them for days. He knew he needed attention from his friends and could not sustain himself much longer. If he should be unable to find them——

But all these gloomy forebodings were scattered a few minutes later by the glimmer of the camp-fire on the other side of the plateau. One of his friends at least must be there, and providentially it proved that both were present.

CHAPTER XXI.

HOW IT ALL ENDED.

A T last the clothing of Jack Dudley was dried, and he felt thoroughly comfortable in body. While he was employed in the pleasant task, Hank Hazletine went away in quest of food. It took time and hard work to find it, but his remarkable skill as a hunter enabled him to do so, and when he returned he brought enough venison to serve for the evening and morning meal. No professor of the culinary art could have prepared the meat more excellently than he over the bed of live coals. The odor was so appetizing that the youth was in misery because of his impatience, but the guide would not let him touch a mouthful until the food was done " to the queen's taste." Then they had their feast.

And yet the two were oppressed by thoughts of the absent one. The attempts of his friends during the day to help or to get trace of Fred Greenwood had been brought to naught, and it looked as if they would have to consent to the humiliating terms of Tozer and Motoza, with strong probability that the missing youth was never again to be seen alive.

"I think, Hank," said Jack, when the cowman had lit his pipe, "that we should run no more risks."

"How can we help it?"

"When you meet Tozer to-morrow morning by appointment, tell him the price he asks will be paid, but everything must be square and above board."

The guide looked at his companion a moment in silence. Then he said:

"If you'll turn the matter over in your mind, younker, you'll see that this bus'ness can't be put through without giving the scamps the chance to swindle us the worst sort of way. They won't give up the boy on our promise to pay 'em the money and no questions asked, for they don't b'leve we'll do it; so we've got to give 'em the money and trust to their honor to keep their part. Trust to their *honor*," repeated Hank, with all the scorn he could throw into voice and manner; " as if they knowed what it means."

"I know from what you have said that Tozer and Motoza are cunning, but——"

In order to receive all the warmth possible, Jack Dudley was sitting within the cavern and facing outward, while his companion faced him, with his back toward the plateau and mountains beyond. Jack suddenly broke off his remark, for in the gloom behind the cowman he saw something move. That something quickly took the form of a white-faced, exhausted youth trudging painfully forward and ready to sink to the ground with weakness.

"Heavens! can it be?" gasped Jack, half-rising to his feet and staring across the campfire. The next moment, and while Hazletine was looking in the same direction, as astounded as the youth, the elder made one bound and was at the side of Fred Greenwood, whom he caught in his arms as he sagged downward in a state of utter collapse.

In the course of the following hour everything was made clear. Under the tender ministrations of Jack Dudley and Hank Hazletine the returned wanderer recovered to a great degree his strength, and to the fullest degree his naturally buoyant spirits. The faint odor of the broiling meat which lingered in the air awoke his ravenous appetite, but knowing how long he had been without food, the cowman would not permit him to eat more than a tithe of what he craved. After a time he gave him more, until his appetite was fairly well satisfied.

"Jack," said Fred, with something of his old waggishness, as he looked across the fire into the face of his comrade, "let's go home."

"You forget that we have a month's vacation, and it is hardly half gone. We can stay another week and then be sure of being back to school in time. You lamented more than I because we could not have a longer playspell. Your sentiments have changed."

The younger lad pointed to his feet.

"There's the reason. If I were like you I shouldn't think of leaving this delightful country until the last day; but I shall need all the vacation to get on my feet again. Do you comprehend?"

"Yes; your demonstration is logical. True, you have lost your rifle and pistol, the same as myself, but we could get others at the ranch, and no doubt meet with plenty more enjoyable adventures, but not as you are. I shall be very willing to start home with you to-morrow morning. What do you think of it, Hank?"

"I'm blamed sorry this bus'ness has to wind up as it does, but there's no help fur it, and we'll leave fur the ranch after breakfast."

"Will you keep your appointment with Tozer?"

"I've been thinking of that; yes, I'll meet him."

There was a peculiar intonation in these words that caused both boys to look into that bearded face, but they could not be sure of his meaning.

It was Fred who spoke:

"Hank, there is one matter as to which I cannot feel certain; I want your opinion of it."

" Wal, I'm listening."

" After Motoza forced me into the cavern at the side of the canyon he went off and has not returned yet, unless he did so after I left. Now, why didn't he go back ?"

" Why should he go back ? He felt sartin there was no way fur you to git out, and if I'd been told that your only chance was to climb the wall I'd 'greed with him, though you struck the spot where I done it myself."

" He must have known I hadn't a mouthful of food ?"

" He couldn't help knowing it."

" The question in my mind is this : what he said to me, as well as what you have told, proves that he understood the whole scheme of my being ransomed. Tozer must have known where I was ; he knew that to bring the ransom business to a head would require several days, even with the use of the telegraph ; they expected me to stay in the cavern all the time. How long would they have left me there without bringing me anything to eat ?"

" They'd never brought you anything."

"Then when the time came to surrender me to my friends I should have been dead."

The cowman nodded his head.

"There ain't no doubt of that."

"And they couldn't have carried out their part of the agreement."

"Which the same they knowed."

"But it seems unreasonable. It would have placed both in peril, from which I cannot see how it was possible for them to escape. If they gave me up after receiving the money they would be safe against punishment. Why, then, should they place themselves in such great danger when they had nothing to gain and all to lose by doing so? That is what I can't understand, and I am sure my brain has become clearer."

It was the same view of the question that had puzzled Jack Dudley, and the two boys listened with interest to the explanation of the veteran.

"Tozer of himself would turn you over sound in limb and body; but, since it was the Sioux who done all the work, as you have showed us, Bill had to make a sort of compromise with the villain, and that compromise was that you should be left with Motoza till the hour come fur you to be produced. That was the price Bill had to pay Motoza fur what he done. It wasn't Tozer, but the Sioux, that was fixing things so as to starve you to death."

The cowman spoke with a deliberation and seriousness that left no doubt he believed every word uttered, and the boys were convinced he was right.

"Bill is as mean as they make 'em," added Hazletine, "but he'd rather grab a pile of money than kill a chap he don't like. It's t'other way with the Sioux. He likes money well 'nough, fur he knows it'll buy firewater, but the sweetest enjoyment he can have is to revenge himself on a person he hates, and from what I've heard he hates you as hard as he knows how."

"There is no doubt of that," said Jack; "I shall never forget the expression of his face when Fred made him give up my rifle."

Fred was thoughtful a moment, and then asked:

"Hank, what do you mean to do about Tozer ?"

"Wal, until I larned your story I was fixed to shoot him on sight."

"But what of the agreement you would have to make before he gave me up ?"

"I'd kept that the same as the other folks, but it wouldn't be long afore I'd git a chance to pick a quarrel with him over other matters, and then it would be him or me ; and," added the cowman, with a grim smile, "I don't think it would be me."

"Do you still hold to that resolve ?"

"I can't say that I do. I don't see that Bill meant any hurt except to make some money out of you, and he couldn't help taking chances on that. If he could have had his way he'd turned you over to us as well as when you left; so I think I'll wait to see what his next trick is to be afore I draw a bead on him. I'll take another plan —I'll give him the laugh."

"Give him the laugh !" repeated the wondering Jack Dudley ; "what do you mean by that ?"

"I'll meet him here to-morrer morning, and, after we've talked a while, let him see you or know how things stand, and then I'll just laugh at him till I drop to the ground and roll over on my back. Won't he feel cheap?"

The conceit was so odd that both boys smiled.

"That certainly is a curious way to punish a man for doing a wrong. It seems to me that, since he had so much to do with abducting Fred, he ought to be arrested, tried, and punished. He should be made to suffer for his crime."

Hank showed his hard sense by replying:

"I don't deny that, but there's no way of punishing him. He hasn't done a thing fur which you could make the court say he's guilty. The younker there that spent more time than he liked in the canyon has never even seed Bill Tozer. What reason, then, has he fur saying Bill had anything to do with the bus'ness?"

"Didn't he admit as much to you?"

"Not a word! He give himself away in

his talk, but whenever he said anything 'bout things he reminded me it was all guesswork."

"Could not Motoza be made to swear against him?"

"He might, and he might not. If he did, why, Bill would swear t'other way, and make it look as if he was trying to play the friend for the younker. It would be like some folks, after the thing was over, proposing to buy Bill a gold medal fur showing himself such a good and noble man. No; my plan is best. When I give him the laugh he'll feel worse than if he was sent up fur ten years."

"It looks as if there is no other way of punishing him," remarked Fred; "but the case is different with Motoza."

"Wal, *rather!*"

It would be impossible to convey a true idea of the manner of Hank Hazeltine when he uttered these words. He nodded his head, clinched his free hand, and his eyes seemed to flash fire.

"Do you mean to kill him, Hank?"

"O, no," was the scornful response; "I'm

going to take his hand and tell him how much
I love him. I'll wipe the paint off one cheek,
so as to make room fur a brotherly kiss. I'll
send him to your folks, that you may have
him for a playmate. He'll be so sweet and
nice among the little younkers. *That's* what
I'll do with dear Motoza!''

It was impossible not to read the terrible
purpose that lay behind all this. The boys
made no mistake. Jack Dudley shuddered,
but was silent. He knew the miscreant
richly merited the threatened retribution, and
yet he wished it were not impending.

Surely, if anyone was justified in calling
down vengeance upon the head of the vagrant
Sioux it was his victim—he who had felt his
hatred, and whose physical sufferings must
remind him of the same for weeks to come.
But Fred Greenwood was in a gracious and
forgiving mood. His heart throbbed when
he recalled what he had so recently passed
through, but he could not lose sight of the
blessed fact that he *had* passed through it all.
He was with his beloved comrade again, not
much the worse for his experience. In truth

he was a little homesick, and was stirred with
sweet delight at the thought that, if all went
well, he should be with his parents within
the coming week.

And yet he was oppressed by the thought
that one of the results of his short visit to
Wyoming was to be the death of a human
being. He was sure he could never shake
off the remembrance, and should he ever wish
to return in the future to renew his hunt under more favorable conditions, the memory
would haunt him. It mattered not that the
wretch deserved to be executed for the crime,
in the commission of which he had been in-
terrupted before he could complete it. He
was a savage, a heathen, a barbarian, who was
following the light as he understood it. Why,
therefore, should not mercy be shown to him?

There are many things which Jack Dudley
and Fred Greenwood have done during their
youthful lives that are creditable to them,
but there is none which gives the two greater
pleasure than the remembrance of the moral
victory gained in their argument with Hank
Hazletine. Fred opened the plea, and his

comrade quickly rallied to his help. Their aim was to convince their guide that it was wrong for him to carry out his purpose regarding the Sioux. That the fellow should be punished was not to be questioned, but it should be done in a legitimate way and by the constituted authorities. Hazletine insisted that the conditions were such that Motoza would never be thus punished, at least not to the extent he ought to be; therefore, it was the duty of Hazletine to attend to the matter himself.

The argument lasted for two hours. The boys were able, bright and ingenious, but they had *truth* on their side, and by and by the grim cowman showed signs of weakening. What knocked the props from under him was the fact which he was compelled to admit that the Sioux was only following the teachings he had received from infancy; that he lacked the light and knowledge with which Hazletine had been favored; that it was the duty of the white people to educate, civilize and Christianize the red men, who have been treated with cruel injustice from the very discovery of our country.

It cannot be said that the guide yielded with good grace, but yield he did, and the victory was secured. He pledged the boys not to offer any harm to Motoza for his last crime, and indeed would never harm him, unless it should become necessary in self-defence.

"But I s'pose you hain't any 'bjection to my giving the laugh to Bill?" he said, with ludicrous dismay; "there ain't nothing wrong in *that*, is there?"

"Nothing at all," replied the pleased Fred; "we shall enjoy it as much as you."

"Which the same being the case, it's time you went to sleep; I'll keep watch and call you when I git ready."

Bidding their friend good-night, the boys wrapped themselves in their blankets and speedily sank into slumber.

The kind-hearted guide did not disturb either, and when they opened their eyes the sun was in the sky. Fred Greenwood was in a bad shape with his swollen and lacerated feet, but his naturally rugged frame recovered rapidly from the trying strain to which it had been subjected. He proved that his appetite was as vigorous as ever, and was eager to reach the ranch with the least possible delay. Hank promised him no time should be wasted.

A lookout was kept for Bill Tozer, the boys remaining in the cavern, where they could not be seen. There was the possibility, of course, that the man had learned of the escape of the young prisoner, but all doubt was removed when, at the appointed time, he appeared on the edge of the plateau and strode confidently to the point where Hazletine, just outside the cavern, awaited his coming.

The two shook hands and immediately got down to business. The scamp felt that he commanded the situation and he was disposed to push matters.

"I've been thinking over what you said yesterday," remarked the guide, "and have made up my mind that I can't do it."

"You can't, eh? It's the only thing you *can* do; Motoza insists that the price shall be ten thousand dollars, but I'll stick by the original agreement and call it half that sum."

"Let me see," said the cowman, thoughtfully; "you promise to give us back the younker safe and sound, provided his friends hand you five thousand dollars?"

"That's it; you understand the whole business. You know, of course, Hank, that I'm only acting as the friend——"

"Don't git over any more of that stuff, Bill. Are we to give you the money afore you produce the younker?"

"Certainly; that's the only way to do business."

"S'pose you bring him, and then I'll ask his folks if they want to make you a present of five thousand dollars—how'll *that* work?"

Tozer broke into laughter.

"You ought to be ashamed to talk such nonsense. The only way by which you can see your young friend again is to hand us the money, give a pledge not to ask any questions or try to punish Motoza or me——"

The jaw of the man suddenly dropped and he ceased speaking, for at that moment he saw Jack Dudley and his limping companion walk out from the cavern and smilingly approach.

The whole truth flashed upon him. He was outwitted as he had never been outwitted before in all his life. Without speaking a syllable, he wheeled around and started at a rapid stride across the plateau toward the point where he had first appeared, with feelings which it is impossible to imagine.

And didn't Hank Hazletine "give him the laugh?" He bent over with mirth, staggering backward until he had to place his hand against the side of the cavern to save himself from falling. It really seemed as if his uproarious mirth must have penetrated a mile in every direction, and it did not cease until some minutes after the discomfited victim had disappeared. Jack and Fred laughed, too, until their sides ached; and who shall deny that there was not full cause for their merriment?

An hour later, the ponies, saddled and bridled, were threading their way out of the foot-hills for the ranch, which was reached without further incident. There the boys remained several days until Fred had recovered to a large extent from his hurts, when they rode to the station at Fort Steele, where they shook hands with the honest Hank Hazletine and bade him good-by.

And thus it came about that on the first Monday in the following November Jack Dudley and Fred Greenwood were in their respective seats at school, as eager and ambitious to press their studies as they had been to visit Bowman's ranch, in Southwestern Wyoming, in which ranch, by the way, they advised Mr. Dudley to retain his half-ownership.

"It's worth all it cost you, father," said Jack, "and perhaps one of these days you will want the V. W. W. to go out and take another look at it."

"Perhaps," was the dubious reply of the parent.

FAMOUS STANDARD
JUVENILE LIBRARIES.

ANY VOLUME SOLD SEPARATELY AT $1.00 PER VOLUME

(Except the Sportsman's Club Series, Frank Nelson Series and
Jack Hazard Series.).

Each Volume Illustrated. 12mo. Cloth.

HORATIO ALGER, JR.

THE enormous sales of the books of Horatio Alger, Jr.,
show the greatness of his popularity among the boys, and
prove that he is one of their most favored writers. I am told
that more than half a million copies altogether have been
sold, and that all the large circulating libraries in the country
have several complete sets, of which only two or three volumes are ever on the shelves at one time. If this is true,
what thousands and thousands of boys have read and are
reading Mr. Alger's books! His peculiar style of stories,
often imitated but never equaled, have taken a hold upon the
young people, and, despite their similarity, are eagerly read
as soon as they appear.

Mr. Alger became famous with the publication of that
undying book, "Ragged Dick, or Street Life in New York."
It was his first book for young people, and its success was so
great that he immediately devoted himself to that kind of
writing. It was a new and fertile field for a writer then, and
Mr. Alger's treatment of it at once caught the fancy of the
boys. "Ragged Dick" first appeared in 1868, and ever since
then it has been selling steadily, until now it is estimated
that about 200,000 copies of the series have been sold.

—Pleasant Hours for Boys and Girls.

A writer for boys should have an abundant sympathy with them. He should be able to enter into their plans, hopes, and aspirations. He should learn to look upon life as they do. Boys object to be written down to. A boy's heart opens to the man or writer who understands him.
—From *Writing Stories for Boys*, by Horatio Alger, Jr.

RAGGED DICK SERIES.

6 vols. By Horatio Alger, Jr. $6.00

Ragged Dick.
Fame and Fortune.
Mark the Match Boy.

Rough and Ready.
Ben the Luggage Boy.
Rufus and Rose.

TATTERED TOM SERIES—First Series.

4 vols. By Horatio Alger, Jr. $4.00

Tattered Tom.
Paul the Peddler.

Phil the Fiddler.
Slow and Sure.

TATTERED TOM SERIES—Second Series.

4 vols. $4.00

Julius.
The Young Outlaw.

Sam's Chance.
The Telegraph Boy.

CAMPAIGN SERIES.

3 vols. By Horatio Alger, Jr. $3.00

Frank's Campaign. Charlie Codman's Cruise.
Paul Prescott's Charge.

LUCK AND PLUCK SERIES—First Series.

4 vols. By Horatio Alger, Jr. $4.00

Luck and Pluck.
Sink or Swim.

Strong and Steady.
Strive and Succeed.

LUCK AND PLUCK SERIES—Second Series.

4 vols. $4.00

Try and Trust.   Risen from the Ranks.
Bound to Rise.   Herbert Carter's Legacy.

BRAVE AND BOLD SERIES.

4 vols.   By Horatio Alger, Jr. $4.00

Brave and Bold.   Shifting for Himself.
Jack's Ward.   Wait and Hope.

NEW WORLD SERIES.

3 vols.   By Horatio Alger, Jr. $3.00

Digging for Gold.   Facing the World.   In a New World.

VICTORY SERIES.

3 vols.   By Horatio Alger, Jr. $3.00

Only an Irish Boy.   Adrift in the City.
        Victor Vane, or the Young Secretary.

FRANK AND FEARLESS SERIES.

3 vols.   By Horatio Alger, Jr. $3.00

Frank Hunter's Peril.   Frank and Fearless.
            The Young Salesman.

GOOD FORTUNE LIBRARY.

3 vols.   By Horatio Alger, Jr. $3.00

Walter Sherwood's Probation.   A Boy's Fortune.
        The Young Bank Messenger.

RUPERT'S AMBITION.

1 vol.   By Horatio Alger, Jr. $1.00

JED, THE POOR=HOUSE BOY.

1 vol.   By Horatio Alger, Jr. $1.00

HARRY CASTLEMON.

HOW I CAME TO WRITE MY FIRST BOOK.

WHEN I was sixteen years old I belonged to a composition class. It was our custom to go on the recitation seat every day with clean slates, and we were allowed ten minutes to write seventy words on any subject the teacher thought suited to our capacity. One day he gave out "What a Man Would See if He Went to Greenland." My heart was in the matter, and before the ten minutes were up I had one side of my slate filled. The teacher listened to the reading of our compositions, and when they were all over he simply said: "Some of you will make your living by writing one of these days." That gave me something to ponder upon. I did not say so out loud, but I knew that my composition was as good as the best of them. By the way, there was another thing that came in my way just then. I was reading at that time one of Mayne Reid's works which I had drawn from the library, and I pondered upon it as much as I did upon what the teacher said to me. In introducing Swartboy to his readers he made use of this expression: "No visible change was observable in Swartboy's countenance." Now, it occurred to me that if a man of his education could make such a blunder as that and still write a book, I ought to be able to do it, too. I went home that very day and began a story, "The Old Guide's Narrative," which was sent to the *New York Weekly*, and came back, respectfully declined. It was written on both sides of the sheets but I didn't know that this was against the rules. Nothing abashed, I began another, and receiving some instruction, from a friend of mine who was a clerk in a book store, I wrote it on only one side of the paper. But mind you, he didn't know what I was doing. Nobody knew it; but one day, after a hard Saturday's work—the other boys had been out skating on the brick-pond—I shyly broached the subject to my mother. I felt the need of some sympathy. She listened in amazement, and then said : "Why, do you think you could write a book like that?" That settled the matter, and from that day no one knew what I was up to until I sent the first four volumes of Gunboat Series to my father. Was it work? Well, yes ; it was hard work, but each week I had the satisfaction of seeing the manuscript grow until the "Young Naturalist" was all complete.

—Harry Castlemon in the Writer.

GUNBOAT SERIES.

6 vols.   BY HARRY CASTLEMON. $6.00

Frank the Young Naturalist.   Frank before Vicksburg.
Frank on a Gunboat.   Frank on the Lower Mississippi.
Frank in the Woods.   Frank on the Prairie.

ROCKY MOUNTAIN SERIES.

3 vols.   BY HARRY CASTLEMON. $3.00

Frank Among the Rancheros.   Frank in the Mountains.
Frank at Don Carlos' Rancho.

SPORTSMAN'S CLUB SERIES.

3 vols.   BY HARRY CASTLEMON. $3.75

The Sportsman's Club in the Saddle.   The Sportsman's Club
The Sportsman's Club Afloat.   Among the Trappers.

FRANK NELSON SERIES.

3 vols.   BY HARRY CASTLEMON. $3.75

Snowed up.   Frank in the Forecastle.   The Boy Traders.

BOY TRAPPER SERIES.

3 vols.   BY HARRY CASTLEMON. $3.00

The Buried Treasure.   The Boy Trapper.   The Mail Carrier.

ROUGHING IT SERIES.

3 vols.   BY HARRY CASTLEMON. $3.00

George in Camp.   George at the Fort.
George at the Wheel.

ROD AND GUN SERIES.

3 vols.   BY HARRY CASTLEMON. $3.00

Don Gordon's Shooting Box.   The Young Wild Fowlers.
Rod and Gun Club.

GO-AHEAD SERIES.

3 vols.   BY HARRY CASTLEMON. $3.00

Tom Newcombe.   Go-Ahead.   No Moss.

WAR SERIES.

6 vols.   BY HARRY CASTLEMON. $6.00

True to His Colors.   Marcy the Blockade-Runner.
Rodney the Partisan.   Marcy the Refugee.
Rodney the Overseer.   Sailor Jack the Trader.

HOUSEBOAT SERIES.

3 vols.   BY HARRY CASTLEMON. $3.00

The Houseboat Boys.   The Mystery of Lost River Cañon.
The Young Game Warden.

AFLOAT AND ASHORE SERIES.

3 vols.   BY HARRY CASTLEMON. $3.00

Rebellion in Dixie.   A Sailor in Spite of Himself.
The Ten-Ton Cutter.

THE PONY EXPRESS SERIES.

3 vol.   BY HARRY CASTLEMON. $3.00

The Pony Express Rider.   The White Beaver.
Carl, The Trailer.

EDWARD S. ELLIS.

EDWARD S. ELLIS, the popular writer of boys' books, is a native of Ohio, where he was born somewhat more than a half-century ago. His father was a famous hunter and rifle shot, and it was doubtless his exploits and those of his associates, with their tales of adventure which gave the son his taste for the breezy backwoods and for depicting the stirring life of the early settlers on the frontier.

Mr. Ellis began writing at an early age and his work was acceptable from the first. His parents removed to New Jersey while he was a boy and he was graduated from the State Normal School and became a member of the faculty while still in his teens. He was afterward principal of the Trenton High School, a trustee and then superintendent of schools. By that time his services as a writer had become so pronounced that he gave his entire attention to literature. He was an exceptionally successful teacher and wrote a number of text-books for schools, all of which met with high favor. For these and his historical productions, Princeton College conferred upon him the degree of Master of Arts.

The high moral character, the clean, manly tendencies and the admirable literary style of Mr. Ellis' stories have made him as popular on the other side of the Atlantic as in this country. A leading paper remarked some time since, that no mother need hesitate to place in the hands of her boy any book written by Mr. Ellis. They are found in the leading Sunday-school libraries, where, as may well be believed, they are in wide demand and do much good by their sound, wholesome lessons which render them as acceptable to parents as to their children. All of his books published by Henry T. Coates & Co. are re-issued in London, and many have been translated into other languages. Mr. Ellis is a writer of varied accomplishments, and, in addition to his stories, is the author of historical works, of a number of pieces of popular music and has made several valuable inventions. Mr. Ellis is in the prime of his mental and physical powers, and great as have been the merits of his past achievements, there is reason to look for more brilliant productions from his pen in the near future.

———

DEERFOOT SERIES.

3 vols.   By Edward S. Ellis. $3.00

Hunters of the Ozark.   The Last War Trail.
Camp in the Mountains.

LOG CABIN SERIES.

3 vols.   By Edward S. Ellis. $3.00

Lost Trail.   Footprints in the Forest.
Camp-Fire and Wigwam.

BOY PIONEER SERIES.

3 vols.   By Edward S. Ellis. $3.00

Ned in the Block-House.   Ned on the River.
Ned in the Woods.

THE NORTHWEST SERIES.

3 vols.   By Edward S. Ellis. $3.00

Two Boys in Wyoming.   Cowmen and Rustlers.
A Strange Craft and its Wonderful Voyage.

BOONE AND KENTON SERIES.

3 vols.   By Edward S. Ellis. $3.00

Shod with Silence.   In the Days of the Pioneers.
Phantom of the River.

IRON HEART, WAR CHIEF OF THE IROQUOIS.

1 vol.   By Edward S. Ellis. $1.00

THE NEW DEERFOOT SERIES.

3 vols.   By Edward S. Ellis. $3.00

Deerfoot in the Forest.   Deerfoot on the Prairie.
Deerfoot in the Mountains.

J. T. TROWBRIDGE.

NEITHER as a writer does he stand apart from the great currents of life and select some exceptional phase or odd combination of circumstances. He stands on the common level and appeals to the universal heart, and all that he suggests or achieves is on the plane and in the line of march of the great body of humanity.

The Jack Hazard series of stories, published in the late *Our Young Folks*, and continued in the first volume of *St. Nicholas*, under the title of "Fast Friends," is no doubt destined to hold a high place in this class of literature. The delight of the boys in them (and of their seniors, too) is well founded. They go to the right spot every time. Trowbridge knows the heart of a boy like a book, and the heart of a man, too, and he has laid them both open in these books in a most successful manner. Apart from the qualities that render the series so attractive to all young readers, they have great value on account of their portraitures of American country life and character. The drawing is wonderfully accurate, and as spirited as it is true. The constable, Sellick, is an original character, and as minor figures where will we find anything better than Miss Wansey, and Mr. P. Pipkin, Esq. The picture of Mr. Dink's school, too, is capital, and where else in fiction is there a better nick-name than that the boys gave to poor little Stephen Treadwell, "Step Hen," as he himself pronounced his name in an unfortunate moment when he saw it in print for the first time in his lesson in school.

On the whole, these books are very satisfactory, and afford the critical reader the rare pleasure of the works that are just adequate, that easily fulfill themselves and accomplish all they set out to do.—*Scribner's Monthly.*

www.ingramcontent.com/pod-product-compliance
Lightning Source LLC
Chambersburg PA
CBHW021340110726
47900CB00005B/1551